DIDO'S REVENGE

Sempronius Scipio and Caracalla. CE 215 to 217.

By Gordon Anthony

ISBN-13: 978-1703148664

Chapter 1
Rhodes

I was enjoying my stay on Rhodes. It was pleasant to relax with no real plans and to appreciate the old city with its meandering streets and welcoming tavernas. I'd taken a room in an out-of-the-way inn, and I'd spent a fair bit of time just wandering around and savouring the atmosphere of the place.

Of course, Rhodes is a bit of a backwater these days. In its heyday it was a major trading port, and its navy was powerful enough to give it a lot of influence. Nowadays, although there is still a fairly sizable flow of merchant vessels coming in and out of the port, and there's a flotilla of fishing vessels going out every day, the only signs of any military fleet are the imperial biremes and triremes in the harbour. The locals don't seem to mind the decline in their status all that much. Being under Roman rule may have its disadvantages, but the Empire has brought peace to this part of the world, and that's always good for trade. Rhodes is often by-passed by the larger merchant ships, but its harbour is still a hive of activity most days.

And then there's the Colossus. I'd heard about it, of course. Who hasn't? But I'd never quite appreciated just how, well, colossal it was. The wreckage is still lying there, some of it on top of the buildings it crushed when it came down. The city couldn't afford to have all that bronze taken away, so the huge statue, now shattered into hundreds of fragments, is still there four centuries after an earthquake brought it down. It will disappear in time, though, because leaving that amount of valuable metal around attracts attention. The city may not be able to pay anyone to clear it away, but bits of it often vanish overnight and probably end up in the metal-workers quarter of the city or in the hold of a merchant ship whose captain fancies an easy profit selling off scrap metal. Nobody minds.

What's left of the enormous statue is still impressive, though. I joined a small gaggle of other visitors to the island to stroll around the harbour and take a look at the wreckage. There was a section of one hand lying in a fairly open bit of ground, so I tried to wrap my arms around one of the fingers. It was so big I couldn't get my hands to meet. That just shows how imposing the finished article must have been when it stood at the harbour's entrance. It was a monument to the power and glory of Rhodes. And now it's a tumbled ruin, although the city hasn't fallen quite that far yet.

As I say, I was enjoying my rest. I felt I deserved it. I wasn't really supposed to be here, but circumstances had influenced my decision, and I felt that an out-of-the-way backwater was just what I needed. You see, I'd recently had a misunderstanding with a Parthian nobleman, and he'd sent some of his thugs after me. I'd reached Antioch ahead of them, and I didn't think they'd dare follow me that far into Roman territory, but you never can tell with Parthians so, after I'd written out my report and delivered it to the temple, I'd taken a boat down the Orontes and then boarded the first ship I could book passage on. It was heading to Rhodes, so that's how I got here. And all because of that little misunderstanding.

Well, truth be told, I don't suppose the nobleman misunderstood what his daughter and I were up to, but I'd certainly misunderstood her when she had told me he was away for a few days. Caught in that situation, I'd made my exit via a first floor window, found my horse and galloped away as quickly as my old nag could carry me.

It was rather an ignominious ending to my mission. Things had gone so well up until then, and I'd been planning to make a quiet and discreet exit from Parthian territory. But I'd spent three months moving around the place, and I was heading homewards when the girl caught my eye. She made it pretty plain she was up for some fun, so what was I supposed to do?

OK, I was supposed to ignore her and continue my quiet and discreet journey back to Roman territory, but I'm only human.

Perhaps I'd better introduce myself. My name is Sextus Sempronius Secundus, although I've never liked the Secundus part of my name and I am generally known as Scipio, which is, in my opinion, a much more prestigious name.

As for my current occupation, I'm an imperial spy. That's why I was in Parthia, posing as a merchant looking for new trade contacts. What I'd actually been doing was gathering information. I thought I'd done a pretty good job of it, even though it had been a stressful few months. Life isn't easy when you are playing a role like that in the knowledge that discovery will end up with you finding your head on a spike. Fortunately, the looks I'd inherited from my Syrian mother allowed me to blend in with the locals, and I speak Aramaic fluently as well as having a smattering of Persian, so I'd been able to move around with no real problems until that last little mix-up.

So I was in Rhodes, and it had been a pleasant few weeks. But even a life of ease can become boring after a while, especially when you are still only twenty-four years old. Not that I was in a rush to stick my neck on the line for the Emperor again, but I couldn't entirely ignore my duties, so I paid a visit to the temple of Serapis every few days and spoke to the chief priest.

I'd introduced myself when I first arrived, and shown him the pendant I wore under my tunic, so he knew I was on the imperial payroll. For the past few weeks, every time I'd visited him, he'd simply seen me, shaken his head and moved on to his priestly duties. This time, though, he gave me a nod and indicated I should wait. He was overseeing some junior priests who were busy trying to learn how to burn incense properly or some such thing. I've never really bothered too much with temples, so they might have been trying to learn how to turn rocks into marble for all I knew. But my reason for visiting the place wasn't to make offerings to the god, but was because my employer had struck upon the very clever ploy of using temples as imperial message centres. Priests know pretty much everything about what is going on in their city. Important people come to them and say more than they should, and the priests take careful notes.

There's an old saying that nobody will ever believe there is a plot against the Emperor until he turns up dead one morning, but our current Emperor was using the ubiquitous temples to keep tabs on who was saying what about him. Perhaps that sounds paranoid, but more than one Emperor has met an untimely death through not knowing who was on his side and who was plotting against him.

So I stood near the side wall, gazing around at the riches adorning the walls and the large statue of Serapis, until a slave came over and handed me a scroll case. I checked the seal and made sure it was my code name on the case, then scribbled a signature on the tablet he handed me to confirm I'd taken receipt.

I shoved the case under my tunic, but not before I noticed it had been re-directed from the temple at Antioch. I hoped the message wasn't urgent, because my unexpected move to Rhodes had probably delayed it by a week or two.

I sauntered back to my room, enjoying the morning sunshine. I was tempted to stop at one of the local taverns and sample some wine because I generally needed a bit of fortification before reading messages from Rome, but I'd had a couple of cups with my breakfast, so I decided it would be better to give it a miss this time.

Once up in my room, I sat on the bed and opened the case to tip out the scroll. As I'd expected when I began to unroll it, there was a second, smaller message hidden inside. My pal, Fronto, often slipped his own missives into the official ones. It was very useful having someone like Fronto at the heart of the imperial spy network. I put his message aside for the moment, then unrolled the official message and began to read.

"To Sigma," it began. "Greetings from your namesake."

That was the usual format. Sigma is my code name, an allusion to my alliterative real name, Sigma being the Greek letter equivalent to our Latin S. So, Sextus Sempronius Scipio – or Secundus if you must – led to my boss giving me the code name Sigma. As for that boss who lurked in his lair on the Palatine in Rome, his name was Sempronius Rufus, hence he referred to himself as my namesake.

He was an odd character, was old Rufus. According to gossip, he was a former actor and juggler who had somehow come to the attention of the old Emperor and had wangled a job in the imperial bureaucracy. Actors are usually regarded as little better than common criminals, so however he accomplished his step up, it was quite a feat. And, once inside the system, he'd moved up to become chief of the current Emperor's spy network.

So Sempronius Rufus was one of the upper class now, although I suspect that, like me, he had acquired his name as a result of one of his ancestors being a slave who had been freed by a member of the Sempronius family. Slaves take the family name of their former master, you see. In my case, it had been my great-grandfather who had been wrested away from a barbarous life in Britannia and had worked as a slave in Rome for more than twenty years before his master died and freed him in his will.

4

My own family is respectable now, although my brother certainly thinks I've not exactly helped that.

Thinking of my brother always puts me in a bad mood, so I turned my thoughts back to Sempronius Rufus. What, I wondered, did he have in store for me now?

"I have read your report and passed a copy to Romulus."

He does love his code names, does Rufus. Romulus is, of course, the Emperor, who represents Rome which was, according to legend, founded by Romulus. It's actually quite an appropriate name because legend also says Romulus killed his brother, Remus, and our own dear Caesar did the same to his own brother in rather bloodthirsty and distinctly odd circumstances. But where the original Romulus left things at one death, our Emperor went on to dispose of around twenty thousand individuals who had formerly expressed love and support for his deceased brother.

That's Roman politics for you. Pick the wrong side and you can expect a terminal outcome.

But I digress. Back to Rufus's message.

"I congratulate you on the detailed information you have provided, and I have commended your report to Romulus."

Oh, that was great! Coming to Caesar's attention wasn't exactly high on my list of personal priorities. I like the pay, and the job is interesting if dangerous, but getting too close to an Emperor can have fatal consequences. Personally, I'd have preferred to remain unnoticed.

Frowning, I read on.

"Another matter has arisen which requires prompt attention but needs to be handled delicately."

Oh, that's just terrific.

Rufus's message continued, "I know you lived in Ephesus for some years, so your local knowledge may help solve the case."

OK, that was better. I liked Ephesus, and the chance to go back would be welcome.

"We are told by one of our Friends that an item has been stolen from the Temple. Also, it seems there was a murder associated with the theft. The item stolen was donated to the temple by Romulus's late father, so he is naturally keen that it be recovered and that the perpetrator is dealt with. You are to proceed to Ephesus with all speed. Contact our Friend who will provide you with all the information and help you will need. I have sent him a note advising him of your arrival, and he will also provide your remuneration."

Well, that was nice. Remuneration is always welcome.

As for the message, it might seem cryptic, but I knew there could only be one temple he was referring to. There are several temples to various gods in Ephesus, but there is only one Temple with a capital T. That's the famous Temple of Artemis. I knew it well, and I also knew it was a secure place, so how anyone could have stolen anything of value was a real puzzle. A puzzle I was supposed to solve.

As for the Friend he mentioned, that would be old Flavius Restitutus, the chief priest at the temple. I knew him pretty well, so that should make things nice and straightforward. To begin with, anyway.

As usual, though, Rufus had left a lot of things unsaid. The man is paranoid about secrecy. I suppose even imperial messengers who criss-cross the Empire transporting his messages can be the victims of accident, but sometimes I find the allusions and code names rather silly.

Fronto, on the other hand, usually says a lot more. The problem is that he uses a code which is a real pain to decipher.

Still, I picked up his tightly-wrapped message and smoothed it out, noting the date at the foot of the message. The numbers of the day and month told me how I should transcribe the letters which were laid out in neat rows and made very little sense when you looked at them. What you needed to do was read them in columns, not in rows, and even then you had to work out which letter of the alphabet should replace the one Fronto had written. This message was dated the third day before the kalends of the fifth month, so that meant each letter Fronto had written needed to be replaced by the eighth letter following it in the Latin alphabet.

Like I said, it's a real pain deciphering these letters, but it's usually worth the effort.

I dug out my wax tablet and stylus and began jotting down the characters as I decoded them. It took a while, although the message was rather shorter than Fronto usually sent. Eventually, though, I had it all down. I'd been reading it as I went, but I always re-read Fronto's letters once they are decoded.

"To my friend Sextus Sempronius Scipio, greetings from Tiberius Sestius Fronto.

You will see from the Juggler's message that you are to investigate a theft and murder in Ephesus. Details of what happened are vague, but the local *vigiles* have been unable to discover how the theft was carried out, nor who was responsible except that the murder victim was found in possession of some other artefacts that had been stolen. The important item, a certain amulet, was not recovered, so we assume that the murder resulted from a falling out among thieves.

"I fear there may be something serious at play here. Stealing from the Temple is not something even the boldest thief would normally contemplate, and the fact that the only item which has not been recovered is one that belonged to our Emperor's father gives me pause for thought. Please take great care when you reach Ephesus as there may be more to this than simple robbery."

Fronto knew perfectly well that I was the last person who needed to be told about the risks involved in stealing from the Temple. The fact that he'd spelled it out suggested he was genuinely worried. He'd given me plenty to think about, but I read on. As usual, Fronto went on to provide me with some news of my family.

"I met your mother last week. She is well, and thinking of you always. It would be a kindness if you could send her a letter to let her know you are well. Your report from Parthia arrived here after I met her, but I will be sure to tell her you are alive and well. It would be better if she could hear this directly from you."

Ouch! Fronto knows how to use a quill to injure you.

"Your brother's business ventures continue to thrive. His wife is pregnant again so, if the gods will it, you will be an uncle to another Sempronius."

I must confess I wasn't too excited about that news. My brother and I have never got on, and I've never met his wife as I'd left Rome before they were married. I knew she came from a good family, but Fronto's earlier messages suggested she wasn't the sharpest quill in the writing case. I already had a niece, and I suppose I should have taken more interest, but the falling out I had had with my brother meant that we virtually ignored each other's existence these days.

Fronto ended with, "Again, take care in Ephesus. It might be best for your health if you failed to discover anything."

Now that was a worrying thought. I could read between the lines. It seemed Fronto thought there might be a plot brewing against Caesar, and tracking down the perpetrators might end up with me on the point of a sword.

On the other hand, failing to find the missing amulet which had belonged to old Septimius Severus, our now-deceased Emperor, might not be the best career move either. I could just imagine Antoninus Caesar hearing the news that one of his spies had failed to recover the stolen jewel. The Praetorians would be on my case pretty swiftly, I reckoned.

So, it looked as if I was facing a no-win situation. All of a sudden, being bored in Rhodes seemed a lot more appealing than it had done earlier that morning.

But orders are orders, so I wiped my tablet clean, stuffed the scrolls back in the case and took it with me until I could find a fire or brazier to dispose of them, and headed down to the harbour to find a boat that would take me to Ephesus and whatever sinister plot was being concocted there.

Chapter 2
The Temple

When I stepped onto the quayside in Ephesus it was like coming home. I may have been born and brought up in Rome, but Ephesus was where I grew from sulky teenager to cynical man, and I loved the place.

It didn't seem to have changed much in the three and a bit years I'd been away. The harbour area was still a riot of colour, noise and smells, with sailors, dockhands, and the inevitable stream of tourists all milling around. The Temple brings all sorts to Ephesus. It is one of the major cities on the Ionian coast of Asia in any case, but the lure of the Temple attracts hordes of visitors all year round.

The first thing I needed to do was find a place to stay. There was the usual bunch of touts lurking around, encouraging the new arrivals to follow them to the best place in town, but I knew better than to pay any attention to them. They'd take the gullible newcomers to the northern part of the city which, because it was close to the Temple, allowed innkeepers to charge extortionate rates for their rooms. The same went, to a lesser extent, to the places near the harbour. A lot of people head for the first garishly painted hostelry they see, and they pay for it.

Determined to maintain a low profile, I slung my bag over my shoulder, looping the strap over my head. I didn't carry a great deal, and it helped add to my low-key appearance. I was dressed in a plain tunic and sandals, with no hat to protect me from the sun. My cloak was stuffed in my satchel, although it, too, would have given the impression of me being either a down-at-heel freedman or a slave.

I didn't have a slave of my own. I'd sold the one I did have when I went off on my first mission for the Emperor. According to the Juggler, spies can't afford the luxury of having a slave tag along with them. Not unless you cut out their tongues to prevent them blabbing, and I wasn't inclined to do that to anyone.

So I lugged my bag and left through the southernmost of the three archways which led out from the harbour and headed into the city.

The place was pretty much the same as I remembered. The streets were crowded and noisy, with people coming and going in all directions, many of them paying little attention to where they were stepping. Avoiding collisions wasn't easy.

The streets still contained the usual mix of three or four storey buildings which provide the crowded avenues with some shade from the worst of the summer heat. Most have domestic residential rooms on the upper floors with shops, taverns and workshops occupying the ground floor. From what I could see, many of these were still the same businesses that had been there before I left. And most were doing a roaring trade, especially the ones selling tatty souvenirs. Artemis is big business in Ephesus, you see. You can buy Artemis ear-rings, Artemis necklaces and pendants, and Artemis just about anything, including brooches which, in my opinion, are a little sacrilegious given how the fastening pin is located on the goddess's rear. There are also hats, cloaks, tunics and even togas decorated with Artemis images around the hems.

But there is also some higher culture in Ephesus, including an army of statues. Every road junction contains a high plinth topped by a statue of a god, goddess, hero or local worthy, although statues of the Emperor obviously outnumber all the others combined.

As for public buildings, some of these are rather grand. Walking through the lesser *agora*, I passed the imposing edifice of the *Bouleuterion*, the city's council Chambers, along with a cool and pleasant *stoa* where philosophers liked to gather to discuss the meaning of life. Further on, there were a few column-fronted temples including the Serapion. Serapis is one of the deities the Emperor likes to cultivate, and he often uses the priests here as local contacts for his spies. In Ephesus, though, the Serapion played second fiddle to the Temple of Artemis, so I didn't bother reporting to the chief priest of Serapis.

Walking slowly and taking in my surroundings, I wound my way in the general direction of the Magnesian Gate to the south-eastern corner of town. Here, I found a room in a disreputable inn I knew from my former stay in Ephesus. It went by the rather unimaginative name of The Resting Place, although the ambience wasn't all that restful. I'd never lodged in this particular dive before, but its seedy reputation provided me with a certain level of anonymity. The innkeeper asked no questions once I'd handed over the required amount of sesterces to book the room for a week, and nobody else paid me much attention once they'd given me a quick look to verify that I had nothing worth stealing.

The room itself was a tiny, cramped space but at least I didn't need to share. Having a room to myself had cost extra. There was a narrow cot, a wooden chest with no lock, and a tiny window which overlooked a squalid and very small courtyard at the back of the building. At least I was on the top floor, so the air wasn't too smelly when I stuck my head out of the window.

I put on a fresh tunic, put my tablet and stylus in a small bag which I looped over my shoulder, dumped my larger bag and went out to find something to eat. It was almost mid-day, so most wine shops and food bars were busy as people took shelter from the worst of the sun, but I managed to find a seat in a small place I knew on the corner of a side street near Trajan's fountain. I ordered a bowl of vegetable stew and a hunk of dark bread. The joint's owner, a large, fat, surly fellow didn't recognise me at all. Neither did his equally fat but always smiling and cheerful wife as she slopped my stew into a bowl. I suppose that was a good thing. I'd been a regular customer here before, but they'd obviously forgotten me. I hoped many others would have done the same, as it would make moving around discreetly that bit easier.

After I'd emptied my bowl, my next task was to have a haircut and a shave. The fashion these days is for men to grow beards, but I was never able to produce much more than unsightly stubble, and the straggly growth I'd developed on the voyage from Rhodes certainly didn't qualify as a genuine beard.

I knew there was a decent bath house near the Magnesian Gate, but it was frequented by people I didn't want to meet quite yet. I didn't want word of my return spreading until I'd had a chance to dig a bit into the theft and murder, so I trekked back towards the harbour where there is a large bath house near the city's largest gymnasium. Here, I sat on a stool while a barber wielded scissors and a razor to tidy me up.

Once I was clean-shaven and had hair that was more Roman in style than the long locks I'd developed during my time in Parthia, I decided I'd better have a proper wash. I had a long, luxurious soak in the warm pool, dunked myself briefly in the cold pool, then dressed and prepared to begin my investigation.

11

By this time, it was the middle of the afternoon. The spring sunshine was blazing down so I relented and bought a floppy hat with a small representation of Artemis sewn into the front. That, I thought, would help me blend in as well as preventing sunstroke. It may not have been high summer yet, but the weather was still hot.

I took a slow walk, looking all around as I recalled the various landmarks on my way to the North Gate. I passed the stadium and yet another of the city's many gymnasiums, then joined the throng trying to squeeze out under the gate arch. There was a bit of a crush, but the mood was good-natured. I noticed a couple of watchmen lounging in the shade nearby. They had clubs, spears and daggers, but their weapons were usually superfluous. The guards were really only there in an attempt to deter pickpockets who always found good business among the tourists.

After a little bit of jostling, I was out of the city and into the countryside. Well, I say countryside, but the first few hundred yards of the road are flanked by the tombs of the city's former citizens, and beyond those elaborately decorated monuments to the deceased, the land is cultivated, with orchards, vineyards and olive groves stretching as far as the mountains which are themselves set aside as grazing land. It's not exactly a wilderness.

The road was busy with visitors heading to and from the Temple. It was thirsty work tramping all the way out there. I'd never taken part in one of the regular Artemis processions where a long column of worshippers walks all the way from the Temple into the centre of the city. I'd seen it often enough, but making that walk in reverse on my own filled me with admiration for the participants who managed to look happy and cheerful despite the heat they must have endured on the way.

Those processions were all part of the attraction of Ephesus, of course. There was music, dancing, bright costumes, jugglers, carts decorated to resemble scenes from history or legend and, as you'd expect, priests and acolytes encouraging the watching public to make donations to the Temple.

Today, however, there was just me and a few hundred others sauntering along the well-trodden road.

The roadway forked, and most people went left. The right fork leads in a great semi-circle around the side of the city, and you can get to the amphitheatre that way, but the left fork takes you to the main attraction which is so huge it was now visible over the tops of the trees which surround its wide gardens.

For anyone who hasn't seen the Temple of Artemis, it certainly deserves its reputation as one of the Seven Wonders of the World. Unlike the Colossus of Rhodes, though, it still stands, dominating the area around it.

I entered through the perimeter gates, passing into the shade of tall trees, then emerging into the lawns of the wide gardens. All around me, spectators were oohing and aahing at the sight that met their eyes.

If you've ever seen the famous Parthenon in Athens, you get an idea of what the Temple looks like, except that this Temple is much, much bigger. Its columns are huge, the statues of gods, demi-gods, nymphs and satyrs which decorate the façade are brightly painted, the roof shimmers like a rainbow in the sunshine, and the Temple seems to go on forever. I remember the first time I saw it, I just stood gaping at it for ages.

This time, I joined the throng for only a few moments. I didn't want to look like I was there on official business, so I stared like everyone else although, to tell the truth, being impressed by this building is very easy indeed.

There are three wide, deep steps leading to the podium on which the Temple sits. These were crowded with sightseers who were gawping up at the immense columns which support that enormous roof. Those columns are so thick it can take three or four men to link hands around them, and they are so tall you get a crick in your neck looking up at them.

After a suitable pause, though, I moved on. I noticed a young priest who was on welcoming duty near the podium steps, so I asked him where I might find the chief priest, Flavius Restitutus. This lad was obviously a new recruit to the service of the Goddess, so he didn't recognise me. He gave me a frown, demanding to know why I wanted to interrupt the busy life of such an important personage.

"I have a message for him," I said, fishing out the small pendant I wore around my neck. When he saw the image of an eagle holding a feathered spear, he quickly changed his attitude and directed me to the rear *cella* of the Temple.

"He has visitors," the priest informed me. "Important visitors."

"Not as important as me," I grinned at him as I left him to his duties and walked along the side of the Temple, taking advantage of the shade the huge edifice provided.

The rear *cella* of the Temple is a smaller version of the huge room you'll find inside the front doors. But where the main *cella* has smaller rooms leading off it, and is also where the cult statue stands, the rear *cella* is a simple, bare room. At least, it was bare when first constructed, but its immensely thick walls and the heavy, iron-studded doors make it an ideal place to store valuables. This is where wealthy citizens bring the loot – sorry, legally acquired riches – they want to keep safe and don't necessarily want to have on display in their homes. The Temple is, in effect, a safe-keeping depository.

The doors are normally kept shut, but they were open today. A bunch of around twenty slaves were sitting on the bottom steps of the podium off to one side, and there was a litter with brightly coloured curtains of blue and gold parked on the ground in front of them.

Two other slaves stood on the top step, barring the approach to the open doors. These two wore short, sleeveless tunics which showed off the bulging muscles of their arms and legs. Their heads were shaved, giving them a pugnacious appearance, and the glint in their eyes was designed to deter any of the sightseers from venturing anywhere near the *cella*. If their appearance wasn't enough, I was pretty sure each of them had a heavy club propped against the rear of the column beside them. I was pretty sure of that because it was a precaution I'd instituted when I was in charge of security here.

I smiled as I made for the steps. One of the large goons made a move to intercept me, but his even larger partner held out an arm to warn him off. This second guard treated me to a wide, friendly grin as I climbed up to meet him.

"By Zeus!" he exclaimed with apparently genuine delight. "It's young Master Scipio! We thought you had gone back to Rome."

"I did. But I'm back for a short visit. How are you, Herakleon?"

"Can't complain, Sir," Herakleon rumbled.

I laughed, "Complaining is what you always did best, Herakleon."

He grinned in acknowledgement of my jibe. I'd always liked Herakleon. He was built like a man-mountain, but there was a brain in his head. He was also a man who knew how to keep his mouth shut when necessary.

"I'm looking for Restitutus," I told him. "Is he inside?"

"The boss? Yes, he's in there. He's got some posh nobs with him. They're putting a load of valuables in for safe keeping while they go to Athens for the summer."

That explained the gaggle of slaves at the foot of the steps. The poor souls must have carried heavy chests of silver and gold all the way out here. No wonder they were taking advantage of a few moments to rest.

"What brings you back then, Sir?" Herakleon asked me.

I wasn't sure whether his companion was someone I could trust to keep things quiet, so I merely said, "I'm just passing through. But I couldn't stop off in Ephesus without coming out here to say hello."

He regarded me with a look that said he knew I was talking bull, but he shrugged, "It's good to see you again, Sir."

"And you. But I'd like a chat with you a bit later if that's all right."

"Any time, Sir," he nodded.

There was a flurry of activity behind him as a man dressed in a white tunic with a narrow stripe of purple emerged from the shadowy depths of the *cella*. He had an elegantly dressed woman beside him. Both were in their forties, I guessed, and both were immaculately turned out, with manicured nails and not a hair out of place. They reeked of wealth and privilege.

"Thank you, Restitutus," the man said as he turned to clasp hands with a balding man in a long robe who was following him out of the Temple.

"My pleasure," the priest replied. "Your goods are safe here."

The man and woman descended the steps, giving me barely a look. They summoned their slaves and both clambered into the litter. Eight of the slaves put their shoulders to the carrying poles and hoisted them high, setting off for the city with the rest of the retinue trudging in their wake.

Restitutus watched them go, his expression betraying nothing. Then he turned to me and gave me a beaming smile.

15

"I am glad to see you, Sempronius Scipio. Thank you for coming, although I had rather expected you sooner."

"I was delayed," I shrugged as I stepped forwards to clasp hands with him.

"You must come to my room so we can talk," he said.

I shook my head.

"Why not talk in there?" I suggested, indicating the open doors behind him.

I reckoned it would be easier to find out what had happened if I was at the scene of the crime.

"Very well," Restitutus agreed.

I followed him inside. The rear *cella* may be a smaller version of the main chamber, but it is still a huge stone-lined vault. It was cool inside, almost chilly in fact. Two oil lamps stood just inside the doors, and Restitutus picked up one of them, holding it high as he led the way further into the dark lair. We passed wooden chests, each one padlocked and clearly labelled, all stacked around the edges of the vast chamber.

Two priests were busy cross-checking the latest deposits, marking details on a vellum scroll by the light of another oil lamp.

"All done?" Restitutus asked them with an intonation suggesting it was more of a command than a question.

"Yes, Sir," they replied before scurrying past us and heading outside.

Restitutus placed his lamp on top of the nearest chest and turned to regard me gravely with his knowing eyes.

"It really is good to see you, my boy. I was delighted when Sempronius Rufus sent word that you were on your way here. But I rather fear your trip will be a wasted one. Too much time has elapsed, and the culprits are long gone."

I liked old Restitutus. No beating about the bush with him. He was getting stuck right into the meat of the matter.

Waving a hand at our surroundings, I said, "Whatever was stolen, it doesn't seem to have ruined your reputation. There's still a huge treasure trove in here."

His lips twitched as he replied, "We did not think it wise to advertise that something had been stolen. Fortunately, we managed to keep the matter reasonably confidential."

I nodded. I didn't want to let slip that Fronto had told me what had been stolen, so I asked, "So what happened? All I know is that something belonging to the Emperor was taken, and that somebody was killed. That's not an easy thing to keep quiet."

Restitutus clasped his hands together in front of him, pausing to gather his thoughts.

I knew he was a very clever chap. You don't become chief priest of Artemis and one of the Emperor's trusted contacts unless you are very bright and very discreet, so his report of the events was as concise as I could have hoped for.

"Technically, the item belonged to the Temple," he informed me. "It was a golden amulet with the image of a bull's head on it. It was donated to the Goddess by our former Emperor, Septimius Severus. He took it from the tomb of Alexander."

That made me blink. I'd heard that old Severus had ordered the tomb of Alexander the Great to be sealed up. I didn't know he'd helped himself to one of the famous conqueror's amulets beforehand.

Restitutus went on, "We discovered the theft just after dawn on the second day before the Ides of February."

I did a quick mental calculation. That meant the crime had taken place over three months ago.

Restitutus continued calmly, "I was present when the Temple doors were opened. As usual, I and several priests went in to offer our morning devotions to the Goddess before holding a formal sacrificial ceremony for the public."

I nodded. This was a daily routine. There were always devotees and even some visitors to the city who would go to the Temple before first light in order to witness the morning ceremony. That was held on the podium in full view of the spectators. Nobody went inside the Temple except the priests. Only after the sacrifice would visitors be allowed to actually view the cult statue which represented the Goddess herself.

"As soon as we opened the doors, I knew something was wrong," the priest explained. "As you know, items donated to the Goddess are displayed all around the main chamber. But many of these had been taken down from their stands and scattered about the floor."

He held my gaze as he added meaningfully, "But everything had been in order when we locked the doors the previous evening."

I nodded to show him I understood the implications of this, and he continued his account.

"I immediately went out to inform the crowd that the Goddess had sent us a signal of her displeasure with us and that a special ceremony of purification would be held later. I did not, of course, tell them what had actually happened."

"Of course," I murmured.

"We then set about putting things back in their proper places. Once we had completed that task, we conducted a thorough inventory of the displays. That was when we discovered several items of great value had been removed."

He sighed softly as he recounted, "There were several small statuettes of the Goddess missing, as well as a necklace of rubies, a bronze dagger of great antiquity which was reputed to belong to Hector of Troy, and, of course, the amulet which had once belonged to Alexander."

"Was there any indication of how someone could have got in?" I asked. "And, more importantly, how did they get back out without you seeing them?"

He nodded as if pleased that I had focused on the central issue of the theft. There is only one way in and out of the main chamber. Someone, somehow, must have hidden themselves inside overnight, selected some small items to steal, scattered other things around to disguise the theft, and then walked back out when the doors were opened the following morning. All without being seen.

Which should have been impossible.

"We were sure that everyone had departed the previous evening," Restitutus confirmed. "There are, as you know, many small nooks and crannies where someone might be able to conceal themselves, but our door slaves were adamant that everyone who had entered was seen leaving."

"Was Herakleon on duty?"

He nodded, "So you can trust his word. We only allow small groups in at any time, and they are watched. Everyone left before the doors were locked shut for the night."

I frowned, wondering what to ask next. As I said, Restitutus is no fool, and I was pretty sure he would have done everything possible to discover who had committed the theft.

He went on, "Pomponius Niger, who has been in charge of security since you left, made enquiries, of course. Everyone who entered the Temple on that morning was searched, even the priests, but none of the items were found. And, before you ask, I trust Niger almost as much as I trust you."

"I'll still need to talk to him," I said.

"Of course. He'll be round at the main chamber. We can go and talk to him soon."

I said, "But I was told there was also a murder. Where and when did that happen?"

"Ah!" Restitutus smiled sadly. "That is how we know who the culprit was, even though we have no idea how he accomplished his feat."

He explained, "Two days after the theft, a rich householder in the city was found murdered. He had been stabbed in the chest several times. When the *vigiles* searched his room, they found all of the items that had been stolen from the Temple. All except the amulet."

"They knew about the theft?" I asked.

"The Tribune did. I felt obliged to inform him, but asked him not to spread the word. He did, though, provide Niger with some watchmen to help scour the city for any signs of the missing valuables. They raided a few places where thieves are known to sell on their gains, but nothing was found until the murder."

"So who was this rich householder?"

"His name was Gaius Aristides. He was a widower who dealt in acquiring and exporting fine arts and items of antiquity. What nobody suspected was that some of the items he acquired were obtained by theft. But the evidence was incontrovertible."

"Perhaps," I remarked, "it could have been a falling out among thieves, but why would whoever killed him leave the loot behind?"

"Because the noise of the killing brought Aristides' head of household running to see what was going on. As I understand it, the killer made his escape but had no time to gather the stolen artefacts."

"And the killer is the man who stole them in the first place? I take it Aristides was not here on the morning of the theft?"

"He was not. But neither was the killer. We do not know who he was, and he has vanished from the city."

I was struggling to keep up here.

Frowning, I asked, "So how do you know who the thief was?"

Restitutus treated me to a weary smile as he told me, "One of the people who was here that morning was a painter by the name of Philippos. He had been doing work for us touching up the statues and frescoes."

"Go on," I encouraged, feeling none the wiser.

"Philippos was recommended to us by Aristides when our regular artist went off to Athens for a few months. He had been working here for over two weeks when the theft occurred, and he came back the following day. But he failed to arrive the next morning, and that was when we heard of Aristides' murder."

"But this Philippos wasn't the man who stabbed him?"

"Apparently not. The description does not match at all. But Diocles, the Tribune of *vigiles,* will be able to give you more information on that."

"So," I said to recap, "Aristides recommended Philippos to you. Philippos was one of the people who was in here on the morning of the theft, then he disappeared on the day Aristides was killed, although the murderer was someone else. Is that about right?"

Restitutus nodded, "You have it."

"And this Philippos was definitely at the Temple on the morning you discovered the theft?"

"Definitely. I spoke to him myself. In fact, he made a point of wishing me a good morning shortly before I unlocked the temple doors."

I pursed my lips, trying to visualise the scene. There would have been several priests, at least a couple of slaves, and this fellow Philippos milling around the doorway when the theft was discovered. Niger, the head of security, would also have been there.

"Is it possible," I asked, "that Philippos stole the items while pretending to help clear up the mess?"

"No," Restitutus shook his head. "He came into the Temple, I remember, because I had to usher him back outside. And he did have a bag over his shoulder, but that was quite normal. He carried his brushes and other things in it. But he had no opportunity to steal anything, and Niger searched his bag later, just as he searched everyone."

"So you don't actually know he stole anything?" I ventured.

Restitutus' nostrils flared a little at that, but he gave a reluctant admission.

"I cannot prove it. But his disappearance must be more than coincidence. Don't forget that it was Aristides who recommended him to us. Philippos was the only person present that morning who lived in the city. Somehow, he must have taken the stolen goods to Aristides. Then the unknown man killed Aristides."

"Unless," I smiled, there was some supernatural power at work?"

Restitutus may have been a priest, but he was well placed to know the limitations of divine interventions.

"Philippos was the thief," he declared. "But he, too, has vanished. Along with the amulet which was donated to us by the Emperor's father."

"OK," I sighed. "I think I remember the amulet, but could you refresh my memory? What did it look like? Did it have any special significance or legends attached to it?"

"It was a golden disc around the size of a clenched fist," the priest informed me. "It was on a chain comprised of large, golden links. When hung around the neck, the amulet would sit on a man's chest. The front image of a bull's head was shown, raised slightly from the disc of the pendant."

I nodded. That sounded familiar, but there were so many treasures in the Temple, I'd not paid much attention to every item. I'd certainly had no idea the amulet had been donated by the old Emperor, but that must have happened before my time here.

Restitutus told me, "Apart from its association with Alexander the Great, it had no special significance as you put it, but that, in itself, is significant, is it not?"

"Yes, I suppose it is."

"There is not much more I can tell you," Restitutus said. "We have replaced all the items we recovered, and nobody other than those who were here and a handful of members of the *vigiles* know what happened. But the Emperor has been informed, and he is most anxious that the amulet is recovered."

That wasn't exactly a comforting thought, but Sempronius Rufus, the Juggler, had already told me what was at stake.

"Can I have a word with Herakleon?" I asked the priest.

"Of course. I will go and find Niger and send him to you as well."

"Thank you."

I held up a hand before he could turn away.

"One other thing."

"Yes?"

"My expenses. I'm overdue a couple of months' pay."

His mouth softened into a sympathetic grin as he said, "I shall see to that. Send Herakleon to me at my room once you have finished speaking to him."

With that, he left, leaving me with the flickering oil lamp and a whole load of things to think about. I trusted Restitutus implicitly, yet the theft he described was impossible. Someone might have been able to conceal themselves inside the Temple overnight, but there was no way they could have walked out the following morning without being seen. As for the murder, there could be several explanations for that, and I wasn't yet convinced that Philippos hadn't also met a grisly end.

Herakleon lumbered into the *cella* while I was mulling all this over.

"So you are here about the missing amulet?" he rumbled with a grin.

"Yes. What can you tell me about the morning of the theft?"

Herakleon gathered his thoughts, then gave me an account which matched Restitutus's story more or less exactly. The only real difference was that he was only vaguely aware that the painter, Philippos, had been in the chamber that morning.

"I honestly can't recall," he admitted. "There was a lot of surprise and concern, as you must imagine. People were running around trying to figure out what had happened. My main job was to prevent any members of the public getting too close, so I can't say for certain that Philippos was there. But if Master Restitutus says he was, then that's good enough for me."

"Me, too," I agreed. "But what can you tell me about Philippos? What was he like?"

"He's in his twenties, I'd say. Roughly the same age as you, Sir. Average height. Short, brown, curly hair. He speaks

Greek with an accent, but that's probably because he's from Macedonia."

"Was he a good artist? He sounds young to be a master painter."

Herakleon shrugged, "I'm no expert, Sir. But he seemed competent enough, although he seemed to spend more time wandering around than actually painting. I was always seeing him walking about the Temple, both inside and out. Maybe that's why I don't recall for sure where he was on that morning. But he'd definitely been in and out of the Temple the day before. I lost count of the number of times he passed through the doors."

"What was he doing?"

Herakleon shrugged, "Usually carrying pots of paint, but sometimes just stretching his legs, so he said."

I frowned. That was certainly odd behaviour, but whether it was suspicious or simply an artist's foible remained to be discovered.

I asked, "And he stayed in the city? Do you know where?"

"No idea, sir. He turned up every morning with that bulging sack of his, and he went off every evening to wherever he was lodging."

"OK. Thanks, Herakleon. Now, could you go and find Master Restitutus in his room. He has something for me, I hope."

The big slave strolled away, but I didn't have long to wait before another man came in.

"Pomponius Niger," he introduced himself as he came into the great vault of the *cella*.

He was about my height, in his late forties or even fifties, and he had the look of a military man. He walked with an erect bearing, and his salt and pepper hair was cut very short. Like many ex-soldiers, he was lean and tough, with a very solid look about him.

"You were in the Legions?" I guessed.

"Third Augusta," he agreed. "Based in Africa. And you had this job before me, is that right?"

"For a short time," I nodded, not wanting to get into any bragging contest. "I'm in the imperial service now."

"So I hear," he said with a trace of a suggestion that he considered me far too young and foolish for such a responsible job. "And you're investigating this theft?"

23

"And the murder," I confirmed.

As I'd feared, though, Niger's story was just another confirmation of what I'd already learned. He'd been present, and agreed that Philippos had been one of the first into the chamber when the doors were opened.

"But I searched his bag a bit later after he'd been ushered outside. He was clean at the time."

"Could he have stolen the artefacts and dumped them outside?" I asked.

"No way. He had no time to steal anything, and there's no place to conceal a stash near the Temple. There are too many people around."

"So the only real reason for suspecting him is his initial connection to Aristides and his disappearance on the day of the murder?"

"Isn't that enough?" he challenged.

"Maybe," I replied. "But it's possible the unknown murderer could have disposed of Philippos as well, isn't it?"

After a moment's thought, he agreed, "It's possible, but then there is no explanation for how the amulet was stolen."

"There's no explanation for that anyway," I smiled.

The look he gave me suggested he wouldn't have minded knocking my teeth out for that comment, but he managed to keep his temper in check. I suppose he felt that the theft having taken place on his watch and me being brought in to investigate was a black mark against him. I'd probably have felt the same if I'd been in his sandals.

I said, "It's a real puzzle. Your security is as tight as it can be, and I have no idea how anyone could have stolen anything without being caught."

That mollified him a little, so I took the opportunity to check a few things with him, although I obtained nothing new.

"What about your regular painter?" I asked. "He went to Athens, I believe? Would that have been old Leonides?"

"That's right. He's been coming here for years, so I'm told."

"I remember him. Taciturn fellow, but a good worker and a dab hand with a brush and paints."

I'd known Leonides when I'd worked here. The Temple always needed an artist on call because the weather faded the bright paints on the statues and frescoes, so they were in regular need of touching up.

"That's right," Niger confirmed. "He got a job offer and went to Athens."

"It must have been a good offer," I mused. "The Temple pays well."

Niger shrugged, so I went on, "Is he back, do you know?"

"Yes. He came back a few weeks ago. He's been out here once or twice, taking up where Philippos left off."

"Is he here today?"

"No, you missed him. He was here yesterday, but I expect he'll be back in a few days. He fits in this work with his other jobs."

I nodded. Leonides might be a surly so-and-so, but he was in demand as a painter. He and one apprentice could get through as much work as most teams consisting of half a dozen painters.

"Do you know where he stays, then?"

"Somewhere near the theatre, I think," Niger told me.

"OK. Thanks very much. You've been a great help."

He gave me a curt nod but couldn't bring himself to wish me luck.

I picked up the oil lamp and followed him to the main door. Here, he took out the other lamp which stood inside the great doors, then we both stepped out and a slave pulled the doors shut. Niger took a large, brass key from his belt and locked the doors securely.

"That reminds me," I said. "I take it only you and the chief priest have keys to the main doors?"

"That's right," he agreed. "And we never let them out of our sight. There are no other copies. Besides, we have patrols of slaves going round the outside of the Temple at night, so nobody could have got in and out even if they did have a key. Which they don't."

I knew all that, but it was nice to know the procedures hadn't been altered since I'd left.

"Thanks for all your help," I said to Niger, eager to stay on his good side as much as possible. "Before I go, could you show me where the amulet was on display?"

He gave a nod, but Herakleon turned up again, carrying a small pouch which he handed to me with a smirk.

"Master Restitutus says to let him know if you need more."

I opened the draw strings of the satisfyingly weighty pouch and fished out a denarius which I handed to Herakleon.

"Let me know if you think of anything else," I told him. "And keep your eyes peeled."

"Thank you, Sir! You are a proper gentleman."

"I know a few who would disagree with that," I chuckled.

"Can I do anything else for you, sir?" he asked.

I shook my head.

"No, thanks. I suppose I'd better head back into town and speak to a few more people."

Niger now set off around the edge of the podium, making for the main doors. I followed with my head full of confused thoughts. It was three months and more since the amulet had been stolen; the theft had been impossible unless the thief could walk through walls; the murderer and the presumed thief had both long disappeared. And I was supposed to solve this mess? Restitutus may have given me a fairly heavy money pouch, but I felt I wasn't being paid nearly enough for this mission.

Chapter 3
The Tribune

There were still plenty of tourists milling around outside the Temple. Some were clustered near the steps leading to the main doors, but a priest was only allowing them inside in small groups, with each group accompanied by another priest and a couple of slaves to make sure nobody touched anything.

Niger led me straight inside, drawing some grumbling from the waiting devotees. I paid them no attention.

The main *cella* is even larger and more imposing than the one at the rear. With the huge doors open and many torches blazing around the walls, it's a dazzling sight, the daylight and torchlight reflecting off gleaming jewels everywhere you look. There are a few small side rooms, but the main chamber is full of pedestals and tables, each adorned by a bronze or marble statue, or some gift donated to the Temple as an offering to the Goddess. Weapons, jewels, cups and plates abounded, as did more practical offerings such as wine and fruit which were piled on a table near the door.

And, as you step further inside, you cannot but help be impressed by the statue of Artemis herself.

It's an odd thing, really. Some people think it is carved from ebony because it is so dark, but it's actually made of a more common wood, but a wood so old that it looks almost black.

Artemis is depicted as a woman, but her torso has multiple breasts, or perhaps representations of grapes or melons clinging to her front. Nobody is quite sure. The priests say that, whatever you believe these oval mounds to be, they represent fertility and plenty.

Her arms are bent at the elbows, hands stretching out to greet visitors with her palms facing inwards. It's as if she's offering an embrace to anyone brave enough to touch her. Few people try.

Her eyes are lapis lazuli of dazzling blue, and she wears an odd headdress which has golden plates dangling at either side of her face, each plate decorated with images of prancing animals like horses and cattle.

To be honest, it's quite a spooky sight. The Goddess has an unearthly aspect, with a stern expression of disapproval and her beady eyes blazing a challenge as if she is ready to strike down any mortal who is foolish enough not to grovel at her feet.

This is Artemis, whose fame has spread all around the Empire and beyond, and whose presence here brings the thousands of visitors who help keep Ephesus rich. There had been some trouble recently when the local Christians had objected to the Temple's very existence, but even the most devout Christian must have known that, without Artemis and her magnificent temple, the city's prosperity would suffer.

I couldn't help admiring the cult statue even though I'd seen it hundreds of times before, but Niger tapped my arm and led me to the rear of the chamber, behind the statue. This was where some of the most valuable artefacts were displayed, and there was another priest and slave on hand to keep watch over them. I couldn't see any blank space where an amulet might have been placed, but Niger pointed to a low pedestal containing a bust of the Goddess.

"We've put another necklace around it now," he explained. "But that's where the amulet used to be."

I remembered it now. A golden disc with a bull's snout and horns projecting out from the front. And a fairly substantial gold chain. Searching my memory, I recalled it as a rather chunky and unattractive thing, its value being in its gold content rather than the artistry. But, if my memory served me correctly, its sheer bulk meant that it would have needed a bag to conceal it. Hanging around your neck, the large links of the chain would have been visible even if you had stuffed the pendant under your tunic.

I spent a little while looking around, but the truth was there was nothing to see.

"The thief must have had a light," I suggested. "Did anyone find it?"

"There are torches, candles and oil lamps all over the place," Niger replied scornfully. "All he needed was a flint to light one."

"True enough," I agreed with an embarrassed grin. "I don't suppose you know where he hid?"

He shook his head.

"There are a few places. He could have slipped behind one of the larger pedestals, probably in a side room. Except that Philippos didn't hide in here. He was seen leaving after the doors were locked on the evening of the theft."

I gave a rueful nod. Somehow, a man who had been locked out had got back in, then walked out without being seen. It wasn't possible, and I was beginning to think that Niger's claim of there being no spare key must be wrong. Someone, somehow, must have got hold of a copy.

I didn't voice my suspicion because I knew how Niger would react, so I offered him my hand and said I'd be in touch once I'd spoken to a few more people.

He didn't say anything. His expression suggested he was torn between hoping I'd recover the amulet in order to avert the Emperor's wrath, and wishing to see me fall flat on my face.

I left, heading back towards the city. Outside the Temple grounds, I stopped at one of the many kiosks and bought a cool fruit juice and a pastry. I drained the drink in one go, then chomped on the pastry as I made the long walk back to town.

As I sauntered along, I mulled over what I had learned. So far, everything seemed circumstantial, but there was a likely scenario forming in my mind. Aristides, the crooked dealer in antiquities, had placed his man on the inside, and somehow this fellow Philippos must have got hold of a spare key and used it to sneak into the Temple at night.

Precisely how he had done it didn't matter for the moment. What mattered was that Aristides got the loot, then someone killed him for it. But that someone only got away with the amulet. Whether Philippos had kept that as his share, or whether the murderer had taken it was still an open question. As was the matter of what had happened to Philippos. Was he in cahoots with the killer, or had he already left when Aristides died? Or was he, too, dead?

I needed more answers, and the best place to start was with the Tribune of the *vigiles*.

By the time I'd reached the city gates, I'd devised a plan of action. My low-key approach had worked at the Temple because people there knew me, but I didn't know the Tribune. Restitutus had said his name was Diocles, which meant that old Polybius must have retired. I'd had a healthy respect for Polybius who often worked the night shift with his men whose duties included extinguishing fires as well as keeping the peace. But it was possible Diocles preferred the day shift. Polybius had certainly always needed to be on call during the day because crowd control and apprehending pickpockets was the order of business during daylight.

That's actually quite unusual. In most cities, the *vigiles* are not responsible for keeping order. Their task is to put out any of the fires which are all too common in a place where thousands of meals are cooked using open flames. But Ephesus had no army garrison, and the Temple attracted a great many visitors, which meant that maintaining law and order was important for the city's prosperity. So the Temple paid a contribution to ensure that the *vigiles* were on hand to discourage those of a light-fingered persuasion.

Since I didn't know this new Tribune, I decided I needed a bit of clout. I returned to The Resting Place, climbed the stairs to my room and retrieved another of my spare tunics. This one, though, was a lot more prestigious than the old ones I'd been wearing up until now. I shoved it in my little bag along with my writing tablet, then went to the baths again.

It was a long walk back to the harbour, but I still didn't want to visit the local bath house in case I ran into some old friends. The folk at the Temple might know I was back, but I didn't want word spreading too quickly. If rumours of an imperial investigator got out, I'd be inundated with every Marcus or Brutus pestering me for rewards for information of dubious worth.

So I left my bag in a cubicle, took a quick bath, then went out and changed into my good tunic. This one was of white linen and had a thin purple stripe, denoting me as a man of equestrian rank.

I wasn't entitled to wear it, so I was running quite a risk if anyone in authority challenged me. The penalties for impersonating a knight can be severe, but I reckoned it was worth the risk because it was a handy disguise. My brother, Primus, is now legally entitled to wear the equestrian garb, so I suppose I could have stretched a point and claimed familial rights, but the truth was the Juggler would back me in the unlikely event of anyone complaining. He didn't care how I got information, and an equestrian tunic was as good a disguise as any. It denotes the wearer as a man of wealth and distinction, which equates to having influence with the powers that be. I hoped the Tribune would be impressed enough to tell me what I needed to know.

The office of the *vigiles* is near the *Bouleuterion* where the local Council meets. It's a large building just off the lesser *agora* which is a small open space used for public meetings and as a market of sorts.

I swaggered in, as a man of my assumed rank would do, and spoke loudly to the poor watchman who was on reception duty. In moments, I was ushered through to the back and into a large office where Tribune Diocles met me with an appropriate amount of respect.

"Sempronius Secundus?" he asked.

"That's right," I confirmed, wincing a little that I'd used my formal name. "Although most people refer to me as Sempronius Scipio."

He smiled, clearly never having heard of me.

"Do sit down," he invited. "I have some wine if you would like?"

I liked. He poured, and we sipped politely while I gazed around the room.

Diocles was, I guessed, in his mid-thirties. Dark-haired, he had fine, chiselled features which would no doubt endear him to the female section of society. He exuded a manner of bluff confidence which I'd seen in others and which all too often seemed to be more bluff than actual confidence. He spoke Greek with a refined accent, showing he was an educated man, but then he would need to be to rise to the position of Tribune. It was a political office as much as anything, and I doubted very much that Diocles had risen through the ranks of the *vigiles*. More likely, he'd put himself forward when old Polybius retired and had been elected to the post.

The walls of his office were adorned with rotas and letters of commendation, while a stand in the corner behind him held a polished breastplate and a plumed helmet along with a short sword in a gleaming, leather scabbard. That would be his official uniform when he went out and about. For the moment, however, he wore a simple tunic.

The office was very warm, almost oppressively hot, in fact, and I could see beads of sweat on Diocles' face which matched the ones I could feel on my own skin. I'd probably need to visit the baths again after this meeting.

He sat facing me across a wide desk which had a couple of piles of wax tablets and another bundle of scrolls, but he pushed them aside to clear a space.

"Paperwork," he explained. "It never ends."

I gave a soft laugh to let him know I sympathised.

"So, what can I do for you?" he asked.

I smiled at him.

"I've been asked to investigate a theft and a murder which took place here in February. The murder victim's name was Gaius Aristides."

His expression became wary as he said, "I remember the case. Who, exactly, has asked you to investigate?"

In response, I tugged out the small pendant I wore under my tunic, and showed him the spear-carrying eagle.

"What's that?" he frowned.

I sighed. This was obviously going to be difficult.

"You don't know what this signifies?" I enquired, keeping my tone polite.

"No. Why don't you tell me? I've got a lot to do, you know, Sempronius Secundus."

It didn't take much to detect his new hostility.

I said, "I've been asked to look into it by someone in Rome. Someone with an office on the Palatine."

It was actually quite amusing to see his expression change again. This time he seemed more than a little nervous.

"Rome? The Palatine?"

"That's right. My employer is a man who has the ear of the Emperor. And he wants me to send him a report of what happened to Aristides. I was hoping you could help. Can you?"

Even Diocles detected the threat implicit in my words, but he wasn't done arguing.

"Why would anyone in Rome be interested in this?" he asked cautiously.

It was only then that I realised he did not know the significance of the missing amulet.

I told him, "Rome is concerned that anyone should steal from the Temple. But this is not a public enquiry, merely a quiet investigation to establish the facts. Can you help me?"

"Of course I can!" he blurted, almost spilling his wine.

"Excellent. I know a little, but perhaps you could explain the full story to me?"

"Yes, well, of course I can," he repeated nervously. "Aristides was stabbed. The killer escaped and we haven't been able to find him."

I sighed inwardly. As I'd feared, this was proving to be hard work.

"Perhaps we could go back a bit," I suggested. "Who was Aristides and where did he live?"

Diocles managed to pull himself together.

"Oh, right. Well, he's lived in Ephesus all his life. A rich man who dealt in fine arts and ancient artefacts. He moved in the highest circles in the city, you know. Well, nearly the highest. He was essentially a merchant, after all."

I smiled and nodded. Engaging in trade isn't favoured by Roman elites. Land is how the really top echelons earn their wealth. Engaging in trade may be essential for the economy of the Empire, but it isn't viewed as the occupation of a member of the senatorial class. Not that there were many Senators in Ephesus, so Aristides' profession probably didn't hinder him all that much. Money talks, after all.

Diocles informed me, "He has ... had a big house up in the north-eastern part of town, just the other side of the stadium."

"Was he married?" I enquired.

"His wife died a few years ago. Since then, he'd taken to having one of his female slaves run the household and help him entertain guests."

I frowned, "That's unusual, isn't it? He didn't free her and marry her?"

Diocles shook his head.

"No, he kept her as a slave. He was a lot older than her, you see."

I nodded. The old goat probably hadn't wanted a younger woman inheriting his wealth.

"How old was he?" I asked.

"Oh, nearly sixty."

"And the slave?"

"Just turned eighteen," Diocles said with a smirk he couldn't quite conceal.

"Well, it's not the first time that's happened," I reflected. "It's not as if the slaves have much choice in the matter."

Diocles gave a careless shrug in response to that, so I moved on.

"As for his business dealings, I take it everyone thought he was a respectable operator?"

"Oh, yes! There was never any suggestion he'd been involved with anything murky. Not until we examined his ledgers after he died, that is. We found a few odd things in there."

"So he'd been carrying on an illegal business for a while?"

"It looks like it. I'm not much of an expert when it comes to Accounts, but the Council put one of their scribes onto it, and he found ledgers containing records of dodgy deals going back forty years or so."

"Any names in there? Anything that would provide a clue as to who killed him?"

Diocles shook his head.

"I'm afraid not. He used initials to record who he'd done business with. All we found was that someone with a name beginning with D asked him to place someone called P within the Temple. It seems they paid him well, and also promised a share of the proceeds."

"The P would be Philippos, I presume?"

"That's what we think."

I nodded. The circumstantial evidence against Philippos was mounting up.

I asked, "But there is no clue as to who D might be?"

"Nothing at all."

"OK, so what about the night he was murdered? How did you hear about it, and what went on?"

Diocles took a gulp of his wine before beginning his account.

"We have watchmen on duty at the North Gate every night. You know, checking the wagons coming in and out."

I gave another nod. Like many cities, Ephesus has copied the edict passed in Rome which bans large wheeled vehicles from the streets during daylight hours. There is enough congestion as it is without cluttering the place with wagons.

"Fruit, grain and livestock coming in, manure going out?" I guessed.

He nodded, "That's right. The guards were called by a slave who told them his master had been stabbed. They went to the house, but they sent for me when they realised it was more than just a domestic argument."

"What time would that have been?"

He tapped his lips while he searched his memory.

"I was called shortly before midnight," he decided. "So I suppose the murder happened no more than an hour before that."

Which meant, I supposed, that the murderer had been out and about well after nightfall to arrive at the house so late. That raised a few other questions, but I wanted to keep Diocles' account in sequence as far as possible, so I asked him, "And what did you find?"

He took a moment to think before informing me, "Aristides had a room on the ground floor which had its own door leading to an alleyway down the side of the house. It seems he used this to admit people he didn't want seen coming in through his front door."

That made sense. If Aristides was a crook, he'd want to keep the shady part of his business as low profile as possible.

Diocles continued, "He'd told his freedman and one of his slaves to be present until he'd admitted an expected guest. Once that man arrived, he dismissed the freedman and the slave. But the slave stood outside the door. When he heard a crash, he called out to his master but got no answer. He tried to open the door, but it was barred, so he shouted for the freedman. By the time they'd broken their way in, the killer had gone, and Aristides was lying on the floor, covered in blood. He'd been stabbed at least three times. It was the sound of him falling that alerted the slave."

"So the killer got away through the side door?"

"That's right. The freedman rousted the house and sent some slaves to look for him, but he'd vanished."

"Was the murderer alone?"

Diocles looked perplexed, but nodded in the affirmative.

"That's what they said."

"There were no slaves or guards left outside while he came in to talk to Aristides?"

There was a moment's hesitation before he admitted, "Nobody saw them if there were any."

"Was there a moon that night?" I probed.

"I don't recall," Diocles admitted. "What are you getting at?"

"I'm thinking that the streets are usually very dark at night. Anyone who does go out and about would normally take a couple of slaves with torches to light their way. What I'm trying to discover is whether the killer did this, or whether he was on his own."

"Ah, I see. Sorry, I don't know."

Which wasn't much help. However, given the quick escape, I was guessing that the murderer had been on his own or possibly had only one companion. That meant he was either very confident or very foolish. Anyone wandering the streets at night has a fair chance of being robbed or worse. But to kill a man in his own house with a slave standing outside the door suggested the man we were looking for was a cool operator.

"What about the scene of the crime?" I asked. "You found some items from the Temple when you arrived?"

"That wasn't hard," Diocles snorted. "They were lying on Aristides' desk. All arranged as neatly as you like."

"As if he'd been checking to see they were all there?"

"I suppose so," he shrugged.

"But one item was missing?"

"So the High Priest told me when I took the recovered items back to him."

"You knew these things came from the Temple?" I pressed, wanting to check against what Restitutus had told me.

"Oh, yes. Their man, Niger, had told me all about what had been stolen. When I saw the bronze dagger, I knew this was stuff from the Temple theft."

"And is there any chance one of the household slaves or even the freedman could have taken the amulet before you arrived?"

"It's not likely," he assured me. "We searched the house thoroughly to check that the murder weapon wasn't there. You know, in case it had been one of the slaves who killed him and made up the story about a visitor."

That was something, at least, even if it had resulted from the impulsive response to blame the slaves.

Keen to tell me how efficient he had been, Diocles added, "Later, everything in the house was sold, and Pomponius Niger helped the auctioneers make up an inventory. Aristides had some very valuable things in his house, but the amulet wasn't among them."

"So it seems more than likely the killer did take it," I nodded. "In that case, what can you tell me about him? Do you have a description? The freedman and the slave must have seen him."

Diocles gave me a rueful smile.

"Apparently, he was wearing one of those Arab-style headdresses. You know, a cloth over the head, with a strip across his face. They only saw his eyes, which they both agreed were brown."

"Height? Accent?"

Diocles looked a bit confused, but eventually said, "They said he was quite tall, but not exceptionally so. They never mentioned his accent."

Which meant, we both knew, that he hadn't bothered asking them.

I moved on.

"OK, so what did you do next? The victim is dead, most of the stolen items left behind, and the murderer had vanished."

"Well, I alerted all the gate guards and told them to search the wagons as they left town. We kept a watch all the next day, but you can't search everyone. Hundreds of people come in and out of the city every day."

I could sympathise with that. He had tried, but looking for a man when you don't know what he looks like is virtually impossible.

"So he's vanished? And so has Philippos?"

"I'm afraid so. We couldn't even find where Philippos was lodging. It wasn't with Aristides, we know that."

I kept plugging away, although I was losing hope.

"Can I speak to the freedman and the slave?"

Diocles shook his head again. It was becoming a depressingly familiar response.

"The slaves were all sold," he told me. "I was going to torture a few of them to see if they were telling the truth, but the freedman insisted that only he and one slave saw the intruder, so there was no point. The Council decided to sell the household."

"What about the young girl Aristides had taken up with? Didn't he free her in his will?"

"No. She insisted he had meant to do that, but he'd not updated his will for years, so she was sold along with the rest of them. She screamed bloody murder about that, I can tell you. But she's gone, and so have all the others, scattered around the Empire by now, I imagine."

It was hard not to swear out loud. Three months is a long time, and my trail was well and truly cold.

"What about his other assets? The house and belongings?"

"They were auctioned off as well. He had no relatives, so everything was due to the city and the Emperor."

That was fairly standard. The city would keep half of the sale proceeds, with the rest going to the Imperial Treasury.

There were dead ends everywhere, but I had one hope left.

"What about the freedman?" I tried. "What was his name? Is he still around?"

"Hang on. I'll check."

He rose to his feet, walked round to the door behind me and opened it.

"Hammo! Come here a moment."

A rather scruffy watchman soon appeared. Diocles asked the questions, and the man told us, "The freedman was called Eteocles. I've no idea where he went afterwards, though."

"Can you describe him for me?" I asked as patiently as I could.

"He's an old guy," the watchman told me. "Must be near seventy years old. He's worked for Aristides for ages. Small chap, going bald, but with some white hair around his temples."

And that, I was dismayed to learn, was all I could glean from the *vigiles*. I thanked Diocles for his time, but it was hard to conceal my disappointment. He, in turn, was eager to know whether I'd put in a good word for him in my report.

"You seem to have been very thorough," I lied.

He was pathetically pleased at that, and saw me to the main door personally. Perhaps he wanted to make sure I was leaving.

So I stepped out into the late afternoon sun, looking around the bustle of the *agora* and wondering what to do next.

Get something to eat, I decided. Nightfall was only an hour or so away. If all I had to look forward to was a night in The Resting Place, I deserved a decent meal first.

There were several establishments bordering the *agora*, so I had plenty of choice, but I'd only taken a couple of steps to begin checking them out when a burly man in a plain tunic blocked my path. He held his arms out to prevent me circling around him, and he gave me a look which suggested I'd better listen to him. As he was a head taller than me, and a lot broader in the shoulders, I decided to let him have his say.

"Your name is Scipio?" he asked in an accent which I couldn't quite place. Not that it mattered much. The Empire contains people from all over the place, and you can hear dozens of different accents in a city like Ephesus. Besides, his words were clear enough.

"Who wants to know?" I retorted.

"The lady I serve."

"Lady? What lady?"

"She's waiting in that wine shop over there," he told me with a nod to the other side of the *agora*.

"Does she have a name?" I enquired.

"She'll tell you herself. As long as you are Scipio."

I gave him a friendly smile. I had no idea who this lady was, but I had wanted to find a wine shop anyway.

"I'm Scipio," I told him. "Lead on."

Chapter 4
Circe

She was sitting at a table for two in a corner of the busy wine shop. The hulking slave who led me to her remained outside where he joined another brute who was lounging against a wall, absently chewing on chunks of bread and cheese.

The lady smiled in greeting when she saw me, and waved a delicate hand in invitation.

I didn't hesitate. After all, I needed to eat, and she was as agreeable a dinner companion as I could have hoped for.

I guessed she was in her early twenties and, while she might not have been stunningly beautiful, she was certainly very pleasant to look at. She had a tanned complexion which would have shocked many upper class Roman matrons but which I thought looked amazing. She also sported a mane of dark hair which hung loose to indicate she was unmarried, and a pair of dazzlingly attractive blue eyes. She wore an expensive looking dress of pale blue, cut in the Greek style, and she wore silver Artemis ear rings as well as having several narrow, jangling bangles on her bare forearms. She was, in effect, a strange mixture of Greco-Roman conservatism and eastern exoticism.

She greeted me with a smile as I pulled out the wooden chair and sat opposite her. When she spoke, though, she took me by surprise by talking in Latin. Most people in the eastern half of the Empire speak Greek, and I wondered whether her use of Latin was because her Greek wasn't fluent or whether it was an attempt to keep our conversation more private. If it was the latter, she was probably wasting her time since most people are comfortable speaking either of the Empire's two main languages.

What she said was, though, just as surprising as her use of Latin.

She smiled, "I am glad to meet you at last. Fronto's description of you was very accurate."

I relaxed a little. If Fronto had spoken to her, that suggested she could probably be trusted.

"You know Fronto?" I asked.

"I work for him," she replied with a smile which set my pulse racing. "Or, rather, for the Juggler. Just like you do."

I smiled back at her. This was getting better all the time.

"His taste in employees is certainly improving," I said.

She ignored the compliment. Perhaps she was playing hard to get, but I wasn't going to be put off that easily.

She said, "So you are Scipio, also known as Sigma. You can call me Circe. Fronto asked me to help you with your investigation."

This was getting better all the time, but my brain still managed to override my more basic responses. I'd been in the imperial service long enough to know it was best to be cautious.

Carefully, never taking my eyes from her, I pulled out my identity pendant.

"Do you have one of these?" I asked her. "I've shown you mine, so you should show me yours."

She smiled sweetly as she replied, "It's not a very suitable item for a woman to wear, is it? But I do have this."

She raised her left hand, displaying what I had thought was a signet ring. It bore the same insignia as my pendant, although the design was so small the details were difficult to make out.

"On open display?" I queried.

She shrugged, "It saves half undressing to get a pendant out from under my robe."

That was a response which did nothing to decrease my heart rate.

"So your name is Circe? Are you going to turn me into a swine?"

She gave me a blank look which suggested she might never have heard of the spell her legendary namesake had placed on the crew of fabled Odysseus, but then she said, "You are a man. In my experience, it does not take much to turn any man into a pig."

Ouch, that hurt! Still, I managed to keep smiling. I hadn't had a close encounter with a pretty girl since that unfortunate event in Parthia, so I wasn't going to be put off that easily.

"You haven't experienced me yet," I pointed out.

That brought me a cool, appraising look.

"We are here to talk business," she reminded me.

"Here? It's a bit public, isn't it? I don't think speaking Latin will remove the risk of being overheard."

She looked around at the noisy, bustling wine shop, with its tables crammed close together and serving staff squeezing through the narrow gaps bearing platters and cups.

"Perhaps you are right," she agreed. "Then let us get to know one another while we eat. Later, we can go somewhere more private to discuss your investigation."

Every word she said seemed designed to tease me, but I had little option except to go along with her. We ordered wine and food. I plumped for spiced minced lamb served in scooped-out flour dumplings, while Circe opted for strips of pigeon and larks' eggs accompanied by a large bowl of olives and figs.

While we ate, I said, "So why don't you tell me about yourself? Fronto never warned me he was sending anyone to help me."

"I think it was a late decision. I'd been on Crete, so perhaps he thought I was close enough to get here in time."

She cocked her head to one side as she added, "I was very surprised I couldn't find you when I arrived. I've been here for five days now."

"Fronto's message to me was delayed," I explained. "But I'm here now."

She paused to allow herself to chew delicately on a morsel of food. Then she asked, "So what do you want to know?"

"As much as you feel able to tell me. If we are to work together, we should know each other, don't you think?"

"So tell me about yourself," she invited.

"You first," I countered. "You're the one who invited me here."

She considered this for a moment, then smiled again, revealing a set of perfect teeth.

"Very well, but there is not much to tell. I normally live in Carthage. It's unusual for me to go anywhere else. My parents were Roman citizens, but they both died. I had an older sister, but she died too, so I was raised by a friend of my father's who also happened to know Fronto's father. He used to do some work for Fronto, and that's how I got involved."

"Is that why you were on Crete?" I probed.

42

She returned another smile as she said, "As a matter of fact, yes. But it was a very simple business. Nothing like your mission here."

"And can you tell me your real name? I assume Circe is your code name?"

"Tertullia," she said softly. "Tertullia Tertia, but I much prefer Circe."

I could understand that. Roman parents have no real choice when it comes to naming their daughters. They are simply given the feminine version of their father's family name, and if there is more than one daughter, they are merely numbered. So Tertullia Tertia was the third daughter of a man whose *nomen* was Tertullius. My own *cognomen* of Secundus resulted from a similar laziness on the part of my father, so I understood why this glamorous girl preferred to use an alias.

I smiled, "If that is what you prefer, then I shall call you Circe."

She hadn't told me much, but it was a start.

She said, "And you are Scipio, but you are not part of the Cornelius family? I thought only the Cornelii used the Scipio *cognomen*?"

I laughed, "It's a nickname I like. I was given it here in Ephesus, as a matter of fact."

"Oh? How did that happen?"

"It was at a gymnasium I used to visit regularly. There was a *pankration* instructor who went by the name of Hannibal. I managed to put him on his back during one practice bout, so he gave me the name Scipio because, just like the famous general, I'd defeated Hannibal. It stuck, and I liked it, so I kept it."

"*Pankration?*" she asked with a flirtatious smile.

"It's an ancient Greek style of fighting," I told her. "It involves wrestling, punching and kicking. Pretty much anything goes in *pankration*."

"And you are an expert in it?" she asked, her gorgeous eyes widening with apparent interest.

"Not really. I did it as a bit of exercise. I just got lucky one time with Hannibal. He rarely lost a bout, which is why my nickname became popular with the others who attended the sessions."

She continued to smile as she said, "Fronto told me your real name is Sextus Sempronius Secundus. He said you prefer Scipio, but he didn't say why."

She was probing now, but this was no real secret.

I explained, "It's a bit of a long story. My father was the grandson of a freedman. He had full citizen rights, but he was determined to be more Roman than the Romans because he felt that having British ancestry might be held against him. It was a daft notion, of course, because nobody in Rome bothers about your ancestry as long as you behave like a Roman."

"And have money," she put in with an unexpected but refreshing flash of cynicism.

"Yes, I suppose so. Anyway, my father joined the Legions and rose to become a Centurion. He was based in Syria, which is where he met my mother. He brought her back to Rome when he retired from the service."

"You must get your looks from her," Circe observed.

I couldn't deny it. My pale olive skin and dark hair was definitely not inherited from my father.

"And your name?" Circe prompted. "How did you come to be known as Secundus?"

"As I say, my old man was ultra-Roman. My brother was born in August, so he was named Sextus because, in the old calendar, August was the sixth month. Four years later, I was also born in August, so I was given the same name."

I grimaced as I recounted, "My father didn't have much imagination. I expect it was beaten out of him during his stint in the army."

"So both you and your brother were called Sextus?" Circe grinned cheekily.

"Which is why," I nodded, "he was given the cognomen Primus and I was called Secundus."

"Now you know how women feel," Circe said, softening her words with an amused smile. "But I detect some bitterness. Is it simply that you don't like being Second while your brother is First?"

"It wasn't just the name," I told her. "But what it signified. Primus had everything lavished on him, and my father even spent a huge portion of his pension setting him up in business."

"And you, poor Secundus, got nothing?"

"I had my mother," I replied. "But my father died when I was twelve years old, and Primus, who was officially a man by then, inherited everything."

I tried to portray a carefree attitude as I told her, "As you've guessed, Primus didn't like me any more than I liked him. So, as soon as I was old enough, I packed up and left home."

"And you ended up in Ephesus?"

"After a short stay in Athens," I confirmed.

"So how did you get involved with the Juggler? Equestrians don't usually do this sort of work, do they?"

I glanced down at the purple stripe on my tunic.

"Ah," I sighed. "That. Well, let's just say I'm in disguise."

I could tell that amused her.

"Fronto said you liked taking risks. So how did you get involved with him?"

"That's easy," I told her. "I've known Fronto since I was a boy. When he discovered I had been taken on as head of security at the Temple, he contacted old Restitutus and recruited me."

"And now you are back," she smiled. "And we need to work out how to recover what was taken."

We'd finished eating by this time. Outside, the sun was sinking quickly. I'd heard my father claim that in the far north of Europe the evenings last a long time and the sun takes an age to set. Here in Ephesus, though, the transition from daylight to full darkness takes only a few minutes.

Many of the wine shop's patrons were heading for home. Others, who presumably had slaves nearby to light their way, were still chatting, laughing and drinking. As far as I was concerned, I could have sat there all night. Circe fascinated me in a way few other women ever had, and I felt incredibly relaxed in her company. For someone like me who is always playing a role, that was a very unusual situation especially because she, too, seemed genuinely interested in me.

But I managed to retain some degree of professionalism even though it was very hard concentrating when I looked into her wonderful eyes.

"So where do you propose we go to talk?" I asked her.

"Where are you staying?" she responded.

"The Resting Place. It's down near the Magnesian Gate."

"What is it like?"

"It's a dump," I assured her.

"Then we shall go to my house."

"You have a house?"

"I am renting it."

I said, "The Juggler must be paying you a lot more than he's paying me."

She gave me yet another disarming smile which threatened to turn my knees to jelly.

"Did I forget to tell you I am very rich?"

My heart began thumping again. She could very well be the woman of my dreams. But there was one other thing I needed to know.

"You don't have a husband I should know about, do you?"

"Not at the moment," she replied with an enigmatic smile.

I didn't press her. Perhaps she was widowed or divorced, so it was a subject which might upset her. I couldn't believe she had never had a husband because most Roman girls are married by the age of sixteen if not earlier, especially rich ones.

But it seemed my path had been cleared, which only added to my mounting excitement. Still, I retained sufficient manners to pay the bill before escorting her to the door. I couldn't help noticing that, once she was on her feet, she was quite tall for a woman and very slender in build. But she moved with a grace and elegance that spoke of a wealthy upbringing.

Outside, her two slaves had lit a couple of torches. They led the way when Circe told them we were going to her home.

The streets were fairly quiet, the rumble of wagon wheels on cobbles not yet having started, while most citizens had retired to their homes for the night.

As we walked, with her hand on my arm, we spoke as naturally as if we'd known each other for years, although our conversation was limited to the delights of Ephesus and the glory of the Temple. It seemed that Circe had spent most of her five days here doing a lot of sightseeing, and she was enamoured by the wonders of the city.

"It's a lovely place," she said.

I couldn't disagree. And it was getting lovelier by the minute.

The house she was renting was not far away, down near the Gate of Herakles in the south section of town. It was a large home, occupying almost an entire block on its own. A door slave opened up for us, barring the door behind us. Circe dismissed the two slaves who had lit our way, and then led me through the atrium to what was obviously a peristyle garden in a central courtyard. It was too dark to make out very much, but we followed a gravel path to the rear of the building which obviously had two storeys. I could see the dim glimmer of lamps in a couple of rooms, but most of the place seemed dark and unoccupied.

"You are staying here by yourself?" I asked in amazement. The place was big enough for a large family plus an army of slaves.

"It's only for a short time," she replied dismissively. "And it provides plenty of privacy."

A short, squat, elderly maid holding an oil lamp appeared in the doorway ahead of us.

"Good evening, Domina," she said in deferential greeting to Circe.

"Good evening, Helena."

There was no other exchange, but the slave woman seemed to know Circe's intentions. After giving me only the briefest of incurious glances, the old woman led the way inside, then up a narrow flight of steps.

My heart was doing gymnastics again. It may have been dark outside, but the evening was still young. I'd expected us to go into one of the ground floor reception rooms where we would be able to discuss the investigation into Aristides' murder, but as I followed Circe's swaying hips up the stairs, my hopes began to rise.

I was not disappointed. The maid showed us into a spacious bedroom where oil lamps had already been lit. She closed the door once we had stepped inside, and Circe turned to face me, stepping close to wordlessly wrap her arms around me. She reached up to kiss me on the lips. Naturally, I responded eagerly, and I know she could feel just how eager my body was.

In moments, her robe was on the floor, revealing her slim body, small breasts and inviting hips. Then my tunic followed her robe, and we staggered to the bed which was piled high with thick blankets.

There was no talking as we joined together, her body arching beneath me as I moved in rhythm with her.

I must admit it was an intoxicating experience. I'd only just met this young woman and already we were making love in a frenzied yet passionate way, both of us gasping and moaning until we shuddered almost simultaneously and I slumped down on top of her.

We lay like that for a long time, her arms and legs holding me to her. Then we moved to lie side by side.

"That was nice," she whispered as she nibbled at my ear.

"It was more than nice," I assured her.

It was nice the next time, too.

Chapter 5
Teamwork

We shared another boisterous encounter the following morning which left me feeling both elated and sated. Afterwards, Circe led me back downstairs and out into the garden where the dumpy old maid, Helena, served us a breakfast of bread and honey.

I'd expected that there might be a sense of awkwardness between us after the events of the night, but Circe was relaxed and affable, delighting in the arrival of a few small birds who hopped around the garden in search of any snacks we might drop in their path.

While she crumbled pieces of bread and tossed them to the grass to entice the birds closer, I looked around. The garden contained several trees to provide shade over and above that given by the surrounding colonnaded walkway. Small shrubs were dotted around in a seemingly random way which was nevertheless easy on the eye. The garden was, in traditional Roman style, surrounded on all sides by the house itself. A quick count of the number of shuttered windows confirmed that this place was indeed a very large home.

"So who normally lives here?" I asked.

Circe shrugged, "I have no idea. When I knew I was coming here, I sent one of my freedmen ahead and he arranged it with the landlord."

I hadn't seen any freedman around, but Circe explained that she'd sent him back to Carthage.

"I honestly can't see us being here all that long, can you?" she pointed out.

I was forced to agree, but I made a few more gentle enquiries and discovered that, apart from Helena and the two bodyguards who were named Agon and Diomedes, Circe had brought no other retainers with her. The only other staff on the premises were a cook, the door slave, a housemaid and a gardener.

"They came with the place," Circe explained.

Helena brought jugs of wine, water and fruit juice. I caught her giving me an appraising look, but she turned away as soon as our eyes met. I gained the impression she was evaluating me, and I guessed I was not the first man Circe had brought home. That shouldn't have bothered me, but it did.

I noticed, however, that while Circe had spoken in Greek to the bodyguards, and had continued to talk to me in Latin, her few words to Helena were in a language I was not familiar with.

"That sounds like some eastern tongue," I remarked casually.

"It's Punic," she informed me. "A lot of people in Africa still speak it."

"Ah, that explains it. I learned Aramaic from my mother, and the languages might be related. The first settlers in Carthage came from Tyre, after all."

"That was hundreds of years ago," Circe replied. "I expect the languages have moved apart since then."

"Yes, I expect they have. I certainly can't follow what you say to Helena. Does she not speak Latin or Greek at all?"

"She understands Latin reasonably well," Circe told me. "But she prefers her native tongue. I like to keep in practice with it myself."

"And you speak Greek," I pointed out. "So why do you switch to Latin when we are talking?"

Her reply was merely a shrug.

"It's the language I usually speak at home," she explained. Then, becoming more brisk and abandoning her attempts to lure the tiny birds, she said, "Now we need to discuss your investigation. Why don't you tell me what you found out yesterday."

So I began my tale, starting at the Temple, then moving on to what I had discovered from Diocles, the Tribune of *vigiles*.

She let me talk without interruption, sipping at a glass of pomegranate juice while she listened to my tale.

When I'd brought her up to date, she observed, "You have only been here one day and you've found all that out? I'm impressed."

"Not that it's done me much good," I replied, although I was secretly delighted by her compliment. "The trail is cold, and I've only got a couple more leads I can follow."

"The painter and Aristides' freedman?" she guessed.

"That's right. I don't expect I'll get much from Leonides, the painter, but I'd like to find out a bit more about the job he was called away for. It seems more than coincidental that he just happened to be away when Philippos turned up."

"It was planned, then?" she asked.

"I think it probably was, but I'd like to check."

"Does it matter?" Circe challenged.

"Not directly in helping find Philippos and the amulet, but if that level of forward planning went into the operation, it suggests there must be something really important about that amulet."

"Apart from its historical significance, you mean?"

"I'm not sure what I mean. There are too many unanswered questions at the moment."

She pointed out, "It could simply have been that Aristides was greedy. If he'd been dealing in stolen artefacts for years, maybe he found a client who wanted the amulet and he recruited Philippos."

"Aristides was the brains behind it, you mean? Yes, that's possible, although it doesn't explain where his killer fits in the picture. Who was he, and why didn't he take all the stolen items when he left the murder scene?"

"Perhaps he didn't have time?" Circe suggested. "If the slave was hammering on the door, maybe he took fright and ran away without them."

"Maybe," I frowned, unconvinced. To me, the killer seemed like a very cool character indeed. I doubted he'd be scared off very easily.

"Perhaps we should consider the amulet," Circe said. "Why would someone take that but leave behind Hector's dagger which must be more valuable? Stealing from the Temple was a huge risk, so somebody must want that amulet very badly. The question is why?"

"That's a good thought," I nodded. "What possible reasons could there be?"

She smiled as she held up a hand, lifting her fingers to enumerate the points she listed.

"First, there's simple greed. Rich people like having antique objects, especially if the objects are linked to a famous person, and they don't come much more famous than Alexander."

"True, but Hector's dagger belonged to a famous person as well."

"If it is genuine," she countered. "The amulet definitely belonged to Alexander. It also has intrinsic value because it is made from gold."

"That's a fair point," I agreed.

She went on, "Second is the amulet's symbolic meaning. Perhaps someone wanted to upset the Emperor."

"That's dangerous, but I see what you mean. If they get away with it, they can gloat about stealing something which had been donated by an emperor."

"It seems unlikely, though," Circe decided before moving on. "Third, we should consider the amulet's history. Before Alexander obtained it, where had it come from, and what did it signify?"

"I have no idea," I admitted. "And I don't think anyone knows for sure."

"You should ask your friend, the High Priest."

"I did ask him about it. He didn't mention anything about its history. I doubt he knows."

"Bulls are important in many myths and religious beliefs," Circe reminded me. "Especially in the east, which may well be where Alexander found it."

"So a bull-worshipping cult stole it, you mean?"

"It's not impossible," she said.

"There aren't that many around now, though," I pointed out.

"There used to be bull worship on Crete," she reminded me. "They were famous for it. Remember the legend of the Minotaur."

"That's so ancient it's more like fable than history," I argued. "But there was also bull worship in Egypt."

"Apis, you mean? That died out as well. Once the first Ptolemy took over, he merged Apis worship with a Greek god and called the new deity Serapis. I dare say some Egyptians still hanker for a bull-headed god, but I doubt any modern devotees of Serapis would welcome you reminding them of the bull worship. It's too strange for most people's beliefs. No, I think you are missing the obvious one."

"Mithras?" I replied. "Yes, it is the obvious one, but I can't see any of his followers stealing from the Emperor. Mithras is most popular in the Army."

Circe nodded, "And it's a most secretive cult in any event. If a local Mithraic group are behind it, we'll never find out who they are."

"We're struggling as it is," I sighed.

Circe brightened as she told me, "To be honest, the simplest solution is probably the correct one. I'll wager Aristides was behind it. He could have arranged for the painter to be lured away, then hired Philippos to steal a load of small items from the Temple. He probably had a buyer lined up, but there was a falling out when it came to sharing the loot, and Aristides was killed during the argument."

I chewed my lower lip while I considered that. It was, in truth, difficult to argue against. Aristides was probably rich enough to have funded a scheme like that. But it still left the nagging question of why the killer had left most of the stolen items behind. If he'd been prepared to kill Aristides for them, why hadn't he taken them with him when he ran?

"I'd really like to talk to Aristides' freedman, Eteocles," I said. "He might be able to shed some light on what happened."

"But you don't know where he is."

"I'm afraid not."

Circe gave me a broad, beautiful smile as she suggested, "Then why don't you go and see the painter while I ask around and see if I can track down Eteocles?"

I had no better ideas, so that was what we did. With Agon and Diomedes walking a few steps behind us, we left the house and headed towards the centre of town and the main *agora*. Circe had decided to start by visiting Aristides' house and speaking to the new occupants. There was an outside chance they might know what had become of the old freedman. Since Aristides had lived in the north-west corner of the city, she had to go past the *agora* in any case.

"It's a marvellous place," she enthused when we reached the huge, ornamental archways which led onto the wide, open space of the *agora*. This main plaza was much larger than the one which housed the *Bouleuterion,* and it was surrounded by many magnificent buildings. A little further on was another plaza in front of the city's column-fronted theatre.

I must confess I enjoyed that walk. The weather was warm, the streets alive with sights and sounds which seemed even more vibrant than usual, and I had a gorgeous girl with me. What more could I ask?

Well, a solution to the crimes, obviously, but I didn't really think about that until Circe pecked me on the cheek and said farewell, heading further north, while I scouted around the side streets beside the theatre plaza in search of Leonides.

After making enquiries in a few of the local shops, I found his home and studio in a narrow alley just south of the main plaza. There was a bored-looking woman in the studio. She was sitting at a table, reading a scroll which seemed to be part of a book, but she put it aside when I entered the small establishment.

"Good morning, Sir. What can I help you with?"

She was, I guessed, well past forty and looked as if every year had taken a heavy toll, but her smile seemed genuine enough.

"I'm looking for Leonides, the artist," I told her.

"This is his workplace," she said, gesturing around the walls.

It was, indeed, the sort of place an artist would produce. It smelled of fresh paint, and the walls were covered by frescoes portraying all sorts of designs and images. One wall showed mythical figures and gods, with satyrs prancing, Athena and her owl, Zeus casting thunderbolts and Herakles strangling the Nemean lion. Another bore abstract designs in both modern and ancient styles, while a third showed scenes from the legend of the Trojan war. Every image was magnificently drawn and coloured. Crammed around the floor were small pedestals bearing statues which had been painted in a riot of bright colours. Miniature gods, goddesses and heroes stared back at me with bright eyes, daring me to impugn the skill of the painter.

Leonides had a reputation, and it was well deserved.

"Is Leonides here?" I asked her.

"He's working," she informed me. "It's a routine house job, but he'll be away all day."

I clucked my tongue in disappointment.

"Could you tell me where he is? I really need to talk to him."

She regarded my equestrian tunic and clearly decided I was one customer she didn't want to let go.

"If it's a quote for a job you are after, give me your details and I'll send him to see you first thing tomorrow."

"No, it's not that. I'm not looking for his artistic skills. I need to talk to him about the job he did in Athens recently."

She pulled a sour face.

"That! It's just as well it paid good money. The whole thing was ridiculous if you ask me!"

"Oh? What was ridiculous about it?"

I guessed this was Leonides' wife. She certainly seemed to be very familiar with his business affairs.

"Well, going off like that for six weeks. And just to paint some frescoes. And then the woman who hired him ran out of money and sent him packing before he'd finished."

"A woman?"

"A young floozy if you ask me," she muttered darkly. "It's just as well I trust Leonides, but she was a bad influence on Pollio."

"Pollio?"

"Our grandson. He's Leonides' apprentice. The woman turned his head completely."

That was the voice of a protective grandmother speaking, I knew.

"Do you happen to know this woman's name?" I enquired.

She frowned, her already wrinkled brow developing deeper furrows, before saying, "Julia. Julia Petronia."

I thanked her, although it did little more than apply a label to a person. But it was another person in the wider scheme of things, and I wondered what relationship, if any, this Julia Petronia had to Aristides.

"So where can I find Leonides?" I asked her.

She obviously wasn't keen on letting me visit her husband while he was working, but the equestrian tunic worked its magic again.

"He's at the home of Marcus Porcius. It's near Hadrian's Gate. Big house with a blue door and a couple of cypress trees outside."

"Thanks. That's a big help."

I left the central area and followed one of the main streets down towards Hadrian's Gate. It's quite near the Magnesian Gate in the south-east of town, both gates giving access to the city from the hinterland where most of the produce the citizens rely on is grown.

55

I found the house easily enough. A blue door and some cypress trees. The door slave who answered my knock listened to my enquiry, then went off to consult his master.

Marcus Porcius grudgingly admitted me, no doubt because I was still wearing the equestrian tunic with its thin purple stripe, but he wasn't happy about it.

"I'm having my dining room redecorated," he informed me sulkily. "I need it finished quickly, so I'd rather you didn't take Leonides away for very long. I'm paying him a lot of money to get this job done on time."

I promised I wouldn't disrupt the work any longer than a few minutes.

"This is an official enquiry, though," I told him pompously. "Tribune Diocles knows all about it."

The name-dropping worked, so I was shown to the dining room which had been emptied of furniture and was now full of trestle tables, pots and brushes, with a grey-haired, broad-shouldered man busy working on a depiction of Achilles fighting Hector, while a teenage lad was stirring a pot, obviously mixing more paint for the craftsman. From the look of things, Marcus Porcius need not have worried. It looked to me as if the frescoes were almost done. Dolphins and sea nymphs decorated one wall, dancing around an image of Neptune – or Poseidon as he was known in these parts – while hunting scenes were played out on another wall, and Dionysius sat at table on the main wall. Again, I was impressed by the standard of Leonides' work.

The man himself grunted at me to wait until he'd put the finishing touches to Achilles' armour. I didn't argue, but stood admiring his work. Leonides is a big chap, a bit taller than me, and certainly broader in the shoulder. His broken nose suggests he was not averse to fisticuffs in his youth, and his manner, as I knew from past experience, was usually less than friendly. But most patrons put up with his manner because he was one of the best artists around when it came to frescoes.

Eventually, he put down his brush and turned to me.

Marcus Porcius, who was obviously intent on listening in to my interview, introduced me.

"I know young Master Scipio," Leonides rumbled before giving me a nod and adding, "Nice to see you again, young Sir. You've gone up in the world."

I smiled, concealing my embarrassment. I'd forgotten that Leonides had known I was no knight.

"It's a recent thing," I told him, gesturing down at my striped tunic.

"So what can I do for you?" he asked pointedly.

"It's about your recent job in Athens," I told him. "I'd like to know who hired you, how it was done, and what happened."

He sighed, shot a brief look at his grandson who lowered his head to avoid meeting his grandfather's gaze, then began his account.

"I was approached by a man who said he worked for an Athenian merchant. This merchant had recently married a young wife and she wanted her house decorated by me. He said she'd seen me working at the Temple and wanted me to create the same designs as the frescoes there."

He snorted, "Daft idea! But he offered a ridiculous amount of money, so I took the job. Me and young Pollio here sailed across and started work."

"What was the name of this merchant?" I interrupted.

"Petronius something or other. He was Italian, but was based in Athens, so his wife said. But he was away, sailing all the way to Hispania, and she wanted the work done while the house was relatively empty. That's what she said, anyway."

"That would be Julia Petronia?" I enquired.

He gave a nod, his face growing stern.

"Aye, that's her. A flighty young thing if you ask me. Flirted with poor Pollio here something rotten, even though she must have been ten years older than him."

Young Pollio, who I guessed was around fifteen, kept his head firmly lowered, but I could see his ears turning red with embarrassment. He looked as if he wanted to hide beneath the sheets that had been laid down to protect the floor mosaics.

I asked Leonides, "Can you describe her?"

"She's in her twenties, I'd say. I didn't pay her much attention, but she's got dark hair."

That didn't help much.

"Do you know if she was Athenian herself?"

"I have no idea," he replied with a shrug. "She spoke Greek with an accent, but I couldn't place it."

"And whereabouts in Athens is the house?"

57

"Just outside the city, on the road to Marathon," he informed me.

"Can you describe it for me? In case I want to find it for myself?"

He gave me a weary look, but nodded, "It's a big old place. A former farm turned into a country mansion, with lots of extra rooms added on piecemeal. It was a strange place, though."

"Strange?" I prompted, knowing Leonides would not elaborate unless asked directly.

"It was like a mausoleum," he grunted. A great big place with lots of rooms and hardly anyone there. Most of the rooms had no furniture either. The woman said they'd only bought it recently and she wanted it decorated before her husband came back."

"That sounds sensible," I observed, wanting to keep him talking.

He snorted again, saying, "It still seemed weird to me. I mean, they hardly had any domestic staff at all. Just a handful of slaves who spent most of their time lounging about. And she never had any visitors the whole time we were there."

It sounded eerily similar to the situation in Circe's rented home, but it seemed to me exactly as it would if a newly married couple had purchased an old property and were trying to do it up, so I moved the conversation on.

"So you finished the job?"

"No!" he grunted. "She kept finding more and more work for me to do, and I went along with it, but then one day she comes and says she's run out of money. She was very sorry, shedding tears and all, but the upshot was we packed up and came home."

"With unpaid bills due?" I asked.

"No, she paid for what we'd done, but she said there was no more, so could we please leave her."

Marcus Porcius, who had been listening with avid interest, interjected, "Never allow a woman to control the household budget! They have no concept of proper financial control."

I ignored him, but I couldn't think of anything else to ask Leonides except the important question.

"Do you happen to know whether she knows anyone in Ephesus?"

After a moment's thought, he said, "She never mentioned it."

"Are you sure? I wondered whether she might have known Aristides."

He frowned at that.

"Who?"

Marcus Porcius gasped, "Aristides? The man who was murdered?"

I shot him a dark look, but gave a nod of agreement.

"That's the one."

"I never heard her mention him," Leonides told me.

I looked at Pollio who retained an intense interest in the pot he was stirring.

"What about you, lad? Did you ever hear her mention anyone in Ephesus?"

"No, Sir," the boy responded in a quiet voice, his face blushing a furious red.

So that was that. Another dead end. I could always go to Athens and try to track down this Julia Petronia, but I wasn't convinced it would be worth my while. It would be a last throw of the dice if I had to resort to that.

I thanked the painter and his apprentice, told Marcus Porcius I was immensely grateful to him and would mention his cooperation in my report, then headed back to Circe's house. I was tempted to pop into The Resting Place to collect my things, but I didn't think walking in there wearing a purple stripe was a good idea. That's how rumours get started.

So I plodded all the way across town once again, hoping Circe had had more luck than I had.

Chapter 6
Seeking Inspiration

Circe was already back by the time I reached the house. She was sheltering from the blazing sun in the shade of the portico which surrounded the garden, sitting at a small, folding table on which sat a tray of bread, cheese, olives and succulent sausages. It looked almost as delicious as Circe herself.

She gave me a look of resignation as I crossed the garden towards her.

"I hope you had more luck than I did," she said with an air of weary frustration.

"I found Leonides," I replied as I took a seat opposite her. "Not that it did me a great deal of good. But I take it you had no luck tracking down Eteocles?"

She paused because Helena had magically appeared at my shoulder. Circe spoke to her briefly in what I knew now must be Punic, and the old servant shuffled away again.

"She'll bring some more food," Circe explained.

I had already grabbed a sausage and a chunk of bread, so I acknowledged her implicit accusation of theft with a guilty smile.

Helena soon brought extra dishes to top up the table, then poured me a cup of watered wine. She vanished inside the house almost before I had time to thank her.

While I devoured another spicy sausage, Circe informed me, "Nobody at the house knew anything about what had happened to Aristides' household. The new owners bought the place in an auction, just as Diocles told you. It had been cleared out by the time they moved in."

"I can't say I'm surprised," I shrugged through a mouthful of bread.

"I even asked some of the neighbours," she went on. "But all they could tell me was that all the property had been sold, including the slaves. Some of them knew Eteocles, of course, but none of them would admit to knowing what had become of him. I get the feeling Aristides wasn't regarded quite as well as Diocles led you to believe."

"Oh? The neighbours suspected his dodgy dealings, did they?"

"I suspect it's more that they simply didn't like him all that much."

"Did any of them say anything specific?" I asked.

She shook her head, setting her Artemis ear rings swaying in a delightfully appealing way.

"Nothing specific. It's just a feeling I gained. None of them really wanted to talk about him at all."

"Being murdered lowers the tone of the neighbourhood, I expect."

She folded her lips in disapproval of my levity, and quickly changed the subject.

"What about you? What did Leonides tell you?"

Between mouthfuls, I gave her the details of what I'd learned from the old painter.

"At least you got a name and a location," she said once I'd finished my account. "That's something to follow up."

"Except I'm not sure the Juggler would want me to go to Athens to investigate such a tenuous lead."

"It's the only lead we've got," she pointed out with ruthless logic. "And going to Athens might not be such a bad idea."

"What do you mean?"

Her smile told me she'd had an idea which she was about to enjoy revealing.

"I've been thinking," she told me. "I still believe Aristides was the brains behind the operation, but I've been wondering who his buyer might have been."

"And?"

"And it occurred to me that we've missed the obvious connection."

"Which is?"

"Macedonia."

I shot her a quizzical look. Whatever she was driving at wasn't all that obvious to me.

I said, "Macedonia is where Alexander came from, but I don't see a connection with our case."

"Philippos," she reminded me. "You said the slave at the Temple told you Philippos was from Macedonia."

I had forgotten that. Yes, Herakleon had mentioned it.

"So you think Philippos was sent by someone in Macedonia to recover an amulet which had once belonged to Alexander the Great?"

"Why not? It makes sense, doesn't it?"

"I suppose there could be a link," I said warily, not wanting to dismiss her idea out of hand. After all, it was better than any idea I'd come up with.

I asked her, "But why would the amulet be important to someone from Macedonia? There's no history of bull worship in Macedonia, is there?"

"I have no idea," she replied, "but that's not the point. The point is that it belonged to Alexander. Most of his treasure was appropriated by his generals after his death. There was probably a lot placed in his tomb, but that's been sealed up now, and the amulet is the only artefact with any known link to him. I can see some rich man in Macedonia lusting after it solely because of that."

"What makes you think it's a man?" I challenged, smiling to soften the question.

"Because it's usually men who collect things like that."

That was me told.

"All right," I conceded, "let's say you are right. How would I go about finding this man? Macedonia is a big place."

"I can't help you with that," Circe said with disarming honesty. "But maybe Fronto could give you some names to check out. I'm sure the Juggler has a list of names of people who are kept under surveillance."

That was true enough. Emperors are many things, and one of those things is paranoid. They suspect everyone of plotting against them, so they like to know who has been saying or doing what.

"So," Circe went on, warming to her theme, "I think your next step should be to go to Athens. It's easy enough to get a boat from here. You can write to the Juggler and ask for a list of possible suspects, and you can look up this Julia woman while you are waiting for a reply. From Athens, it's easy enough to travel up to Macedonia."

"I notice you are talking about this as if I'm going on my own," I remarked.

"I'm afraid you will be," Circe said apologetically.

She leaned across the table to place a warm hand on my forearm.

"I need to get back to Carthage, my love. I'm not really supposed to be here at all, you know. In fact, the Juggler doesn't know I'm here. It was Fronto who asked me to help you."

I put my other hand on top of hers, squeezing gently.

"I'm glad he did," I told her earnestly.

She smiled, "I think he was worried you might be walking into some deep plot against the Emperor. At least now you'll be able to tell him it was probably just a robbery and that any plot will likely be found in Macedonia."

I thought she was jumping to a few conclusions, but I nodded because I couldn't think of any argument against her theory. There were a lot of unanswered questions, but Athens was indeed the only lead I had left.

"I'd prefer to stay around here a bit longer," I told her, looking into her inviting eyes.

"So would I. But I really do need to get back to Carthage."

"You could come to Athens with me," I suggested hopefully.

She gave me a smile full of regret.

"No, Scipio. I'm sorry. Like I said, I'm not supposed to be here. In fact, when you write to the Juggler, please don't even mention me. I'd rather he didn't know I didn't go straight back to where I'm supposed to be working. You can tell Fronto if you like, but don't let it go any further than that."

I was feeling rather despondent by this time. My investigation had not really uncovered much in the way of hard evidence, and I'd only spent one night with Circe. It wasn't nearly long enough. And if she returned to Carthage, I might never see her again. The Juggler knew my particular skills meant I was of most use to him in the east. With relations with Parthia always on a knife edge, I doubted he'd let me sail half way along the coast of North Africa just to meet up with a girl.

She must have seen my dismay, because she said, "I can stay another few days, perhaps. It depends on how long it takes to find a ship to take me to Carthage."

I brightened at that.

She smiled sweetly as she went on, "And you should write out a report. Take it to the Temple, and you can let the High Priest know what you intend to do next."

"Yes, I suppose I need to do that in any case."

"So we will have a few days together," she assured me. "What would you like to do with that time?"

I looked up as if considering the question deeply.

"Well, I would like to go to the gymnasium."

She slapped my hand.

"The gymnasium!" she laughed. "What on earth for?"

"To do a bit of exercise."

"In that case, I shall come with you."

"No, you won't. They don't let women into the gymnasium."

"Why ever not?"

"Because of all the naked men who pose and strut around, I expect. Women aren't allowed to see any of that in case they develop hot flushes."

She regarded me with a teasing smile as she said, "In that case, why don't you come upstairs and you can show me what I'll be missing. Then maybe we can do some exercising of our own."

That was the best offer I'd had since before breakfast, so I put aside all thoughts of Athens, Macedonia, amulets and the gymnasium and practically carried her up the stairs.

Chapter 7
Hannibal

We spent the rest of that day in bed, taking only a short break to lounge on couches in the dining room and enjoy a dinner of wild fowl served with a date and wine sauce, with honeyed pastries to follow. It was an over-indulgent waste of time which should have been spent on my investigation, I know, but the thought of losing Circe when I'd only just met her meant I could not bear to let her out of my sight that day. I didn't dare admit it, but I think I was in love.

Circe was much more practical. She obviously enjoyed our love-making, but she was quite pragmatic about the limited time we had left together.

"Let's enjoy it while we can," she told me.

We certainly did, but by the following morning, I knew I needed to get back to the outside world.

"I'll need to collect my things from The Resting Place," I told her. "I haven't slept in the room I rented for two nights now. I'll be lucky if my stuff hasn't been stolen or thrown out."

"And I will need to send Agon to the harbour to find a ship," she sighed.

Giving me a gentle prod on the chest with one beautifully manicured finger, she added, "And you need to write that report. Do you want some parchment and ink?"

"I'll write it at the Temple," I replied. "I need to talk to Restitutus and Niger anyway."

"Good, but don't take all day. I want you back here."

I grinned at that. Rising from the bed, I picked up my old tunic which had been washed and neatly folded by Helena.

"Aren't you wearing your purple stripe today?" Circe asked.

"Not today. There's no need, and it would look out of place in the inn. I think I'll also go to the gymnasium. There's an old friend I'd like to catch up with."

She responded with a smile which suggested she thought the idea of the gymnasium was funny, but all she said was, "I'll get Helena to wash your striped tunic then. You never know when you might need it again."

She rose from the bed, moving seductively towards me and pressing her naked body against me as she wrapped her arms around me and placed her lips against mine in a deep, passionate kiss.

"Hurry back," she breathed when she at last pulled away.

"Stop it!" I hissed, slapping her backside playfully. "I'll never get out of this room if you keep doing things like that."

She laughed happily, giving me a gentle shove towards the door.

"Go on, then. Go and strut around in the nude. But don't forget to write that report and send it off."

I left, feeling relaxed and happy, and stepped out into another hot day in Ephesus. The streets were as crowded and noisy as ever, but I was in no real rush. I began mentally composing my report to Sempronius Rufus as I strolled my meandering way to The Resting Place.

To my delight and surprise, my few belongings were still in the room I'd rented. I'd half expected the landlord to let the room out to someone else seeing as I hadn't been back since my first day in Ephesus, but my bag was still there, and its contents unmolested. Not that those contents were of much value anyway, but it was nice to know I wouldn't need to replace them. There was another tunic, my old cloak, a spare pair of sandals, a razor and a small mirror of polished copper, a wooden bowl and spoon, and a spare wax tablet for taking notes. I shoved my small bag into the larger one, slung it over my shoulder and went down the stairs to ask the landlord for a refund seeing as I was leaving earlier than planned. He declined, but I didn't argue. For one thing, I didn't want to make a scene which would bring me to people's attention, and for another thing he had a brute of a slave standing at his shoulder whose function was clearly to resolve all disputes in a quick and straightforward manner.

Ah, well. I had a heavy purse now anyway, so it was the Emperor they'd stolen from, not me.

Glad to be out of that flea-ridden dump, I walked eastwards towards the Magnesian Gate. The cobbles were wet here, the overnight flow from Trajan's Fountain having spilled out and created a shallow stream. Now that the sun had risen, people were collecting water in buckets, so the fountain, fed by one of the city's aqueducts, was barely able to keep up with the demand, and

I knew the street would be bone dry within an hour or two as the temperature rose.

I eased my way through the crowd who were waiting patiently for their turn to collect water, and headed down to the gymnasium.

There are several gymnasia in Ephesus. In that respect it is a traditional Greek city. The Romans may have influenced house styles and brought an amphitheatre where the citizens could watch men and beasts being bloodily slaughtered for their entertainment, but many Greeks still preferred the traditional facilities of a gymnasium.

I'd been a regular visitor to this particular establishment when I'd first stayed in the city, having rented a room in the next block, and the place hadn't changed much. I went in, paid my entrance fee and left my stuff in the care of one of the gymnasium's slaves. I asked him his name, then asked whether Hannibal was in today. The slave replied in the affirmative, which told me two things. First, that my old friend was still here and, second, that the slave knew I knew the boss, so pilfering any of the silver I'd stuffed into the bottom of my bag would not be a good idea.

Naked, I strolled through to the main exercise area. This was essentially little more than a very large chamber where Greek men and boys met to test themselves against each other or simply to keep themselves fit. There are spaces set aside for running, for jumping, for lifting heavy weights, for wrestling and, my personal favourite, *pankration*.

As I'd expected, the place was busy. A few dozen men, mostly young but with a few older types still flexing their muscles, were engaged in a variety of exercises, all of them basking in the bright sunlight which streamed in through the high windows. The chamber echoed to their grunting efforts and their shouts of triumph or dismay as they engaged in various competitions.

There were other men sitting around on benches in alcoves let into the walls. Still dressed, they were either talking, or reading scrolls. One even had a lyre and was entertaining a small audience who clustered nearby to listen to him recite one of Homer's epic poems.

I scanned the room and found Hannibal easily enough. He's not particularly tall, no taller than me, in fact, but he's brawny with a thick chest and broad shoulders. His arms and thighs are pure muscle, and there's not an ounce of fat on him. He has dark skin, a trait inherited from some Nubian ancestor, and his head is completely bald. I guessed he must be about forty years old now, but he still looked as tough and menacing as ever. Newcomers to the gymnasium are often intimidated by Hannibal, but he has a strong sense of justice and was as good a friend as I'd ever had, so I couldn't help smiling when I saw him.

I stood to one side, watching him prowl around the *pankration* area, offering encouragement and criticism to two young men who were grappling with one another, each trying to throw the other to the wooden floor.

Pankration is, at first glance, quite similar to wrestling, but the big difference is that it has no real rules. Contestants are allowed to use any part of their body in any way they see fit in order to overcome their opponent. In the practice bouts, head-butting, genital grabbing, eye-gouging and biting are usually forbidden, but pretty much anything else goes.

The contest ended when one of the men used a sideways kick to knock his opponent slightly off balance. Taking advantage, he twisted his body, gripping the other man's upper arm tightly and ramming his shoulder into the man's chest. With a heave, he spun the unfortunate combatant to the ground, slamming him down hard.

"Well done!" boomed Hannibal above the noise of the busy gymnasium. "Polyclitus, you need to watch your footing. You should have been able to block that kick."

The two fighters, sweating and with their bodies gleaming with oil, clasped hands, the victor reminding his defeated opponent that he now owed him a jug of wine.

Hannibal turned just then and noticed me. He blinked, stared, then revealed his gleaming teeth in a wide smile of genuine delight.

"Scipio!" he shouted, holding his arms wide and coming to meet me. "What in Hades' name are you doing here? I thought you were in Rome."

"Hello, Hannibal," I grinned as he crushed me in a naked embrace which might have suggested to some onlookers that we were more than mere friends.

When he released me, I said, "I'm only here for a day or two, but I thought I'd come and say hello. And maybe test my fitness."

"Come on, then," he invited, gesturing me towards the *pankration* area. "Let's see how rusty you are."

I was very rusty indeed. In only a few minutes he had floored me four times. I barely managed to land a punch or a kick, never mind knock him off balance. When I hit the floor for the fifth time, I groaned and sat up slowly, rubbing the back of my head which had come into rough contact with the floorboards.

"I think that's enough," I told him. "Can we talk now?"

"If you like. Let's bathe and then we can have some wine."

There was a small bath house attached to the gymnasium, so we scrubbed away our sweat, then we both donned our tunics. I checked my bag to make sure the pouch of silver was still there, then Hannibal and I went outside.

"Do you remember Meristides' place next to the library?" he asked.

"Yes, of course."

"Good. Let's go there."

The wine shop was a large one, and very busy, but Hannibal is well known there, so we were quickly provided with a table. We soon had a jug of wine, two beakers and a chance to talk.

I added a lot of water to my wine, not wanting to become too intoxicated this early in the day. Hannibal did likewise. He was always careful about his diet.

The son of a former slave, he'd always been tough and good in a fight. He had once confided to me that he'd almost been tempted to become a gladiator, but he'd found *pankration* much more to his liking. He'd won a lot of money in competitions and, when the owner of the small Magnesian Gate gymnasium had died, he'd put all his money, plus a lot more he had borrowed, and bought the place. He'd since turned it into one of the most popular gymnasia in the city. It might be smaller than most of the others, but its reputation was second to none, and everyone knew Hannibal.

That's not his real name, of course. As far as I know, he's never been anywhere near Carthage where the famous general of that name hailed from. But his early fights had shown him to be a wily competitor who often tricked his opponents into making mistakes. That trait, combined with his obvious African ancestry, had earned him the nickname and it had stuck. His real name is Critias, but hardly anyone calls him by that name nowadays. He's just Hannibal.

"So how is your family?" I asked as we sipped at the watered wine and nibbled on the complimentary olives. "How many kids do you have now?"

He grinned with pride as he replied, "Four now. Three girls and a baby boy."

"Congratulations. Phaedra must be six or seven now, is she?"

"She's eight. Kritia is six, Glykera is three, and Thymon is only six months old."

"And Maria?"

"She's tired," he admitted. "She insists on nursing the babies herself rather than use a wet nurse. She has a small army of slaves to help look after the older ones, but the children are a handful."

"I bet they run all over you," I grinned.

"Naturally. I'm just a big softie. You know that."

It was true that Hannibal was gentle and considerate, even full of fun, when dealing with children, especially his own, but I knew plenty of adults who had been on the wrong end of his disapproval, and few of them would have considered him soft. I'd once seen him single-handedly quell a scuffle in the agora when half a dozen drunken youths had set upon some unfortunate passer-by who had said something out of turn. By the time the *vigiles* arrived, four of the six were on the ground nursing injuries of one sort or another, and the other two had fled.

"Are you still living above the gym?" I asked him.

"Yes. It's like a big nursery now, though."

He was obviously full of paternal pride, but he didn't want to talk about his family. Instead, his curiosity about my doings led the conversation the other way.

"So how's life in the imperial service?" he asked me. "Have you met the Emperor yet?"

"No, not yet. I work for one of his household departments. I'm not likely to ever meet the man himself."

"That's probably a good thing from what I hear," Hannibal murmured softly. "Lots of people have ended up on the wrong end of a sword since he became sole Emperor."

I couldn't argue with that assessment. Our beloved Antoninus had originally been joint Emperor with his half-brother, Geta, but the two of them had hated one another. Eventually, Geta had been killed, dying in his mother's arms after what Antoninus Caesar claimed was an attempt by Geta to lure him into a trap. Nobody really knew the truth of it except perhaps the Emperor and his step-mother, and they weren't saying. In fact, rumours suggested that they had more than just a pact of silence, but I certainly wasn't going to voice any suggestions about how intimate their relationship might be. That's just too dangerous a topic.

"So what are you doing here?" Hannibal asked me.

"I'm supposed to be investigating a recent murder," I told him, wishing to keep the theft from the Temple as confidential as I could. The murder was well known, so there was no harm in mentioning it.

"Which one?" he asked.

"Gaius Aristides. He was stabbed back in February."

"Oh, yeah. I remember that. But why are you looking into it? What's it got to do with the Emperor?"

"Hopefully nothing. That's what I'm trying to find out. But I'm not really getting anywhere."

"The *vigiles* didn't get anywhere with it either," said Hannibal. "That peacock of a Tribune might be able to strut around and impress the women, but he hasn't got much idea when it comes to tracking down criminals."

I smiled at that. Hannibal clearly didn't have a great impression of Tribune Diocles either.

"It's not just that," I grumbled. "The trail has gone cold. It's been more than three months, and I'm running out of people to talk to. Aristides had no family, and all his slaves were sold."

"I know," Hannibal nodded. "I bought one of them."

"You did?"

I was suddenly energised again, failing to prevent myself from becoming excited.

Hannibal noticed my interest and nodded, "Yes. The lad who was on duty in the changing room. He's not the brightest, but he's trustworthy enough. I got him pretty cheap, too, because

71

Aristides had a large household. Young Barnabus was one of the last on the block."

"Can I talk to him?" I asked, almost spilling my wine as I leaned forwards.

"If you like, although I don't think he'll be able to tell you much. I know he was asleep when the murder happened. He told me that much."

"I'd still like to talk to him. I'm trying to track down Aristides' freedman. A fellow called Eteocles. Maybe your slave knows where he is."

Hannibal's mouth widened in a grin as he said, "You don't need to speak to Barnabus for that. I know where Eteocles is."

"You do? Where?"

"He's working in one of the knocking shops near the harbour. I don't know exactly which one, but I remember a few of the patrons at the gymnasium talking about it shortly after the auction. They thought it was hilarious. Quite a come down for the old guy."

He shook his head, his expression disapproving as he added, "I thought it was a bit sad. From what I gather, Eteocles was with Aristides for a long time. He's too old to be of much use to anyone now, so he's had to take what he could find."

"Are you sure about this?" I pressed.

"Positive. You know how it is in the gymnasium. Guys get together and they talk, bragging about what they know. Aristides' murder was the only topic of conversation for a good couple of weeks. I'm sure I heard someone say his freedman was working in a brothel. I can't tell you which one it is, but it's definitely near the harbour."

That didn't narrow it down a great deal. The dock area has plenty of brothels.

I said, "Look, Hannibal, I need to go and find him. I'm sorry to dash off, but it's important. But I'd like to come back and talk to your slave later if that's all right."

"No problem," he said. "In fact, why don't you come for dinner tonight? Maria would love to see you, and you can talk to Barnabus at the same time."

I hesitated for a moment, and he shot me an inquisitive look.

"What's wrong?" he asked.

"Nothing. Well, I'd love to come, but there's a girl, you see."

"A girl? Here in Ephesus? Anyone I know?"

"No. She's visiting. Like me."

"And you have only been here a few days?" he smirked. "That was fast work."

"It just sort of happened," I told him, reluctant to reveal the true nature of Circe's reason for being in Ephesus.

"Well, bring her along. Unless you had other plans?"

"I'll ask her," I promised.

"Come at the fifth hour after noon," he invited. "Then we can have a proper talk."

"I will."

"Good. Now, be off with you. I should get back and make sure my gymnasium hasn't been wrecked."

I drained my cup, shook his hand and we left, him heading back for the gymnasium and me setting briskly off across the city towards the harbour.

I turned right, then left into the theatre plaza, then straight on along the main street which bisects the town and leads directly to the harbour. It's a very busy street, but it's the shortest route, and I was in a hurry.

"Eteocles," I whispered to myself, "I'm coming."

Chapter 8
The Freedman

I dismissed the notion of going to fetch Circe. Visiting brothels wasn't the sort of thing I felt appropriate for an educated young woman like her. Fortunately, finding the right place wasn't all that difficult. The people who run the dockside brothels know who their competitors are, and the first place I entered gave me the information I needed.

"Eteocles?" growled the manager of the tiny, smelly place. "You'll find him at the Green Door. Turn left when you go outside, then take the second left and it's on your right."

"It's got a Green Door?" I guessed.

"You're quick," the man grunted.

It did indeed have a green door, with a picture of a phallus painted on it in graphic detail. There was also a phallus etched into the paving stones of the street outside the door in case anyone who was so inebriated they were reduced to crawling along the street needed directions.

I went inside. It was basic and functional. I was in an ante-chamber which had a desk to my right behind which sat a pudgy sleazeball of greasy aspect. There was a closed door behind him, and a curtained doorway at the far end of the narrow room. The walls were decorated with erotic pictures of couples engaged in all sorts of sex, and there were two beefy slaves whose task it was to keep order and extort the appropriate fee if anyone argued with the manager.

This fellow was middle-aged, balding and fat, with a seedy and unpleasant air about him. I was glad the atmosphere inside the room was filled by the smell of incense because I could see the dark stains of sweat under his armpits and could still detect a strong whiff of garlic on his breath.

He offered me a gap-toothed smile of welcome as he asked, "What would you like?"

"I'd like to see Eteocles," I replied, thinking my equestrian tunic might have intimidated him rather more than my scruffy ordinary tunic obviously did.

"The boss?" he shot back in surprise. "What do you want to see him for?"

"Private matter," I told him, concealing my amazement at the title he had given Eteocles. Hannibal had felt sorry for the old freedman, but it seemed Eteocles might actually be running the place rather than scrubbing out the lavatories.

"You'll need to tell me more than that," the manager told me, adjusting his seat in a failed attempt to appear more intimidating. "He's a busy man."

"It's official business," I told him. "Tribune Diocles said I could find him here. I need to talk to him. I just need some information. That's all."

Dropping Diocles' name into my little lie didn't quite have the effect I'd hoped for.

"Diocles has no right to send anyone here," the man growled. "We've paid our dues this month."

I suppose I shouldn't have been surprised that Diocles, or some of his watchmen, were taking bribes to turn a blind eye to what went on here. Extortion isn't exactly uncommon in Roman business affairs.

I sighed. I briefly considered invoking the Emperor's name and threatening to come back with a cohort of Praetorians if I didn't get to see Eteocles, but I knew that was a hollow threat. I needed to keep this low-key if possible.

I said, "Look, could you just tell him I need to ask a few questions concerning an amulet that belonged to the Temple. That's all I'm interested in. I don't care what you get up to in here. I'm sure he'll see me if you tell him that."

The man didn't look convinced, and I noticed the two slaves were already flexing their muscles in anticipation of throwing me out. One of them put his hands together and loudly cracked his knuckles. This could get nasty, and I was already aching from my bout with Hannibal, so the prospect of landing head first on the cobbles outside didn't appeal to me at all.

Still, I stood my ground and waited. The manager studied me for a long, thoughtful moment, then reached a decision.

"What's your name?" he demanded.

"Sextus Sempronius Scipio."

"All right. I'll tell him you are here," he conceded. "But that doesn't mean he will see you."

I swallowed a sharp retort and gave him a smile and a nod of thanks.

The manager stayed in his chair, but he nodded to one of the slaves who turned and went through the door behind the desk. He was back a few moments later; moments during which I studiously ignored the manager and spent examining the various pictographs which decorated the walls. They weren't up to Leonides' standard, but what they lacked in style and grace, they made up for in graphic detail.

When he returned, the slave said, "He says to come up."

I gave the manager my brightest smile, then followed the slave through the door and up a flight of stairs to the next level. Several doors led off a long corridor, and the nearest one opened as we approached. A scantily-clad girl came out, her head lowered as she scurried past us. I caught only a brief glimpse of her face, but she seemed quite pretty and couldn't have been more than fifteen years old at most.

"In here," the slave told me, indicating the door the girl had come from.

I stepped into a spacious room which seemed to combine uses as a study, office and meeting room. There was a large desk with a rack of cubby holes containing scrolls and tablets on the wall behind it, while to my right was a low table flanked by a long, comfortable couch and a couple of padded chairs.

A small, grey-haired, slightly built man stood facing me, adjusting his tunic as if he'd just pulled it back on. It was pretty clear what he'd been up to, and I felt even more sorry for the poor girl who had just left because this man must be at least fifty years her senior.

My instant dislike of him was not alleviated by his smarmy manner when he greeted me.

"Sempronius Scipio, is it?" he asked with a barely disguised sneer. "I'm Eteocles. I'm the owner here."

"Thanks for seeing me," I said as pleasantly as I could. "I won't take up much of your time."

He guided me over to one of the comfortable chairs, seating himself opposite me and gesturing to the wine jug and cups which sat on the table between us.

"Would you care for a drink?" he offered.

"No thanks. I've just had one."

Even though it was true, that was a convenient excuse. I wouldn't have put it past the little mobster to put something unpleasant in my wine. That may seem harsh, but I'd already worked out that, to become the owner, Eteocles must have invested a fair amount of cash in this place. That meant he'd been salting away money for years. And much of that money must have come from Aristides' dodgy dealings in antiques.

I'd need to be careful here. I was aware that the slave had not left the room but was standing by the door behind me. I didn't like that one bit, and Eteocles' manner did nothing to ease my sense of trepidation.

"Can we talk privately?" I asked the brothel keeper.

"This is private enough," he said. "My staff know how to keep their mouths shut."

He regarded me with suspicious eyes.

"You said something about an amulet?"

"Yes, one that belonged to the Temple. It was among the items stolen by your former employer. I'm trying to find out who killed him and what they did with the amulet."

His face became a mask.

"I can't help you," he told me flatly. "I told the *vigiles* at the time. I wasn't in the room, and I never got a good look at the killer. He wore a hood and a face mask. I know nothing about any amulet."

"I've spoken to Tribune Diocles," I informed him. "I know what you told him. But I want to know if there is anything else you may have remembered since."

"There's nothing!" he snapped abruptly. "I've said all I have to say."

"Why so defensive?" I pressed. "I'm not accusing you of anything. I'm trying to find the murderer. I know you didn't see him well, but did you notice whether he had an accent when he spoke?"

"I barely exchanged two words with him!" Eteocles insisted.

"So you have no idea where he came from?"

He shook his head, then demanded, "Who are you anyway? Why are you interested in Aristides' murder after all this time? I don't need to tell you anything."

I lowered my voice as I replied, "I work for a man in Rome. His office is on the Palatine. And his boss wants to know what happened to his property. Do I need to say more?"

I put as much menace into my words as I could, and I could see Eteocles pause as he tried to work out whether to cooperate or have me chucked out.

In the end, he saw sense. He scowled deeply as he muttered, "I still can't help you. I know nothing."

"Perhaps not. But I'd like to hear it from you directly rather than second or third hand."

"So what do you want to know?" he sneered, clearly having decided that answering my questions was the easiest way to get rid of me, but determined to do so with as little grace as possible.

I ploughed on, "So you don't know where the killer came from, but what about the painter, Philippos? Did you ever meet him?"

"Only once," he said grudgingly.

"And do you know where he came from?"

"Macedonia, or so he said."

"And how did your former employer come to know him?"

Eteocles hesitated, and I could see his mind working as he tried to figure out how much to tell me. He had something to hide, I was sure, but it was probably his own involvement in Aristides' nefarious dealings. He must have known what was going on, but he wanted to distance himself from the theft of temple artefacts. Or so I hoped.

I was right.

He said, "He came to the house with another man. He was tall, with an Arab or maybe Berber look about him, although he told Aristides he was also from Macedonia."

That was interesting, although the man's appearance didn't mean all that much. Alexander had conquered so vast an empire that men from all over had joined his army. It wouldn't have surprised me if Arabs or Persians had travelled back to Macedonia and settled down. Their descendants might still look like their ancestors. Or, more likely given the Roman Empire's willingness to embrace people from any culture, he might well be a recent arrival in Macedonia. Either way, it backed up Circe's theory.

"Did this man have a name?" I asked.

"If he did, I never found out what it was. All Aristides told me was that he represented a client who wanted an important job done."

"You don't know the client's name?"

"No. Just that it was a woman and that she wanted the amulet."

"A woman?"

"That's what Aristides said."

I wondered if that woman might be the mysterious Julia Petronia who had lured Leonides away to Athens.

"And she is in Macedonia?"

Eteocles shrugged, "I really couldn't say. But that's where her men said they came from."

"So Philippos was with this other chap, and they both worked for a woman? Is that right?"

He nodded, "And that's all I know. Aristides wouldn't let anyone in the room when the hooded man arrived that night. He was excited, I know, but I didn't know why."

I smiled at that. He knew why, all right. Aristides was expecting to receive his share of the loot from the Temple.

"But things went wrong?" I prompted.

"Obviously. By the time the slave called me and we smashed through the door, Aristides was dead, and there were all those stolen things laid out on the desk."

"But no amulet?"

I was treading on dangerous ground here. If Eteocles had seen the treasures, he could easily have helped himself. Of course, with Aristides dead, he'd known the *vigiles* would be snooping around, so maybe he was smart enough not to be found with stolen Temple goods on his person. But he must have been tempted.

He gave me a frown as he asked, "What amulet?"

I wasn't sure how good an actor he was, but his puzzlement seemed genuine.

"There wasn't a golden amulet among the items on the desk?"

He growled, "At the time, I was more concerned about Aristides' fate to check what was on his desk. But no, I don't recall seeing an amulet."

Cautiously, I asked, "So why didn't the killer take everything? That's the big puzzle here."

"I have no idea," he replied coldly. "You would need to ask him that. If you ever find him."

"I will," I assured him. "But, getting back to the stolen items, is it possible the slave could have pilfered the missing amulet?"

Eteocles stared at me. He knew what I was driving at. I hadn't actually accused him of stealing anything, but he knew, and I knew, that he had had the opportunity.

"It was all very chaotic," he said at last. "But I told him to go after the killer, and I warned the other slaves who were arriving by that time not to touch anything."

"Very commendable," I smiled.

His hard expression didn't waver as he demanded, "What's so special about this golden amulet anyway?"

"Only the fact that it's missing. My boss doesn't like it when valuable items are stolen from important temples."

I couldn't be sure he believed me, but that was the end of our conversation in any case. Eteocles rose to his feet, extending one arm towards the door.

"I really am busy. I have nothing else to tell you, so please be on your way."

He may have been a small, wizened little creep, but he knew how to strike a pose like an autocrat, and I knew that in his own lair he was as powerful as any Emperor, so I didn't protest. In truth, there wasn't much more I could ask him without prying into Aristides' illegal business, and I knew he would clam up if I went down that road.

"Thanks for your time," I said as I pushed myself out of the chair.

I didn't shake his hand when I left.

Once outside, I pondered what I'd learned. I'd added a little bit more to the puzzle, but not much.

What seemed clear now was that a woman had wanted the amulet for reasons unknown. A woman who had lured Leonides to Athens to allow her employee, Philippos, to gain access to the Temple. Somehow – and I still didn't know how – he'd stolen a few items.

I wasn't entirely sure of the next bit, but the most straightforward explanation was that the killer was the same man who had first visited Aristides with Philippos. This Arab, or Berber, or possibly Persian, had delivered most of the stolen loot to Aristides, but there had been an argument. Aristides had been stabbed to death, and the killer had run off, leaving the loot behind.

That still struck me as strange. Could it be that the woman behind the plot was only interested in the Alexander amulet? Even if that were true, a man prepared to knife one of his accomplices would surely have no scruples about taking stolen treasures? It was a real puzzle, but I did have a lead of sorts. Two witnesses had told me the plotters were from Macedonia, and that fitted with Circe's idea that it was the symbolism of ownership of the amulet which was behind the theft. Of course, the men could have been lying, but it was the only lead I had. As Circe had told me the previous day, I needed to go to Athens, and then on to Macedonia.

I worked all this out while I walked all the way back to the Temple. Here, I was taken to Restitutus' private chamber in one of the buildings which sits apart from the Temple, screened by hedges and rows of trees.

Pomponius Niger, the head of security, joined us as, over a lunch of sweetmeats, I explained everything I had discovered.

"So there may well be a plot against the Emperor," Restitutus said with a grim expression on his lined old face.

"Possibly. The amulet seems to have been the main target. Whether because of its connection to Alexander, or because it had been donated by the Emperor's father is hard to say. Personally, I'm inclined to think it is someone who is simply greedy to have an object which once belonged to Alexander. Once she discovered it was on display, she contacted a local dealer in stolen art and antiques to help her place her thief in the Temple."

Restitutus mulled that over for a while before saying, "I hope you are right. I have certainly heard no whispers of plotting from anyone in Ephesus."

"If there is a plot, it's probably in Athens or Macedonia," I shrugged.

Niger rasped, "Whatever the reason, Caesar will want their head."

He was probably right about that. Our beloved Emperor has a vengeful streak a mile wide, but I wasn't about to say so out loud.

"You have done well, Scipio," Restitutus told me. "You had best write it all down. I will ensure it travels to Rome as soon as the next imperial messenger arrives."

So I sat in his plush room, quill in hand, and wrote a long, detailed report, omitting only Circe's presence. If she didn't want the Juggler to know she was here, that didn't matter to me.

When I was done, I rolled up the parchment, dribbled hot wax onto the join and pressed my pendant insignia into the wax, adding my Sigma sign in ink just beside the seal.

As I handed the report to Restitutus, I told him, "I made sure the Juggler will know there is no fault at the Temple. Aristides was well-regarded by everyone in Ephesus, and the security here is as good as it can be. I still don't understand how Philippos managed to steal those things, but I don't see how you could have prevented it."

"Thank you," he smiled. "It is not a pleasant feeling to be taken in by someone you believed to be honest."

He asked me, "What will you do now?"

"I'm going to Athens," I told him. "I'll see if I can find this Julia Petronia woman. Then, depending on what reply I get from Sempronius Rufus, I'll probably be going to Macedonia. Unless he sends someone else there and I'm sent back to Parthia. There's trouble brewing there."

"There is always trouble brewing with Parthia," Restitutus opined.

"But this evening," I told him with a happy smile, "I'm going out for dinner with friends."

Chapter 9
Dinner

Circe was rather put out when I told her what I'd been up to. She had given me a rather alarmed look when I explained how I'd tracked down Eteocles and what had happened when I met him.

"You should have told me," she scolded. "It was dangerous going into a place like that on your own."

"It would have been even more dangerous for you," I pointed out.

She pulled a face as she said sharply, "I meant you could have taken Agon and Diomedes along with you."

That hadn't occurred to me, but I simply shrugged, "It turned out to be no real problem. I'll bet Eteocles is a bit of a tyrant, and he certainly employs thugs, but once he realised I wasn't after him, he told me enough of what I needed to know."

After I'd recounted what I'd learned, Circe agreed with my assessment of the most probable sequence of events.

"Aristides must have built up a network of contacts all over the eastern Empire," she reflected. "And he was well known enough here in Ephesus to make a recommendation to the Temple about taking on Philippos."

"Yes, Restitutus still feels annoyed about that. Aristides tricked him, and he's not happy. If I thought it would do any good, I'd ask him to put a curse on the thieves."

"I think you are more dangerous to them than any curse," Circe assured me. "Look at how much you have learned in only a few days."

"I haven't really learned all that much," I sighed. "But at least we have a lead to follow up. Tomorrow, I'll need to find a boat which is going to Athens in the next few days."

She placed her hand on mine as she said regretfully, "I will be leaving the day after tomorrow. Agon found a ship bound for Alexandria. It's not ideal, but it will take me part of the way home, and there are always plenty of boats travelling from Alexandria to Carthage."

My heart lurched. Two days. That was all the time we had left.

We decided to make the most of it, so we were a little late arriving at Hannibal's home. I'd been worried that Circe might not want to meet some of my old acquaintances, but she was delighted when I told her of the invitation. With Agon and Diomedes escorting us, we walked across town and then climbed the sturdy, wooden staircase which ascended the side of the three-storey building which housed the gymnasium on the ground floor. We could still hear the noises of exercise from inside, but Hannibal was at home rather than overseeing things.

He welcomed us with a broad smile, sent Agon and Diomedes upstairs to the slaves' quarters where he told them they would be fed, then took Circe and me inside a warren of rooms and passages, many of which betrayed the signs that young children lived here. Several toys, including more than a few dolls, were scattered around, and I half expected to hear the sounds of high-pitched, squealing voices, but Maria had the three girls lined up for our inspection while baby Thymon was sleeping in a wicker basket beside her chair.

Maria was a buxom woman, and feeding her new baby had resulted in her breasts being even larger than I remembered. She'd often joked that they were the two main reasons Hannibal had married her, although anyone who did not know her well would be surprised that she could ever say such a thing. She was a shrewd woman with long, brown hair and a face which could have been sculpted from marble. She was not only pale of complexion, her expression rarely gave anything away. I knew that appearance was deceptive, and her smile softened her features when she introduced her children to us.

"They will be going to their rooms soon," she informed us. "But we wanted you to meet them."

I'd never been all that good with young children, but Circe rose to the occasion, complimenting the three youngsters on their dresses, their hair and how lovely they looked. Phaedra, Kritia and Glykera responded with bashful smiles and words of thanks, then a slave woman took them off to their rooms.

"Now, let's go through to the dining room," Maria said, picking up the wicker basket.

Circe insisted on cooing over the baby. While she did so, Hannibal nudged me. When I looked at him, he jerked his chin to indicate Circe, then gave me a wink of approval.

The dining room was a spacious area with a large window admitting the evening sun which illuminated a long table set with several chairs. Some Greeks have adopted the Roman style of dining while lounging on couches, but Hannibal and Maria preferred the Greek custom of sitting at table.

"We don't often have the chance to entertain guests," Maria explained as she showed us to our seats. "This room hardly ever gets used."

"That's because Hannibal doesn't have any friends," I told Circe.

She was surprised at this comment, but Hannibal burst out laughing.

"I've got friends," he chuckled. "I just don't like any of them."

"Do be quiet, Critias!" Maria scolded him, using his real name. Turning to Circe, she said, "It is just that we like to spend a lot of time with our children. Entertaining guests is not high on our list of priorities. We only do it for special friends."

"And Scipio is a special friend?" Circe asked, arching her eyebrows.

"He lived in the next block for five years," Hannibal informed her. "We got to know each other pretty well, even if he was just a silly youngster himself back then."

"Tell me more," Circe asked with rather too much keenness for my liking.

"He wanted to learn how to fight," Hannibal explained. "I've never seen anyone practise *pankration* as much as he did back then."

"Not that it did me much good," I put in.

"No, but your dedication was impressive, even if your ability wasn't."

Circe said, "I thought it was you who gave him the name Scipio?"

Hannibal laughed aloud again.

"I let him win one bout because he was beginning to get depressed about always losing," he explained.

"I beat you fair and square!" I protested.

Circe glanced at each of us in turn, then shot a worried look at Maria who told her, "They are always like this when they get together. They'll argue and tease, finding constant fault with one another, but do not let it fool you. They really are good friends."

"Yes, but you can go off people," I muttered.

Hannibal laughed again.

"Behave, or I will pick you up and bounce your head off the floor. Anyway, we don't want to talk about you. We want to hear all about the lovely Tertullia Tertia who has so smitten you."

I squirmed a bit at that, but Maria took up the baton and began asking Circe all about herself. The story she gave was much the same as she'd told me, so I didn't learn any more of her background, although she did tell us a little about her home.

"We had a big villa just outside Carthage," she explained. "We bred horses, and we grew olives, grapes and figs. But when my older sister died, I was taken in by a friend of my father's who lived in the city. But the villa is mine now, and I've moved back out there. I have a trusted freedman who ran the place for me while I was growing up."

"She's very rich," I put in.

"Then she should steer clear of you," Hannibal declared. With a warning shake of a finger to Circe, he told her, "He'll scrounge off you if you let him. And he's always living hand to mouth, although I expect he's a bit better off now he's working for the Emperor."

Slaves had served wine which I diluted only a little, and they now began filling the table with a variety of dishes containing various sorts of seafood and vegetables. We continued chatting while we ate.

Hannibal asked me, "Did you find the man you were looking for?"

"Yes. I can't say I took to him. He's a nasty piece of work."

"Really?"

"Yes. Your information was a bit off. He doesn't work in a brothel; he owns the place. And I don't think he treats the girls all that well."

"None of them do," Hannibal frowned.

Maria, obviously keen not to discuss such unsavoury aspects of city life, said, "Critias tells me you are investigating that dreadful stabbing. Did you learn anything useful?"

"Not really. But he confirmed a few things I'd heard elsewhere, and that means I'll need to move on as soon as I can."

"Where to?" Maria asked.

"Athens. That's where the trail leads. After that …?"

I gave a shrug to indicate that my fate would be determined by others.

"The Emperor keeps you busy," she observed.

"I don't think he even knows I exist," I told her. "I work for one of his secretaries. And I've only ever met the secretary a couple of times."

"And what about Rome? Do you like it any better than you did when you first came here?"

I paused to consider my answer, then said, "Most of my work tends to be out here in the east. I've only been back to Rome a couple of times, and I can't say I'm all that keen to go back any time soon."

"So where have you been?" Maria asked.

"Here and there," I shrugged.

Hannibal interjected, "Wife, he either can't say, or he's trying to be mysterious to impress us."

"You've found me out!" I grinned.

Maria pulled a face at Hannibal, but said to me, "So you have no tales of the Emperor? I hear he's been in Germania for the past year or so."

"Putting down some fractious tribes," I agreed. "But that's a full time job in that part of the world. The Germans love fighting."

"Just like those fearsome Britons," Hannibal said, looking directly at me to let me know he was having a dig at my ancestry on my father's side of the family.

"There is fighting around most of the Empire's borders," I shrugged. "But, in all honesty, I haven't heard anything about the Emperor recently. I've been away for a bit."

Circe put in, "I heard he is on his way to Armenia. There's another civil war there."

"There's another civil war in Parthia, too," I added, just to reinforce my earlier point about the borders of the Empire being war zones.

Hannibal smiled broadly as he said, "Then it seems I know more about Caesar's doings than you. There's a chap from

Ephesus who serves with the army. He's back, recuperating from a wound he took in Germania. He was down at the gymnasium the other day, and he told me the Emperor is on his way to Parthia."

"So there is going to be another war?" Maria asked with undisguised dismay.

"No. There's going to be a wedding. Apparently, Caesar is going to marry a daughter of the Parthian king."

That was news to me. I'd been in Parthia for months, gathering all sorts of information on military strength and political goings-on, but I'd had no inkling our Emperor was carrying on diplomatic negotiations of that sort while I'd been risking my neck for him.

Hannibal went on, "But, naturally, our Antoninus is still playing at soldiers. Apparently he stopped off in Macedonia and raised a Legion of spearmen who use the old-fashioned *sarissa*."

Circe and I looked at each other when he said this.

"What is it?" Hannibal asked. "Did I say something important?"

I shook my head.

"No, it's just that Macedonia has come up once or twice during my investigation. It's just a coincidence, I'm sure."

I don't think he believed me, and I was sure Circe knew it must have been more than coincidence, but I tried to move the subject on.

"Does he really think using the *sarissa* is a good tactic?" I wondered. "Alexander may have conquered Persia using the long pikes, but the Roman Legions made short work of the phalanxes when Greece was absorbed into the Empire."

Hannibal gave a shrug.

"I'm no soldier," he said. "But one thing you can say about the Emperor is that he knows his stuff when it comes to warfare. If he's raised a Macedonian phalanx, he must have a use for it."

I couldn't argue with that. One thing Antoninus Caesar knows about is war. He'd been fighting ever since he was a teenager, and he'd learned from his father, Septimius Severus, who had won more campaigns than many Emperors.

Hannibal gave a throaty chuckle as he told us, "Apparently, he's got a new nickname as well."

"Oh?"

"Yes. This chap I was telling you about said Caesar has insisted his troops all start wearing a long, hooded cloak which he first saw in Gaul. He claims it will protect them from the sun as well as wind and rain, and he's gone on about it so much, they are calling him Caracalla after the type of cloak."

I grimaced, "I wonder what he thinks about that?"

"Apparently he loves it," Hannibal assured me. "So now he's Emperor Caracalla."

I said, "Well, if I ever do meet him, which I doubt I will, I don't think I'll call him that to his face."

"Trust me!" Hannibal laughed.

"I know your sense of humour, my friend. That's precisely why I don't trust you on things like that."

"It's true! I swear!"

"Well, whatever people call him, I'm surprised he is looking to make peace with Artabanus of Parthia. I thought he'd be more likely to try to take advantage of the weakness caused by the civil war to invade Parthia. That's his usual style."

"You would know more about that than I do," Hannibal shrugged.

Circe had been very quiet while we'd been talking about Caesar and his methods, so Maria switched the subject and began telling her all about Ephesus. She asked whether she'd seen the Temple, and what she thought of the theatre and the library.

The conversation moved on, and Hannibal gave me another surreptitious wink, warning me to stay off the subject of war and politics. Maria was far more interested in domestic issues and didn't care who was in charge as long as there was peace and stability in her home town.

Circe then moved the topic on to Maria's children, a subject on which Maria could talk for hours.

Still, although this domestic bliss was something I was totally unfamiliar with, the evening passed pleasantly enough. The sun set, the slaves closed the large shutters on the window and lit oil lamps, at the same time removing dishes and bringing other sweetmeats to the table.

It was late in the evening by the time I announced we should be going. I'd had more wine than I ought to have done, and I noticed Circe was a little tipsy as well. That, and the sight of the elegant contours of her body beneath the expensive dress she was wearing reminded me that we might have only one more night together, so I told Hannibal we would need to head for home.

"You still haven't spoken to Barnabus," he reminded me.

"Who? Oh, the slave you bought from Aristides?"

To be honest, I'd almost forgotten about that. Having found Eteocles, I didn't think there was much more a slave could tell me.

Circe frowned, "You didn't tell me Critias had bought one of Aristides' slaves."

"It slipped my mind," I admitted. "But he said he was asleep when the murder happened, didn't he?"

"Yes, he was," Hannibal confirmed.

"Still," I sighed. "I'd better have a quick word with him. I've already sent my report in, but I'd kick myself if I wasn't thorough."

So Hannibal sent for Barnabus, dismissing the other slaves. Maria picked up baby Thymon who had woken at last and was beginning to demand a feed of his own. She invited Circe to accompany her back to the family room, but Circe said she would like to hear what Barnabus had to say.

He arrived a few moments later, looking rather nervous. He was a young lad, of average build, with a rather plain face and not much liveliness showing in his eyes.

Hannibal explained to him that I was investigating the murder of his former owner, and that I had a few questions which he was to answer truthfully.

Telling myself to remain professional despite the wine flowing in my veins, I asked the slave, "Did you happen to see the man who stabbed your owner?"

"No, Sir. I was asleep. I woke when I heard the shouts and the banging on the door, and I ran to the room, but he was gone by then."

"What did you see in the room?"

Barnabus had to think about that for a while, but he eventually told me, "It was all a bit strange. Everyone was shouting and yelling. The master was on the floor beside his desk, all covered in blood, and there were all these things spread out on the desk."

"Things?"

"Jewels and stuff."

"Did you see anyone touch them?"

"No, Sir. Eteocles, that's the freedman, told us not to touch anything."

Well, that confirmed what the little brothel keeper had told me. Eteocles might be a nasty piece of work, but he was smart enough to know that the *vigiles* would have asked questions if they'd found stolen items from the Temple being hidden in the house. By leaving them on open display, all the blame would fall on Aristides.

I asked the slave, "So what happened next?"

Again he needed to concentrate to recall the events of that night.

"Glaucus, the slave who had gone after the man with the knife, came back and said he couldn't find him. And Eteocles had already sent someone else to fetch the *vigiles*. When they arrived, they took over and sent us all back to our rooms until their Tribune arrived."

I sighed. As I'd expected, there was nothing new to be learned here.

As a last throw of the dice, I asked him, "Did you ever see the man named Philippos? He was a painter who came to see your master with another man who might have been an Arab or Berber."

"Oh, yes, I saw them," Barnabus nodded eagerly.

I sensed Circe tensing beside me. Had we caught a break here?

I tried not to let my expectations rise too far as I said, "What can you tell me about them? When did you see them?"

"It was a few weeks before the murder. I served them some refreshments while they were waiting for my master. They were sitting in one of the rooms off the atrium. He had someone else with him at the time, so they sat around for a while."

"I don't suppose you heard them say anything important?"

"Like what, Sir? What's important?"

"Did they call each other by name, for example?"

His brow furrowed as he searched his memory.

"I don't think so. Not that I can recall."

I gave Circe a quick glance and saw her shoulders slump in resignation.

Turning back to Barnabus, I tried, "Did they say anything about where they were from or mention anyone else's name?"

91

There was another long delay while he gathered his thoughts.

"I don't remember them saying a name, but they did mention something about a place."

He seemed to be having trouble recalling what he'd heard. I supposed it had been several months ago.

I suggested, "Macedonia, by any chance?"

A look of confusion crossed his face as he shook his head.

"Oh, No, Sir. Well, yes in a sort of round about way."

"What do you mean? Did they mention Macedonia or not?"

"Well, Sir, the Berber did. He told the artist not to mention those other people because he was supposed to be from Macedonia."

I felt my senses tingle, and Circe was also on edge.

"What other people?" I asked.

For once, Barnabus seemed fairly certain of what he'd heard.

"Well, Sir, I was outside the room, just out of sight but waiting in case they needed something, so I could hear them pretty well even though they were speaking softly. But the artist chap definitely said something about 'Our people in Alexandria', and that's when the other man told him not to mention them or Alexandria because he was supposed to be from Macedonia."

Circe let out a gasp of surprise, and I slumped back in my chair.

"Alexandria?" I asked, "Are you sure about that?"

"Oh, yes, Sir. Very sure. I heard Eteocles say later that they were from Macedonia, but I knew that was wrong. They were definitely from Alexandria. Also, I recognised the artist's accent. I'd once accompanied my master on a trip to Alexandria, so I know what the accent sounds like."

I took a deep breath and turned to look at Circe whose expression was one of astonishment.

"Can you book me passage on that ship?" I asked her.

Because I knew now that I would not be going to Athens or Macedonia.

I was going to Alexandria. With Circe.

Chapter 10
Voyage

The sea was calm for the first part of the voyage, the season having brought good sailing weather. Our ship was one of the usual merchant vessels which were the lifeline of trade all across the Mediterranean. It was based out of Alexandria and had sailed up the Ionian coast bringing supplies of papyrus, spices and the skins of exotic beasts such as crocodiles and hippopotamuses. Now it was making the return journey, carrying amphorae of olive oil, plus valuable silks and spices from the east which had reached Ephesus along the famous Silk Road, a journey of thousands of miles.

We sailed during the hours of daylight, the vast, linen sails catching the breeze and pushing the fat-bellied boat southwards. Like most merchant vessels, our ship relied solely on the wind for propulsion. Oarsmen cost money even if they are slaves, and they take up valuable space in the hold, which reduces the profit margin, so a small crew of sailors kept the vessel moving under the watchful eye of a surly captain.

Seafaring has always been a bit of a mystery to me. The sailors who dealt with the rigging and maintaining the ship spoke to one another in a strange language of their own, using words which meant nothing to me. They were a rough lot, but there were no more than a dozen of them, so they were kept permanently busy. Again, the profit motive determined the crew size; the fewer men who needed to be paid, the more profit for the captain and the ship's owner.

Each night, we docked in one of the many coastal towns which line the Ionian coast of Asia Minor. There was little opportunity to go ashore, for the ship set sail again at first light, so Circe and I saw very little of the towns we stopped at. Even Halicarnassus was in virtual darkness by the time we docked, so we had no chance to see the famous tomb of King Mausolus which, like the Temple of Artemis, is counted as one of the Seven Wonders of the World. I wasn't too bothered since I'd seen it before, but it would have been nice to visit it again with Circe beside me.

I reflected that this mission seemed to be bringing me into close proximity to the famous Seven Wonders. I'd known the Mausoleum and the Artemis Temple before, but now I'd seen what was left of the Colossus of Rhodes, and I was on my way to see the famous Pharos lighthouse at Alexandria. That was four of them marked off the list. It would be nice if I could find a chance to travel further into Egypt to see the famous Pyramids. It didn't seem likely, but in my line of work you never knew where you would end up. If I did manage to see those ancient Pharaonic tombs, there would really only be the statue of Zeus at Olympia left for me to see.

If you are thinking I've only listed six so-called Wonders, I should explain that I've been to Babylon once, in the guise of a wandering beggar. I'd spent a few days there, but I hadn't seen any sign of the famous Hanging Gardens. Babylon is a much reduced place now compared to what it was allegedly like in its heyday, but I still thought it odd that even the locals could not point to where the gardens had been. It made me wonder whether they'd ever existed at all.

As far as I was concerned, though, there was already another Wonder to replace those legendary Gardens. That was Circe. Even dressed in a long-sleeved robe with a broad-brimmed hat to protect her from the blazing sun, she looked gorgeous. Even so, her mood was sombre. We'd had a little bit of a falling out over my accompanying her on this trip. She'd insisted I ought to stick to my plan and go to Athens to find Julia Petronia, but the Alexandrian lead was just as strong, even if we had no specific location to search for. The clinching factor for me was that we would be able to be together for a few more days, so I told her I was going to Alexandria no matter what she said. That had rather put her out, and she'd sulked for a while.

I must admit I thought her reaction was a little odd, but I put it down to her being upset that her pet theory of a Macedonian connection had been seriously challenged. But the new information was too good to ignore, so I'd stuck to my decision despite her irritation.

I'd scribbled a quick note to Sempronius Rufus to advise him of my change of plan, then hurried up to the Temple to deliver it before rushing back down to the harbour and joining Circe on board the merchant ship.

I'd hoped she would have regained her normal temperament, but she remained moody, although she did at least talk to me. For my part, I was just happy to be around her.

Not that we were able to be together at nights. There were only two cabins on the main deck, and the captain occupied one of those. Circe and her maid, Helena, took the other.

"I can't have an old woman like her sleeping out on the deck even if she is a slave," Circe had told me firmly.

That left me with the choice of either sleeping on deck under an awning which was stretched between the ship's two masts or taking a bunk in a dark, squalid cabin below decks along with two other passengers.

I initially opted for the deck, lying on a mat of woven reeds beneath the awning. I selected a spot near the starboard side which kept me clear of the huddle of slaves who accompanied the paying passengers. It wasn't the most comfortable bed I'd ever slept in, but it wasn't the worst either. Until I was woken one night when I felt someone kneeling down beside me.

Fortunately, I'm a light sleeper. I sensed the furtive nature of whoever it was, and knew they were up to no good. Rolling to my side, I flashed out my arm, knocking a probing hand aside, and sat up.

"Get lost!" I snarled.

I caught a glimpse of steel in the moonlight, and only then did I realise the figure, who smelled like one of the sailors, had a knife. Much to my relief, he darted away into the darkness. I think he had been almost as surprised as I was, and I reckoned he'd been trying to relieve me of my purse while I slept. I was tempted to chase him, but the thought of stumbling around in the darkness looking for a man with a knife didn't appeal to me, so I bundled up my mat and made my way down to the cabin below decks where I could close the door. All I needed to put up with down there was the fetid atmosphere and the snoring of my fellow passengers. These were a fat scribe who was carrying messages on behalf of some wealthy aristocrats, and a young man who was heading to Egypt to join the Governor's service. I'd barely exchanged a dozen words with either of them, but I felt I could probably trust them not to rob me while I slept. Still, the attempted theft had given me a scare, and it was some time before I eventually managed to doze off.

I decided not to tell anyone about the attempted theft, not even the captain. What could he do in any case? I hadn't seen the man's face, and all it would have done was create a nasty atmosphere if I went around accusing the crew of trying to rob me. We only had another few days to go, then I'd be on firm land again. In the meantime, I vowed to watch my back.

The days at sea were a lot more pleasant than the nights. I spent these on deck, standing or sitting with Circe while we kept a watch for sea monsters. Circe was adamant she'd seen a whale spouting far off in the distance, but I doubted that. The glare of the sun on the water was so bright it hurt the eyes to look too far beyond the ship's gunwales.

We did see a pod of dolphins one day. They came close alongside, jumping and breaching joyously as they cavorted all around us before diving deep and vanishing beneath the waves.

"It must be wonderful to swim like that," Circe smiled happily as she looked for more signs of the friendly beasts.

But, other than those few moments when Circe deigned to talk to me, the voyage was, as usual, rather boring. The sailors occasionally threw nets over the side in an effort to catch fish, but the captain was more interested in making the best speed to Alexandria.

Beyond Halicarnassus, he had a choice to make. He could stop off at Cyprus or Crete, but both of those required changing course before doubling back towards Alexandria. As his hold was full of cargo, he opted to head directly for Egypt, which meant we would have a few nights out at sea.

It was on the third of those nights that I realised the thief who I thought had been trying to cut away my purse had probably had a far more sinister aim.

The sun was setting quickly below the western horizon, and the ship was bobbing slowly along, the two huge sails catching a strengthening breeze. Most people had retired for the night, but I needed to relieve myself, so I went to the prow where, over the low gunwale were some wooden steps protruding from the hull. It was a precarious foothold, but the men on board clambered down here to relieve themselves into the ocean. The women were permitted to use clay pots in the privacy of their cabin, but we males were afforded only the privacy of being out of sight below the height of the decks.

I moved carefully past the massive sails as I headed towards the prow because the sea had become a little choppy, and I needed to adjust my gait to counter the rolling motion of the deck. I must admit I wasn't looking forward to clambering out over the gunwale and perching on the narrow step, but my bladder was telling me I couldn't leave it until morning.

There was a solitary crewman up at the front of the ship. He stood beside an oil lamp which was hung out over the prow. Its purpose was to alert other ships to our presence, and the sailor's job was to look out for other ship's lanterns. Running aground wasn't a concern so far out at sea, but collisions with other vessels weren't impossible, so most ships hung lanterns at their prow and stern.

I gave the man a friendly nod, but I didn't think he'd noticed. The gloom was gathering quickly as the last rays of the sun sank redly below the western horizon, turning the sea to our starboard a frothy blend of orange and black.

It was only as I reached the rail that I sensed him coming quickly up behind me. He'd not said a word, so I spun around just in time to see his raised hand holding what looked like a metal spike set in a long, wooden handle.

In the rapidly fading light, I saw the gleam of murder in his eyes, but that same light was dazzling him and made it difficult for him to gauge his attack. That allowed me a split second to react.

I flashed out my left hand, grabbing his right wrist as he struck down, then twisted my body, turning into him and seizing his right arm with both hands. In a move Hannibal had taught me years before, I bent my knees, hunched my head and used the man's own momentum to lift him over my shoulder.

I threw him with as much force as I could, my only thought being to disarm and disable him. In a gymnasium, he'd have hit the floor hard and I'd have won the bout, but we were not in a gymnasium. Even as I hurled him over my shoulder, the ship rolled, adding impetus to his fall. He let go of the spiked club which tumbled over the gunwale, and he followed it, letting out a startled yell of shock and fear which was cut off when he splashed into the sea.

I took a deep breath, clamping both hands on top of the gunwale and looking down at the water, but there was no sign of him at all. I listened hard, but there were no cries for help, nor any distressed splashing. The man had simply vanished beneath the surface. Perhaps, like a surprising number of sailors, he couldn't swim.

But somebody had noticed. I heard shouts of alarm from the stern of the ship where I knew the steersman was manning the rudder from his post on top of the cabins. He would not have been able to see the attack because the enormous sails blocked his view of the forward deck, but he must have seen or heard the splash.

I moved quickly, crossing to the port side and climbing down over the gunwale where I completed the task I had originally come here for. It was an eerie sensation standing there with dark, menacing waves surging just below me, and I confess I felt my legs begin to tremble as reaction set in. It wasn't the first time someone had tried to kill me, but I hadn't expected that sort of danger on this voyage. It took a while before I was able to compose myself and clamber back over the rail onto the deck.

I'd been aware of footsteps and voices. Now, in the faint pool of light from the prow lantern, I saw several shadowy figures looking out over the starboard rail. The sun had set by now, and stars were beginning to appear in the sky, so it was impossible to make out who was there, but I did recognise the captain's voice as he cursed the idiocy of his lookout.

I had a decision to make. Had the sailor who attacked me been working on his own, or were the rest of the crew in on a plot to do away with me? Then I realised that, if they were, I had nowhere to hide, so I may as well confront them now.

Moving up behind them, I asked, "Is something wrong?"

They all spun round to look at me.

The captain said, "Oh, it's you, Sir. We think our lookout must have fallen overboard. Did you happen to see anything?"

I gaped at him in what I hoped was a suitably astonished response, although I doubt he could make out my expression very clearly.

Shaking my head, I told him, "I was over the other side having a piss. I did hear what I thought was someone shouting."

Moving to the ship's side to take a look for myself, I added, "How could that have happened? Has he drowned, do you think?"

"All we know is there was a shout and a splash. And Sisycus isn't at his post. He must have been leaning over the side looking at the sunset and lost his balance. I've seen it happen before. The sea can have a mesmerising effect if you stare at it long enough."

"Oh, dear!" I sympathised. "Can you go back for him?"

"No point," the captain told me. "We'd never find him at night. And we think he went straight down. He couldn't swim."

I expressed a suitable amount of shock and sympathy, but it was clear there was nothing to be done. The captain detailed someone else to stand watch at the prow, and I made my way towards the rear deck, holding onto the rail with one hand to counter the increasingly noticeable movement of the deck.

I ducked beneath the foresail. Under the great awning, another dark figure loomed up in front of me, and I tensed, anticipating another attack, but it was only Agon.

"What's happening Sir? Are you all right?"

"I'm fine," I assured him. "But it seems one of the crew fell overboard. He's probably drowned."

I couldn't see Agon's face in the dim light, but he clucked his tongue.

"Best be careful yourself, Sir," he warned. "The deck isn't exactly steady tonight."

"I'm heading below," I told him. "But you make sure you keep a good eye on your mistress's cabin. Don't let anyone sneak in."

"Of course, Sir," he replied, his tone sounding offended. If he wondered why I was giving him that warning, he didn't say anything.

Without another word, I moved on, passing the rear sail and descending the steps into the murky depths of the ship. Another oil lamp hung here, swinging from side to side, lighting my way to the cabin door, but I was not able to relax until I'd slipped into my bunk.

Once there, I tried to reason out what had happened.

Had it been another attempt to rob me?

No, it couldn't have been that. If that blow with the spike or whatever it had been had hit me on the head, I'd possibly have died immediately. I'd certainly have fallen into the sea, putting me out of reach of my assailant.

So, if not robbery, then what?

The look I'd seen in the sailor's eye told me the answer to that question. Someone wanted me dead.

But who? I couldn't believe a member of the crew would have taken such a serious dislike to me, so it seemed obvious he'd been bribed to do away with me.

But hardly anyone knew I'd been in Ephesus, or that I was going to Alexandria. I ran through the list of the people I had spoken to and eliminated them one by one.

Restitutus and Herakleon I knew of old. They were friends, even if Herakleon was a slave. I didn't know Pomponius Niger, but Restitutus trusted him, and that was good enough for me.

Hannibal was an old friend, so I barely even considered him except to wonder whether anyone in the gym or wine shop might have overheard us. I soon discounted that as well.

Working for Sempronius Rufus had taught me to question everything, so I even reviewed my meeting and subsequent love affair with Circe. Women are often painted as villains by bards and poets, but Circe worked for the Juggler too, and Fronto had recommended she help me, so that was as solid an alibi as anyone could have.

Diocles the Tribune was a pompous ass, but I doubted he had any reason to want me dead. I'd promised to put in a good report of his investigation and, even though I had been critical of him in what I'd actually written, he couldn't possibly know that.

Leonides the painter? No, he had no reason to want me dead. And, unless he had failed to complete his work in the dining room of Marcus Porcius, neither had his current employer.

Which left only Eteocles the freedman.

That slimy little sod had decided to get rid of me after all!

I wondered why he hadn't simply sent some of his boys round while I was in Ephesus, but perhaps he had wanted me to be well away from his city so there could be no connection made.

That meant he had something more to hide, but I fell asleep long before I could figure out what that might be.

I told Circe about the attack the next morning, playing down the danger and assuring her that the sailor had been so inept he had fallen over the side all by himself.

She was still horrified.

"We must tell the captain!" she said.

"No, we must keep it quiet. The captain thinks it was an accident, and I'd like to keep it that way. So we say nothing, sit tight and watch our backs in case the assailant has an accomplice. We'll be in Alexandria in a couple of days anyway."

She was not happy with this decision, but she grudgingly agreed to go along with it, although she fretted all day.

"I can't believe Eteocles would want to have you killed!" she repeated several times.

"I'll get even with him when I go back to Ephesus," I told her. "But forget him. We're nearly there."

And we were. Two days later, the southern horizon darkened as land came into sight, and a bright spark of light showed where the famous Pharos stood at the entrance to Alexandria's harbour. The fire at the top of the lighthouse is kept burning constantly, even during the day, because the shore around here is rather featureless, so the beacon of the lighthouse shows ships where to find the great harbour. Enhanced by polished mirrors behind the fire, sailors say the light is visible for miles, guiding them into the port even on the darkest of nights.

This wondrous edifice grew clearer as we drew closer. It stands on a long island which protects the harbour entrances, and it must be as tall as the Colossus ever was, rising in several layers to the bright flame at the summit.

Circe and I stood alongside the other passengers and slaves, each one of us gazing up in awe at the incredible sight of the famous lighthouse.

Then, accompanied by screeching gulls who whirled overhead, we rounded the Pharos island and edged towards the western harbour. But even as we approached, I looked to the other, greater harbour because I knew that was where the famous grain ships docked to be loaded with the supplies Rome needed. These massive ships, far bigger than any other vessel on the sea, plied the route between Alexandria and Ostia, Rome's port, day after day, supplying the Empire's capital city with the grain it needed to feed its vast population. Egypt was Rome's bread basket, and I was interested to see one of these magnificent ships.

What I saw instead left me speechless.

101

The great harbour is massive, so large that it has an island in its centre where the famous Cleopatra is said to have had a palace. Now, though, the harbour was crammed with what were unmistakably vessels of the imperial fleet. Row after row of them told me something out of the ordinary was going on.

Circe had seen them, too, and she grew worried about what it might mean.

"Why are they here?" she wondered.

I didn't answer, although I had a sneaking suspicion I knew the reason.

We found out as soon as we disembarked, because the entire city was full of the news.

"The Emperor is here!" was the reply to our question. "His Legions are camped outside the city, and he is in the Governor's palace."

"The Emperor?" Circe gasped, putting a hand to her mouth in astonishment. "Why is he here?"

I had no idea, but I did know one thing. I would need to go and report what I'd discovered in Ephesus.

First hand.

To the Emperor himself.

Oh, Jupiter!

Chapter 11
The Prefect

I'd never been to Alexandria, so I had no idea of how to go about finding a decent place to stay. What the city presented as we left the harbour area was a bewildering riot of noise and sights, with crowds of people milling around, many of them holding conversations at the tops of their voices or trying to gain the attention of newcomers like me and Circe.

"I usually find it's best to ignore the touts and head into the centre of town," I told her.

She nodded absently as she, too, gazed around in wonder at the bustling scene around us. Standing behind her were Helena, Agon and Diomedes, each of them carrying a heavy bag of Circe's belongings, while several porters she had hired were manhandling the trunks which contained the rest of what she assured me were essential belongings. It was no wonder I'd never seen her wear the same dress twice.

She shot me a frown as she asked, "Don't you need to go and report to the Emperor? You did say you ought to do that."

"I know, but maybe we'd better find somewhere to stay first."

She reached a decision, telling me, "You go and do what you need to do. I'll find rooms for us. Then I'll send either Agon or Diomedes back here. They can bring you once you are finished at the palace."

Agon started to say something, but Circe cut him short with a barked, "That is what we will do."

I said, "I have no idea how long I'll be. I doubt the Emperor will drop everything just to see me."

"Come when you can," she replied. "If you are not here by dusk, then I'll send one of them to meet you here first thing tomorrow."

That, I realised, was as sensible a plan as I could think of. There was every possibility I might be sitting around for hours waiting for an audience – and that was if I ever got close enough to speak to the Emperor himself. More likely, he'd have one of his secretaries interview me. It wouldn't be Sempronius Rufus, I was

103

sure, because the Juggler rarely emerged from his lair on the Palatine in Rome, but I had no doubt the Emperor would have a veritable army of quill-pushers with him.

"OK," I agreed. "I'll come back here as soon as I can."

"Give your bag to Diomedes," she told me. "You won't need it."

She was probably right, so I tossed my bag to the slave. It didn't add very much to the burden he was already carrying.

Turning back to Circe, I bent my head to kiss her goodbye. She didn't pull away, but her response was not as enthusiastic as I'd hoped. It seemed I was still not back in her good books.

"Go," she whispered softly. "And stay safe."

I gave her my most confident grin, assuring her I'd be back before too long, then set off eastwards towards what the ship's captain had told me was the palace district.

I did glance back over my shoulder, but the streets were so busy I couldn't see any sign of Circe because of the press of people all around me.

Alexandria, as everyone knows, was founded by Alexander the Great when he brought Egypt into his empire. The city is built on a limestone ridge between the vast harbours and a lake to the south which provides the city's water. I knew that much, and I'd heard a lot of stories about the magnificence of the city, but the reality was almost too much to take in. Marble shone everywhere, with tall buildings all around, the architecture combining Roman and Greek styles with a definite dash of Egyptian thrown in for good measure. Columns, porticos, statues and obelisks vied for attention as I wound my way along the wide main avenue, constantly dodging the hundreds of other people who thronged the place.

Of course, it is the people of Alexandria who are even more famous than its incredible buildings. In the pre-Roman days, several unpopular rulers were dragged out of their palace and torn to shreds by the Alexandrian mob, and the place had once rioted for several days when a visiting Roman official accidentally killed a cat.

Such riots had consequences for the structure of the place too. Alexandria had once been home to the greatest library in the world, but that had burnt down during the riots when the people had besieged Julius Caesar in the palace when he had made

Cleopatra sole ruler instead of her more popular younger brother. Of course, what Julius meant by "sole ruler" was that Cleopatra would rule under his supervision, and the people knew it. Their protest had ultimately proved futile, and a great many people had lost their lives until Rome eventually took firm control under Julius' heir, Augustus. In cultural terms, though, the loss of the Great Library was an immense blow to the city. It does still have a library, but it is a shadow of the original.

The other main thing I knew was that Alexandria contained the tomb of the great conqueror himself, brought here by Ptolemy after Alexander's death. Ptolemy had claimed Egypt as his personal province when the Macedonian empire had fragmented as each of Alexander's generals grabbed whatever piece of territory they could hold. Legend has it that, when asked on his death-bed to whom he bequeathed his empire, Alexander had said, "To the strongest."

It was a statement typical of the man. He cared little for civilisation and culture, conquest being his only real aim, and his lack of foresight resulted in decades of wars between the various generals and their successors. Only in Egypt was there relative calm. Protected by sea and desert, the Ptolemies held onto it and, aside from a short-lived occupation by the Persians, had retained power until the Romans came along and took it from them.

The result, or what my first impression of Alexandria suggested was the local result, was a real mix of a place. Like everywhere in the Empire, I could see people from all sorts of backgrounds, with the usual variety of skin and hair colours, but it was the languages that struck me. I heard Greek, of course, because the upper classes, that is those who were descended from Ptolemy and his original army of Macedonians, spoke Greek, and many of their subjects had adopted the language. There was, though, a distinct accent audible, and I understood what the slave, Barnabus, had meant.

The same went for Latin, which was also prominent, but there was another tongue much in use which I guessed must be the local language.

It was obvious, though, that even the poorest local had a smattering of Greek. I passed one young urchin who couldn't have been more than ten years old who asked me whether I'd like to make love to his sister. He phrased it rather more crudely than that and, when I declined, he trotted after me to inform me that he had a brother as well if that was more to my taste.

I told him where to go. Not politely, but in a phrase I knew he'd understand.

He did go, but not before confirming that he had quite a vocabulary of crudities.

All in all, Alexandria buffeted the senses.

I quickly discovered that the city was laid out in a grid pattern, with streets running north to south and east to west. That made navigation a bit easier. Besides, beyond the massive warehouses and public buildings which bordered the harbour district, I could see the tops of other grand buildings on the far side of the great harbour. That, I supposed, would be the palace district, where the Governor's residence would be found. And that, I hoped, would also be where I would find Marcus Aurelius Antoninus Augustus Caesar, Emperor of Rome and, if my pal Hannibal was to be believed, now being referred to as Caracalla.

As I slowly eased through the crowds, I tried to think of a reason why the Emperor would have come here. But with his campaign in Germania concluded, and with Parthia being occupied by discussing a marriage alliance, I supposed it made some sense for the Emperor to visit Egypt. This place is, after all, the source of a great deal of wealth, not to mention the grain supplies without which the Roman plebs would no doubt riot. Egypt is so important to the empire, in fact, that no Senator is allowed to visit without the express permission of the Emperor himself. No Emperor wants a powerful and influential man grabbing hold of Egypt and so holding Rome to ransom. The Governor is always someone of Equestrian rank, and few of them are left in office long enough to develop any thoughts of setting themselves up as local magnates. As an added precaution, the Governor has only two Legions at his disposal. At any given time, despite all the demands placed on our army by the immensely long borders of the empire, the Emperor can muster several Legions if he feels the need to stamp his authority anywhere.

It was pretty clear that his authority was on display now. The closer I came to the peninsula which housed the palace district, the more soldiers were in evidence. Some dressed in chainmail, others in the traditional *lorica segmentata* armour, they were standing around in small groups on nearly every street corner, watching the civilians with wary eyes. There is no such thing as uniform equipment in the Roman army, and the Emperor had introduced a number of reforms which meant his men were armed with a variety of weapons, but I did notice that many of the men were wearing a long, hooded cloak, so maybe Hannibal's information had been correct after all.

Mind you, I still didn't fancy addressing His Imperial Majesty as "Caracalla".

As for my own attire, I had considered changing into my equestrian tunic, but had decided against it. For one thing, I wanted to remain inconspicuous until I understood what was going on and, for another, I didn't fancy the idea of having to explain to the Emperor why I was wearing a tunic I was not entitled to. Besides, my pendant should be enough to get me past the guards. I hoped.

I'd also discarded my wide-brimmed hat because walking around with an Artemis badge on my head would have marked me out as a definite tourist, and I knew how locals always targeted visitors.

So I plodded on through the afternoon heat, grateful for the breeze which came off the sea, but I was still tired and sweating by the time I met the first obstacle.

I reached this long before I got anywhere near the Governor's palace. A cordon of legionaries blocked the cobbled street ahead of me, all of them looking suitably grim and imposing.

A Decurion held up a hand and told me, "Turn back. Nobody is allowed beyond this point."

He spoke in Latin, so I guessed he wasn't from one of the local Legions.

Replying in the same tongue, I told him, "I need to see one of The Emperor's secretaries. I have important information."

"Yeah, you and half the bloody city," the Decurion sneered. "Get lost before I get one of my lads to ram a spear up your arse."

I smiled to show him I hadn't taken offence at this threat. Tugging on the thong around my neck, I pulled out the eagle pendant and held it up for him to see.

"Do you know what this means?" I asked him.

He glared at me, gave the pendant a cursory glance, then hissed, "I told you to get lost!"

"It means," I told him calmly, "that if you don't let me past, or at least relay a message to someone in authority, you could find yourself painting the northern side of Hadrian's Wall for the rest of your career."

"Are you trying to threaten me?" he rasped, although I saw a hint of uncertainty in his eyes. He'd been expecting to intimidate me, and my response wasn't that of an ordinary civilian.

"It's no threat," I assured him. "It's a promise. Now, neither of us wants any trouble, do we, so why don't you send one of your lads to find your Centurion? Better yet, have them take me to him."

The Decurion saw a way to save face. With a savage grin, he signalled to two of his troop.

"You two! Arrest this scruffy sod and take him to the Centurion. But search him first in case he's hiding any weapons."

I dropped my pendant, letting it hang outside my tunic, and nodded my thanks. Being under arrest didn't bother me as long as they held off on the beatings until I had a chance to speak to someone with a suitably senior rank.

The Centurion was the man. After roughly patting me down, the two soldiers marched me along the street, round a corner and into a large house which had obviously been appropriated by the army. Here, in a room off the atrium, sat a hot and flustered Centurion. He was wearing his armour, but his helmet with its crosswise plume was sitting on a chair to one side of the room while he dictated orders to another soldier who was busy scribbling on a wax tablet.

The Centurion looked up in irritation when I was frogmarched into his office at the point of two swords.

"What's this?" he demanded testily.

"Assuming he meant to ask, "Who is this?" I replied, "My name is Sempronius Scipio. Also known as Sigma. I need to see the Emperor's senior secretary."

I lifted the pendant again, showing him the golden eagle with the feathered spear in its talons.

Unlike his Decurion, this man knew what the symbol signified. He stood up, moved stiffly around the desk and studied the pendant closely.

"Have you searched him for weapons?" he asked the soldiers who stood behind me.

"He's unarmed, Sir!" one of them barked in response.

"Then take him to the palace and let the Praetorians decide what to do with him."

He looked at me with a gaze like flint as he said, "I hope for your sake that's a genuine token. If it's not ..."

He ran one finger across his throat to tell me what would happen to me if I was not who I claimed to be.

"It's genuine," I assured him.

That didn't seem to endear me to him at all. I suspected that, like many soldiers, he preferred seeing his enemies face to face with a sword in his hand. Spies, informers and secretive plotters were probably little better than pond life to him.

Still, I'd passed the first couple of hurdles. The soldiers, now a little less sure of themselves, escorted me along a wide avenue to a grand building which had an even grander entrance flanked by a pair of Ionic columns and with several garishly painted statues lining its front wall. Marble shone in the sunlight, and the building rose high above us, each level decorated by yet more statues of gods and heroes.

It seemed I had arrived.

There were more soldiers here, and this lot looked even meaner and tougher than the first ones I had encountered.

"Praetorians," one of my escort informed me quietly.

That was all I needed to know. The Praetorians are the Emperor's personal bodyguards. Over the centuries, they had developed a taste for the easy life because they rarely saw any action other than putting down civilian riots. Based in Rome, they had also become accustomed to being bribed by whoever wanted to succeed a dead Emperor. Rich men soon came to realise that paying the Praetorians immense amounts of money was the best way to be elected to the Purple. The Senate might choose their own man to rule, but they always backed down when a candidate was acclaimed by the Praetorians. Not that this had prevented the Praetorians from doing away with several Emperors with extreme prejudice when they felt there might be a better offer in the wings, and more than a few men had come to a bloody end as a result.

When our current Emperor's father, Septimius Severus, had seized the imperial throne, he'd summoned the Praetorians to a parade. They had murdered the previous Emperor, initiating the civil war which Severus had won, and they probably thought they were about to be rewarded. Instead, Severus dismissed every last one of them, exiling them from Italy. Judging by the way he then stamped his authority on the empire, they were probably lucky he didn't have them all executed on the spot.

He'd since instituted his own Praetorians who had remained fiercely loyal to him until his death from natural causes, and now they owed that same loyalty to his son, Antoninus.

To be fair, the entire army loved our current Emperor. He had, after all, just about tripled their pay. Rumour had it that his father's last words to him were, "Enrich the soldiers; scorn everyone else."

He'd possibly used a word other than "scorn", but I'm sure you get the idea. Young Antoninus had certainly followed that maxim, although he'd made his soldiers work for their money. Warfare was his main occupation, and he was never happier than when sending his troops into battle.

We went through the same pantomime again, with me displaying my pendant, a Centurion being summoned, and then me being passed further up the chain and deeper into the palace complex. My original escort were sent back to their duties, and I now had a couple of brawny Praetorians looking after me.

I was stopped a couple more times, with scribes checking their lists of guests, then studying my pendant when I was not on the list. They let me through until I was shown into a small room which seemed to be a study of some sort. There was a polished desk, some comfortable chairs, and racks full of book scrolls lining the walls.

There were several windows set high in one wall, so the room was quite bright, but it was pleasantly cool after the heat of the Alexandrian afternoon.

I sat there for a while, the two Praetorians taking up position outside the door.

After some time, a rather effete scribe came in and asked me questions about who I was and what my purpose was.

I answered truthfully and patiently.

"Is Sempronius Rufus here?" I enquired.

"No," he replied, but I could see that the name meant something to him.

"Then I need to see someone in authority. I have some information which may be of interest to the Emperor."

"The Emperor is busy," the scribe informed me. "He has many meetings, and tonight is hosting a dinner for members of the local Aristotelian school of philosophers plus, of course, all the Senators who have accompanied him."

"I understand," I assured him. "But perhaps one of his secretaries who is familiar with Sempronius Rufus might spare me some time?"

"Could you tell me what it is about?" he asked.

"No. Not unless you can tell me what you know of my mission to Ephesus."

He couldn't, so he went off to find someone who could. He did, though, have a tray of wine and honey cakes sent in, so at least I didn't go hungry.

I waited for a long time, some of which I passed by browsing the scrolls. Eventually, with nothing better to do, I began to read a copy of Thucydides' Peloponnesian War. There's nothing like a bit of history to make you want to sleep.

The room grew darker as the light coming in through the high windows faded. I knocked on the door and swung it open, asking the guards to have someone bring me some light. A slave soon arrived, lighting an oil lamp which he placed on the table. Its dim light, and old Thucydides, was all the company I had for the next few hours.

I was growing tired by the time the door opened again, but the person who entered banished any weariness I might have felt. He was dressed in a toga, and I could smell wine on his breath as he came towards me, right hand extended in greeting.

He was not a large man, quite slim in fact, and a little shorter than me. He had a full beard, and the slightly dusky hue to his skin suggested he was of African or Egyptian descent. I reckoned he must have been around fifty years old, and he was obviously a man accustomed to having authority, for he acted and spoke with complete self-confidence.

I'd guessed at his identity, but when he told me his name I knew exactly who he was.

"Marcus Opellius Macrinus," he introduced himself.

Macrinus. The Praetorian Prefect. Effectively the Emperor's right hand man. The second most powerful man in the empire.

And he was here, clasping forearms with me in the traditional Roman style.

I'd never met or even seen Macrinus before, but I knew his reputation. Many Senators detested him because he had risen through society from the lower ranks. This was thanks to the policies of the old Emperor, Severus, which had been continued by his son, whereby men were promoted thanks to their ability rather than their wealth or their name and ancestry.

Macrinus was of Berber stock, from North Africa, but he was now very close to the top of Roman society. The Praetorians were under his direct command, and he was privy to everything that went on in the empire. Which meant he must be a very capable man indeed.

"Sempronius Scipio," I said in reply to his introduction.

He gestured for me to sit, while he took another chair and pulled it close so that we sat virtually knee to knee.

The two guards were in the room now, barring the way to the door. It wasn't entirely clear to me whether their presence was for Macrinus' protection or to intimidate me. Perhaps it was a little of both. Not that Macrinus' attitude was in any way threatening, but the presence of the two hulking guards left me in no doubt that things could turn nasty at a single word from the man facing me.

"What is your code name?" he asked, getting straight to the point.

"Sigma."

"And your full name?"

"Sextus Sempronius Secundus, but I prefer Scipio."

"No wonder the Juggler calls you Sigma," he said with a soft smile which nevertheless suggested there was steel behind it.

He stared intently at me as he continued his questions.

"What name does Sempronius Rufus use to denote Caesar Augustus?"

"Romulus," I answered without hesitation.

"And what was stolen from the Temple in Ephesus?"

"An amulet belonging to Alexander the Great which was donated to the Temple by our former Emperor."

He nodded, apparently satisfied with my responses, then shot me another question.

"What is your relationship to Tiberius Sestius Fronto?"

So he knew Fronto. I supposed a man like Macrinus would need to know a great many people. But did that mean he knew about me as well?"

I said, "I knew Fronto as a boy. We grew up as neighbours."

"And your mother's name?"

"Zoe."

Now, at last, Macrinus relaxed. His manner had been friendly enough, but I knew he had wanted to be sure I was who I said I was. Where he had obtained his information, I did not know. I couldn't imagine he carried it around in his head because I was a rather insignificant piece of the imperial spy network. Still, he was sufficiently satisfied to tell the two guards to leave the room so that we could talk in private.

"I am familiar with your mission," he told me once the lumbering Praetorians had closed the door behind them. "I had asked Rufus to keep me apprised of developments, but since you are here you may as well tell me now. What have you discovered?"

So I spent the next half hour giving him a concise report of what I had learned. I didn't mention Circe because she might have presented a complication, but I told him everything else, including the fact that someone had tried to kill me on the voyage to Alexandria.

Macrinus did not waste time in drawing conclusions. He had a sharp mind, and he quickly honed in on the main issues.

"I think you were right to come here instead of going to Athens," he nodded. "I suspect that house will be empty by now. I shall write to Sempronius Rufus and have him send someone to check that, but if there is a plot, it is here in Alexandria."

He frowned, rubbing his cheek pensively while he considered the implications.

"The fact that only the amulet was stolen suggests that either the thief has an obsession with Alexander, or that they wished to harm our Emperor's reputation by stealing from him."

"That's what I think," I agreed.

"But which one?"

I shrugged, "I don't have enough information to make that judgement."

"I think you do," he said with a smile. "Why would the freedman want you dead? He knew you were hunting the amulet.

If it were merely theft to satisfy someone's greed, he would surely not seek to have you killed to prevent you discovering the identity of the culprit."

I considered that for a moment before countering, "Or it may be that the person who now has the amulet did not realise it had belonged to Caesar's father. Once they learned that, they may have panicked."

Macrinus pursed his lips, nodding gently to show he acknowledged my suggestion.

"That is possible," he admitted. "But my role is to prevent any harm coming to the Emperor. If there is the possibility of a plot against him, I must consider what to do about it."

"I can't see how stealing an amulet poses a threat," I told him. "I've given it a lot of thought, and while it may be that someone wants to thumb his nose at Caesar, it surely doesn't represent any actual danger."

"His nose? Or hers, perhaps," Macrinus pointed out. "The woman in Athens may have been the principal behind the theft. And do not forget, they have already killed once. Aristides may have been a crook, but they killed him to silence him. The question is why. What did he know that required his death?"

He had me there, so I said nothing.

Macrinus placed his elbows on his knees, clasping his hands together beneath his chin and tapping his fingers together while he pondered what we knew so far.

"There may be more to this than you realise, Scipio," he informed me after a moment's consideration. "You see, Alexandria is a hotbed of potential revolt. Its people have always been volatile, and feelings are running particularly high at the moment. Did you know they recently performed a satire lampooning the Emperor himself?"

"No, I hadn't heard that."

"It was very uncomplimentary to say the least. Caesar was not pleased when he heard of it."

"Do you know who was responsible for it?" I asked.

Macrinus grinned, obviously pleased that I was thinking along the same lines as he was.

"Oh, yes. Half the city was behind it, especially the priests of various cults."

114

"So should I start by looking around the temples to see if I can locate Philippos?"

"Do you know what he looks like?"

"No. He's described as being around my age, I suppose. With dark hair. And he speaks with an Alexandrian accent."

"That narrows it down to a few tens of thousands," Macrinus said with a smile.

"But the temples are a good place to start," I persisted.

"I have no other suggestions to make," Macrinus sighed. "So go and start asking questions. Be as aggressive as you like. See if you can obtain a reaction."

"A reaction like someone trying to kill me, you mean?"

It probably wasn't the sort of question I should have put to the Praetorian Prefect, but Macrinus gave a low chuckle.

"Yes, that sort of thing. Do you want me to assign some Praetorians to accompany you? That might help keep you alive while you are ruffling people's feathers."

I shook my head.

"No, thank you. I work better on my own. But it would be nice if I could have some way of contacting you quickly. It took all afternoon for me to reach you."

He said, "I shall have a pass written for you. That, combined with your pendant, should allow quick access."

He glanced at the scroll I had left lying on the table. Picking it up, he read the title, then shot me a satisfied smile.

"Thucydides? Yes, that should do."

I waited, wondering what he meant.

He told me, "I shall have a man posted outside the Sema every day. He will be reading this scroll, and he will know your code name. You can pass messages to him if needed."

"The Sema?" I asked.

"Where the tomb of Alexander is. It's almost in the centre of the city, so you should be able to reach it reasonably quickly wherever you might be."

"I understand. Thank you."

"Do you want a local guide as well?" he asked.

The more I talked to Macrinus, the more I liked him. He seemed to think of everything. The trouble was that the things he was thinking of meant Circe's presence would soon come to his attention.

I said, "That's a good idea. But not straight away. I'd like to establish a base for myself in the city. I'll tell your contact man, Thucydides, when I need the guide."

"Very well. If there is anything else you need, let me know, either through the man we will call Thucydides or by coming here directly."

"Can I ask how long you will be staying in Alexandria?" I enquired.

"A while yet," he replied. "Probably a few weeks. Perhaps longer."

I nodded, "That should give me plenty of time to find Philippos."

"Good. I wish you luck. Hopefully you will learn it is nothing more than a case of greed and theft, but we cannot be too careful when it comes to protecting the Emperor."

He placed the scroll on the desk, then turned back to me.

"I will have someone find a bed for you here tonight, but I think you should accompany me back to the feast."

"Me?" I blinked in surprise.

"Indeed. We may as well start ruffling feathers now. You see, we not only have some leading citizens from the city as guests, there are rather a lot of Senators here as well, including that pompous idiot, Cassius Dio."

"Senators?" I asked, struggling to keep up.

"Of course. You see, there are many Senators the Emperor does not trust. We find it is easier to insist they accompany him on his travels. That way, they cannot be making secret plots in Rome, and we can keep a close eye on them. It might be useful if you came to recognise them."

"In case any of them are behind the theft of the amulet, you mean?"

He grinned again, clapping me on the shoulder.

"Very good, Scipio. I see Sempronius Rufus chose well when he recruited you. Now, let us join what is left of the feast before everyone succumbs to the effects of the wine and passes out."

Chapter 12
Searching

I left the Governor's palace early the following morning, stepping out into what promised to be another sweltering day. I had spent the night in a comfortable bed, and I now had in my sweaty hand a pass bearing Macrinus' signature and seal. This document allowed me to negotiate my way past the various sets of guards and sentries with no difficulty. Once beyond the final check, I folded the small parchment and tucked it into one of the pockets cut into the inner lining of my belt. This was a trick I'd learned from the Juggler. My belt was wide and made of thick leather, with a solid if unremarkable buckle, but on the inner side were cut several pockets. I normally used them to hold an emergency supply of coins, but they were equally useful for keeping important documents safe.

I felt refreshed and ready to resume my hunt for the mysterious Philippos and the stolen amulet. Macrinus had certainly boosted my sense of confidence that I had done the right thing in coming to Alexandria, although I recognised that he was not a man who would take too kindly to being disappointed if I failed to track down the people behind the theft and murder.

Thinking of Macrinus turned my mind back to the previous evening. As I strolled back into town, I reflected on the meal I had attended at his insistence. It had been held in a huge room which was set with dozens of couches in the Roman style. They were organized in sets of three laid out in the traditional *triclinium* arrangement, with a low table having a long couch on three sides, leaving an open side for slaves to deliver the various dishes. Macrinus had placed me at a free space in a *triclinium* which could not have been further away from the Emperor unless it had been placed outside the room. Two of the couches around this remote table held three Senators, while only two men lay on the one Macrinus pointed out to me.

I was rather nervous of sitting in such exalted company, especially as I was still wearing my shabby tunic. I probably looked like one of the kitchen slaves, but Macrinus stopped beside the couch and, in a voice which was loud enough to be heard by the closest Senators even over the hubbub of conversation which echoed around the great hall, he told me to take my place there.

"There is a space for you here, Scipio," he said imperiously. Then, beaming amiably at the Senators, he told them, "This is one of my spies. He's here to report on anything you say."

Then he burst out laughing and walked off to join the Emperor at the far end of the room.

I felt very awkward, taking my place nervously, trying not to nudge the nearest man as I stretched out and leaned on one elbow in the traditional Roman pose.

"You're a spy?" my neighbour's voice sounded close beside me.

"Actually, I'm part of a diplomatic mission to Parthia," I replied, using the lie Macrinus had suggested. "I'm really just a messenger, but the Prefect said the easiest way to feed me was to bring me here."

"So you're not a spy?" the man persisted, his words slurred by drink.

I twisted my neck to look at him, noting the florid face and heavy jowls. He was, like most Senators, an older man who seemed perpetually angry. He'd obviously been here for a while, for the rumpled folds of his toga were covered in crumbs and bore more than one stain of spilled wine.

"Would it bother you if I was?" I asked him. "Are you planning some dreadful plot?"

I smiled as I said it, and one of the men sitting opposite laughed aloud.

"Caesar and his Berber Prefect have spies everywhere, Titus," he told my immediate neighbour. "I'm sure every word we've said will be known to them by the morning whether this Scipio is a spy or not."

The others smiled or chuckled, although I noticed they were all regarding me warily. Perhaps it was my obvious lowly status that irritated them as much as the possibility that I might really be an imperial spy.

As it turned out, I learned very little except that they were all more than half drunk and all very bitter about being dragged around the empire in the Emperor's wake.

"He insists we attend him every day," my new friend Titus complained, "but then he keeps us standing around outside whichever building he has taken residence in, and sometimes he doesn't bother talking to us at all."

Scowling at one of the men who sat in a position of relative seniority on the third couch at the head of our lowly table, he added, "I hope you'll be writing that down in your damned history, Dio."

I guessed the man named Dio must be the Cassius Dio Macrinus had mentioned. Was it a coincidence that Macrinus had placed me at the same table? I doubted it. Macrinus didn't seem to be the sort of man who was prone to coincidental behaviour.

Dio gave me a thin smile, but said nothing in response to Titus' grumbling.

I affected not to notice. The feast was almost over by the time I had arrived, with the slaves having delivered the sweet courses, but I had one of them bring me a plate of shellfish, so I pretended to concentrate my attention on eating, allowing the Senators to resume their mutual moaning. If Macrinus had expected me to uncover some deep plot, he was going to be disappointed. I thought this bunch of whiners were a load of self-indulgent nonentities. The only one who seemed to have a brain was Cassius Dio, but he rarely spoke and when he did he was very circumspect. I couldn't blame him for that.

I'd made my excuses as early as I could, slipping out of the room and finding one of the household slaves who found a bed for me for the night. I never did catch more than a brief glimpse of the Emperor.

And now I was back on the hunt for Philippos and his accomplices. First, though, I needed to find Circe.

I walked along the wide avenue which crosses the city from east to west, linking the city's two main gates. I took my time because Alexandria was impressive and I wanted to make sure I saw as much as possible. I was particularly enamoured with the two magnificent obelisks which stood outside a large temple to Augustus, their unfamiliar design confirming that Alexandria was not a typical Roman city.

When I reached the marketplace, I eased through the growing crowds to the corner of an adjoining street which ran south from the harbour and market district. This was where I had left Circe the day before and where she was supposed to send one of the slaves to meet me.

119

There was nobody there. Nobody I recognised, at any rate. It may have been early, but the vendors in the market were already setting up, eager to do business before the heat of the day blistered the city again. Their customers were flocking here, too, but there was no sign of Agon or Diomedes.

I wasn't too worried because it was still early, so I took a wander around the market, idly checking out the goods on sale. There was, as they say, everything you could want, including all sorts of foodstuffs, a wide selection of clothing and crockery, along with plenty of fake art objects masquerading as ancient artefacts from the age of the Pharaohs, and all of it being touted by men with loud voices and waving arms.

I didn't bother spending any of my money as I was simply passing the time, but when I returned to the street corner half an hour later, there was still no trace of Circe's slaves.

Now I was beginning to grow concerned. Frowning, I dodged past a street entertainer who was performing acrobatics for the amusement of a small crowd of passers-by, and walked south into the city. As I moved slowly along, I scanned the buildings to either side of the cobbled street, looking for any likely inn where Circe might have gone in search of rooms. I found a couple which seemed reasonably up-market and went inside, but my enquiries about Tertullia Tertia and her caravan of luggage met with blank looks and head shakes.

I turned around, retraced my steps and checked again, but the corner where I'd left Circe still held no welcome for me.

I began to experience those doubts you get when things go wrong, so I walked along the east-west road for a few blocks in case I'd mistaken which street corner was the agreed rendezvous. Then I turned back and walked a few blocks in the other direction. Eventually, I returned to what I had known all along was the right place, and still I was alone.

I glanced skywards, checking the sun. By my reckoning, it was past the second hour of the day, so even if Circe and all three of her slaves had slept in, one of them would surely have appeared by now.

I was feeling very anxious by this time. Alexandria was a busy port, with visitors coming on a daily basis, so it had quite a few inns. That would make searching difficult, especially as I did not know the town, but the really concerning thing was that Circe had not sent someone to fetch me. That could only mean one thing. Something had happened to her.

But what? And how on earth was I supposed to find her?

Telling myself to remain calm, I purchased a bag of figs from one of the stalls so that I could eat while on the move, then decided to begin the mission I had agreed to do for Macrinus. But I'd also drop into every inn I passed so that I could carry out both searches at once. I pushed back the thought that, if something really had happened to Circe, she might not be in any of the inns. So, if I happened to find any *vigiles* or whatever the Alexandrian equivalent was, I'd ask them whether there had been any reports of trouble concerning a young woman and three slaves.

Following the advice I'd given Circe the day before, I headed due south down the main road, aiming for the centre of the city.

Before long, I arrived at the place I'd been looking for. Known as the Sema, there was a wide, tree-lined square of sand and gravel surrounded by many impressive buildings which included the Temple of Isis. And in the centre sat the Tomb of Alexander.

I'd seen a lot of magnificent buildings, including some of the Seven Wonders, and it must be said this one didn't quite match any of them for scale. But what it lacked in size – and it was still an impressively large building – it more than made up for in decoration. It towered above the surrounding buildings, rising high to an incredible pyramid-shaped roof. Its marble walls and columns dazzled with reflected sunlight, and larger than life statues of Alexander wearing military armour flanked what should have been the entrance. I say "should have been" because there was now only a brick wall to mark where the doors had been. I recalled Restitutus telling me that our previous Emperor, Septimius Severus, had sealed the tomb after removing the amulet. It was an odd thing to do, but perhaps he didn't want anyone else helping themselves to the great man's treasures after he'd had his pick. As it was, the bricked-up entrance was a real eyesore compared to the opulence of the rest of the building.

Under the pretence of looking at the Tomb, I glanced around to see whether anyone was sitting reading a copy of Thucydides. There were plenty of stone and marble benches dotted around the square, and the Tomb seemed to be a sort of meeting place, but it was probably too soon for Macrinus' man to have taken up his station.

I took a slow wander around the tomb, admiring the intricate decoration and the sheer magnificence of the construction. Ptolemy had certainly done his leader proud.

The place was teeming with people now. Some were sitting in the shade of the trees, others hurrying past on errands, while some were copying my own admiration of the tomb. But still there was nobody I recognised.

It was growing hot by now, so I headed into the temple of Isis. It seemed as good a place as any to start.

Isis is a major deity in many parts of the Empire. I knew that, while the Emperor had displayed a marked preference for Serapis, he also used Isis temples as message drop locations. When it came to spying and sniffing out subversion, our Antoninus Caracalla was happy to use the services of any god or goddess.

Under the shade of the portico, the temperature dropped considerably, but it became decidedly frosty when I moved inside. Worship of the gods is usually an outdoors affair, and a sour-faced young priest soon made it clear that, unless I was there to offer a donation, he'd prefer me to leave the goddess's sanctuary.

Smiling, I showed him my pendant.

"Tell your High Priest that I need a word, would you?"

He glared at me, but he obviously recognised the symbol, and soon I was being ushered through a side door, down a corridor and into a small but opulent chamber where an elderly, bearded man invited me to sit once I'd shown him the pendant.

"I have not seen you before," he said, his tone polite.

"I'm only here for a short while, I hope," I told him.

He smiled knowingly. The Emperor was in town, so it made sense that a small army of spies would have moved in with him.

I went on, "I am looking for somebody. He was recently in Ephesus. The name he went under was Philippos, and he was an artist and painter."

"I do not know the name," the priest told me.

"It may not be his real name. I'm told he is about my own age, with short, curly, brown hair."

He gave me a helpless smile as he pointed out, "That description could match a great many young men in this city."

122

"I know. But I need to find him. He may be in the company of a man with Arabic features."

Again, the priest's eyes betrayed no hint of recognition.

"That could apply to even more people in Alexandria," he informed me.

I sighed, "Well, if you do see him, or hear about someone who might be him, I need to know as a matter of urgency. The Emperor wants me to find him."

The priest nodded, then asked, "And how shall I send a message to you if I do hear anything?"

"That's easy," I told him, giving him an explanation of the Thucydides' reader Macrinus was arranging. "Tell him you have a message for Sigma."

The priest promised to keep his eyes and ears open, but I wasn't holding out much hope. Still, this was only the first temple I'd tried, so I thanked him and went back outside into the stifling heat.

This time when I circled the tomb, I noticed a middle-aged man sitting on a bench at the tomb's shaded north wall. He was busy studying a scroll which he held in his lap. I couldn't make out the title, but I sauntered over and sat down at the opposite end of the bench. People don't normally plonk themselves right beside a stranger, so I hoped this would look natural enough to anyone who might happen to be watching us. Not that I thought anyone would be watching us out of anything other than idle curiosity, but working for the Juggler does make you careful.

The man hadn't even looked up. He was intent on the scroll.

"It's a hot day," I remarked, as strangers do when they encounter one another.

He glanced over, nodding in a not-too-friendly way, then went back to his book.

"What's that you are reading?" I enquired.

"Thucydides."

"Ah, that's good. I'm Sigma."

He gave me another look, then returned his attention to the scroll.

There was a long silence, but he eventually spoke in a low voice which only I could hear.

"Do you have a message, then?"

"Only to say that I have begun my enquiries. I have informed the high priest of Isis that he should pass messages to you. His messenger will know my name. I'll tell other temples the same thing."

The man nodded, never removing his gaze from the lines of Greek text in front of him.

"Nice talking to you," I said as I rose and moved on.

I suppose I couldn't blame him for being less than amiable. It might be an easy job sitting there all day waiting for me to report, but it probably wasn't the most exciting task in the world.

My own task proved more frustrating than exciting. Criss-crossing the city, I visited three more temples by lunch time, including the fabulously glittering and ornate Serapion, but none of the priests could shed any light on the whereabouts of Philippos. Nor did I find any trace of Circe in the several inns I visited. I even tried asking a gang of street kids whether they'd seen her passing the previous day. They demanded coin for their information, then shook their heads before running off in case I asked for my money back.

By late afternoon, I had walked more miles than I care to remember. My feet were sore, and my spirits low. Five more temples and three more inns had produced precisely the same, negative results.

I ended up back near the harbour, where my last visit was to the temple of Augustus. After the usual response to my enquiries, I came out feeling very low. I decided I needed to take a break.

First, though, I returned to the meeting place in case one of Circe's slaves had turned up.

They hadn't.

Wearily, I trudged over to the market. Here, I invested in a new bag which I could sling over my shoulder by its long strap, then purchased a replacement tunic, some fresh underwear, new sandals, a razor and mirror, a cloak to wear after dark when the heat would be replaced by chilling cold, and a wax tablet and stylus.

I hated doing this, because it was an admission that I had failed to find Circe and that something dreadful had happened to her.

I considered going to Macrinus and asking for the local guide he'd offered, or even for a troop of Praetorians to help my search, but I hadn't mentioned Circe to the Prefect, and doing so now might seem odd. She'd asked to be kept out of my reports, but now I was beginning to regret it. I was imagining all sorts of terrible things that could have happened to her, and it was preying on my mind so much I knew I wasn't concentrating properly on how to solve the problems. There had to be an easier way to find her and Philippos, but I couldn't think straight.

I toyed with the idea of going back to the Governor's palace, but eventually headed back down to the Sema and Alexander's tomb. I found Thucydides still sitting there, although he'd moved to another seat under the spreading boughs of a lime tree.

"No luck," I told him in response to his raised eyebrow. "But I need some information for tomorrow if you can get it."

He gave a slow nod to indicate that he'd heard, but he made no other response. He certainly wasn't the world's greatest talker.

"It may be unconnected," I told him, "but there could be a young woman who might know where to find the man I'm looking for."

He waited in silence, so I went on, "She's in her early twenties. Goes by the name of Tertullia Tertia. She's from Carthage, and she arrived in Alexandria yesterday, coming in on a boat from Ephesus. But I can't find her either. Can you check with the local watchmen to see whether they've heard of any trouble she might be in."

"What sort of trouble?" he asked, breaking his habit of silence.

"I don't know. That's why I'm asking. It's a long shot, but if I find her, I might get a clue as to where Philippos is."

"What's the connection?" he asked.

"I'm not sure," I said, knowing perfectly well there was no connection at all. "Like I said, it's a long shot, but it's odd that she's disappeared so soon after arriving. There may be nothing to it, but I'd like to be sure."

"Anything else?" he asked.

"Not for today. I'll see you tomorrow."

With an exaggerated sigh, he rolled up his scroll, stood, stretched his back and legs, then strolled away without giving me a solitary glance.

Which left me looking for somewhere to spend the night.

I opted for a small inn down a narrow street just off the Sema. It was better than the dump I'd checked into in Ephesus, but not much. I didn't think it was the sort of place Circe would ever use, but I asked all the same, receiving the usual negative replies.

I had to share the room with three other men. Normally, the snoring that filled the cramped chamber would have driven me mad, but that night it was thoughts of Circe that kept me awake. I worried and fretted so much I don't think I managed more than a couple of hours' very poor sleep.

I rose early the next morning, put on my new tunic, stuffed my other things in my bag, and went out to find somewhere to eat breakfast.

There was a little booth near a corner of a street which led onto the Sema Square. I paid for a bowl of spiced gruel and a hunk of bread, along with a glass of what I was assured was fresh water, and joined a few other early diners who were standing around eating their breakfast. I leaned against the wall adjoining the booth, dipping the bread into the gruel and trying to think of a better way to find Circe.

I needed an incredible stroke of luck and, even though I'd made no offerings to any of the gods whose temples I had visited the previous day, one of them must have been listening to my silent pleas, because it was while I was standing there and chewing on the last of my breakfast that I at last saw a familiar face.

She was walking past Alexander's tomb, the handle of a large wicker basket held in the crook of her left arm as she waddled towards where I stood.

I almost shouted her name, but instead I ducked a bit lower, concealing myself behind a couple of other men who were engaged in some heated discussion in the local dialect.

I watched as she kept going along the street, wondering whether I was mistaken, but it was definitely Helena, Circe's attendant slave.

She hadn't noticed me, so I kept my eyes on her and began following her from a distance, keeping to the other side of the street and using other pedestrians as cover whenever I could.

It wasn't long before she stopped at one of the local shops which sold fresh produce. I kept going, moving past her but always keeping her in sight. She haggled for a while, stuffed a variety of food items into her capacious basket, then walked back the way she had come.

I was confused. What was Helena doing out here buying food as if nothing had happened to her mistress? The only conclusions I could reach were either that Circe had sold Helena to someone else, or that Circe was deliberately keeping away from me. The first didn't seem likely, while the second made me feel as if someone had landed a solid punch in my belly.

Naturally, there was only one thing I could do. I followed Helena as she made her way back past the tomb, entering another street which led off to the east. Then she went into an alleyway, vanishing from my sight. I hurried my pace, the hobnails in my sandals loud on the cobbles, then stopped when I reached the alley. Cautiously, I peered round the corner.

The dark lane was empty. It ran between two large houses. I could see high, stone walls on either side. The houses, each with a flat roof three storeys above my head, had courtyards at their rear, but these were guarded by walls which were over ten feet in height.

At the far end, I could see bright daylight between other houses which backed onto these two, but there was no sign of Helena.

I knew she couldn't possibly have reached the far end so quickly, so I ducked into the alley and moved along, squinting as my eyes adjusted to the alternating patterns of light and dark.

The answer, of course, was simple. Helena was a slave, so she wouldn't have used the front door. Once I'd passed beyond the buildings and reached the walls around their courtyards or gardens, I found two gates; one on either side. She had obviously gone into one of these houses through the rear entrance. But which one?

The gate to my right was old and cracked with age, while the one on my left was very solid and had iron bands running across it, as well as a very substantial lock.

So, I reasoned, try the easy one first.

It was then that I heard someone else moving into the alley from the main street. Glad I hadn't been caught red-handed trying to break into a property, I turned to see who was coming in behind me.

The alley was not wide, having barely enough space for two people to walk side by side, and the man who was coming briskly towards me now was big enough to occupy most of that space. As he emerged from the comparative gloom of the first part of the lane, I saw he was wearing a simple belted tunic and sandals. His hair was short, his skin tanned, and I reckoned he must be in his thirties.

"Can I help you, Sir?" he asked in refined Greek.

"Yes, actually I think you can. Can you tell me who lives in these houses?"

He hesitated for a moment, but replied, "Of course, Sir."

Gesturing towards the fragile, ancient gate, he said, "That one belongs to the widow Zenobia. Here on the other side is the house of my master, Dion of Memphis."

"Ah. Thanks. Do you happen to know if either of them has a guest at the moment? A young woman by the name of Tertullia. I thought I saw her slave. She's an old friend, you see."

"I'm sorry, Sir. I know nobody of that name. The widow rarely has visitors, and I know my master has no guests at the moment."

I paused, considering my options. I was absolutely certain it was Helena I'd seen, and she must have gone into one of these homes. I had just decided to head back to the main street and knock on the front doors when I heard a key turning in the lock of what this slave had told me was the home of Dion of Memphis.

Naturally, I glanced towards the gate as it swung open on oiled hinges.

And I stared into the face of Agon.

We gaped at one another, neither of us reacting very quickly. In fact, it was the other slave who moved first, grabbing me and bundling me towards the gate. I yelled as Agon jumped backwards, moving out of the way, then I was shoved roughly down to the paved floor of the courtyard. I heard the gate slam shut behind me, then I felt something very hard and very heavy hit me on the back of the head. It wasn't an expert blow, but it was enough to daze me.

I sprawled on the ground, trying to push myself up, but one of them seized me by the arms while the other ripped my bag away from my shoulder. Then I felt them relieve me of my purse.

"Nice," said Agon as he heard the clink of coins.

I struggled desperately, but that only earned me another clout on the head.

"We should kill him now," I heard Agon say through my dazed senses.

"Not here!" the other slave shot back. "You know the Master does not like that sort of thing here. Take him inside and let the Master decide."

They hauled me upright and bundled me towards another impressively strong door which led to the rear of the house. I was still alive, but Agon battered my head again for good measure.

"You're a dead man!" he hissed in my ear.

Chapter 13
Interrogation

By the time I had recovered my senses, I had been dragged into the house. I heard some voices, their tone surprised and anxious, then I was hauled into a large room and shoved down onto a wooden chair. In moments, burly hands had lashed ropes around my chest and legs, pinning me to the chair while I continued to blink away the stars which were spinning in front of my eyes.

As my vision gradually returned, I saw that I was in what was obviously a large dining area, dominated by a heavy and very expensive-looking table, with sturdy chairs arranged all around it, several of them occupied.

I suppose it should have seemed odd that so many people were here at this early hour of the day, but all thoughts of trying to understand were driven from my mind when I saw Circe among the seated guests. She was sitting on the far side of the table, facing me. In fact, everyone was facing me. I saw three middle-aged and prosperous-looking men, along with two younger men around my own age who were obviously identical twins, although I had to check that twice in case I was seeing double.

Every one of them, including Circe, looked at me with an expectant air, although I should have realised that there was also an element of apprehension on their faces. At the time, though, there was too much to take in.

To my right, at the head of the table, sat an older man with short-cropped, grey-flecked hair. He wore a very expensive robe of fine linen, dyed a shade of dark green that must have cost him a fortune. He wore gold rings on a couple of fingers, and a smile of genuine delight on his tanned face.

I took all this in in an instant, but my eyes were drawn to the objects which sat on the table in front of the grey-haired host. Again I wondered whether I was seeing double, but there was no doubt about it. There were two identical amulets, both made of gold and with golden chains attached. Each amulet bore a bull's face which stood out in relief from the front of the fist-sized golden plate.

I stared at the things with blank incomprehension.

I blinked, seeking Circe, but she simply stared back at me, her face hard and impassive.

"Welcome, Sempronius Scipio," said the grey-haired man to my right. "Or should I call you Sigma?"

"Who are you?" I rasped, my voice thick with anger and humiliation, although my brain was still working sufficiently well enough to recognise that he was the man in charge.

"My name is Dion," he informed me casually. "This is my home."

"And these others?" I demanded, jerking my chin to indicate his other guests.

He smiled a cruel smile which would not have shamed a Nile crocodile as he said, "These are my friends. The ones who will help me free Alexandria from the tyranny of Roman rule."

"You're mad!" I told him.

As ripostes go, it probably wasn't a killer, but it was the best I could come up with because I had a lot of things whirling in my aching head at that moment.

Not least of those things was what Circe was doing here.

"What's going on?" I asked her, annoyed at the sound of self-pity which accompanied my words.

In a cold, quiet voice, she told me, "I warned you not to come to Alexandria. I told you to go to Athens. You would not listen, would you?"

I still did not understand.

Dion's next words confused me even more.

"Dido did her best to send you off on the wrong track," he told me. "If you had followed her advice, none of this need have happened."

"Dido?" I frowned, desperately trying to understand.

Circe shrugged, "It is a name I use."

That set my mind racing.

"Is there any particular reason you use it?" I asked, failing to keep my dismay at her betrayal from my voice.

"You must know the legend," she told me brusquely. "Work it out for yourself."

Her tone left me as helpless as a punch to the belly would have done. I had loved this woman, had spent passionate nights – and days – with her. And now she was telling me she was my enemy and had been in on the plot the whole time.

I knew the legend of Dido, of course. Every Roman knows it.

It began with the sack of Troy, when Aeneas fled from the burning city, carrying his father on his back. Taking ship, he and a few followers had sailed away, eventually reaching the newly-founded city of Carthage which was ruled over by a beautiful queen named Dido. As you'd expect from such a story, they had an affair which was, according to legend, almost as passionate as the one I had had with the woman I knew as Circe.

But Aeneas was driven by destiny, so he decided to leave Carthage. He abandoned Dido and set sail for Italy where, according to some versions of the tale, he founded Rome.

Of course, Rome was also said to have been founded by Romulus and Remus, so the bards have come up with some very inventive and highly convoluted explanations for this apparent contradiction, but tradition holds that Romans are descended from Aeneas and his band of Trojan refugees.

As for Dido, she was so bereft when Aeneas ran out on her that she threw herself on her own funeral pyre and burned to death, all the while screaming eternal hatred for Aeneas. That, the legend says, is why there had been centuries of warfare and enmity between Rome and Carthage. It was eventually ended with the destruction of Carthage which was later rebuilt as a Roman city, but the story of Dido remained vivid in the memory of most Romans.

And what it meant was that Circe, or Tertullia Tertia, or Dido as she was now calling herself, had a grudge against Rome.

I could not fathom any of this, and I kept shaking my head as if to deny the obvious truth of how she had duped me. I did not care that I was tied to a chair, nor that Dion was heading a lunatic plot. All I wanted was for Circe to tell me she loved me and that this was a terrible mistake.

But the mistake had been mine.

Even through my despair, though, an idea flitted into my head, a question which screamed at me for an answer.

"Fronto," I gasped. "You said Fronto sent you to Ephesus."

Circe continued to stare at me. It was evident even to my love-clouded eyes that she was not my Circe now. That person had gone, replaced by a hard, uncaring woman who hated Rome.

She said, "Fronto is as gullible as most men. He told me more than he should have in an attempt to bed me."

I sighed. It seemed I was not the only one who had fallen for her.

I asked her, "Does he know what you are doing?"

"No."

That was something, at least, although it left a lot of questions unanswered.

Amidst all those questions, another thought had struck me. It was, I sighed inwardly, annoying that ideas were now falling into place when it was too late.

I looked at the two young men who sat at the other end of the table. Brown-haired, handsome and smiling, they both seemed highly amused at the predicament I was in.

"One of you is Philippos?" I guessed.

They both grinned, almost as if their reactions, as well as their features, were identical. I certainly could not tell them apart.

Dion told me, "They are both Philippos."

"Actually," said one of the twins, "we are now both Alexander."

This was still going too fast for me, so I focused on the fact that there had been two men masquerading as Philippos the artist.

"Twins!" I breathed. "That is how you stole the amulet! One of you hid inside the Temple overnight. The other one made a point of being seen leaving that evening and being outside the doors before they were opened the next morning."

The twins grinned, the three other men smiled, and Dion said, "Well done, Scipio. That is precisely how it was accomplished."

I took as deep a breath as my bonds would permit, then guessed, "So one of you was outside, but slipped away, probably down the side of the Temple where you could hide between the columns. The other one came out of hiding when the priests rushed in to look at the mess you'd made, then you left, exchanged bags, and went back to be searched. By that time, the stolen items were already on their way out of the precinct."

Dion looked at Circe and said, "You were right, Dido. He is a clever one."

"But why kill Aristides?" I persisted. "Where did he fit in, and what was the point of murdering him?"

Dion, clearly in an expansive mood, was only too happy to show off how clever they had been.

He said, "Aristides was known to me. I'd had some dealings with him in the past. Dealings involving artefacts from the time of the Pharaohs. I knew he was not averse to handling stolen goods. So we asked him to ensure that Philippos was placed at the Temple."

"Which worked because Leonides had been tempted away to Athens."

I glared at Circe.

"You were Julia Petronia?" I guessed.

She gave a curt nod, her expression still hard and unsmiling.

I did not know what to make of this woman of many identities. Who was she? Circe or Dido? Tertullia Tertia or Julia Petronia? Or was she somebody else entirely?

I remarked, "You took a chance going to Ephesus. What would you have done if you'd bumped into Leonides or his grandson?"

"I'd have denied it, of course," she replied stonily. "I doubt they'd have recognised me, but I could always have claimed to have a twin sister who lived in Athens."

She shrugged as she added, "But it did not matter. I never saw them."

Which was why, I realised, she had sent me to speak to Leonides while she allegedly searched for the freedman, Eteocles.

"So what about Aristides?" I asked.

Dion took up the explanation.

"I am afraid he became greedy. He demanded more gold even after he had been presented with his very substantial share of the Temple goods. He threatened to go to the Tribune of *vigiles* if he was not paid even more. So our associate disposed of him, leaving behind the evidence that Aristides had been behind the theft."

I gave a weary nod. That explained why the killer had left the rest of the treasure. Circe had tried to convince me that Aristides was the mastermind behind the theft, and I'd almost fallen for it.

"So where is the killer now? The man who looks like an Arab or Berber? Who is he?"

Circe said, "He is a man I trust. But he is not here at the moment. Forget him."

I lowered my head, letting my chin slump to my chest. I had been fooled all along the line, and now all I wanted was for the floor to open up and swallow me.

But something inside me would not surrender to the despair which was threatening to drown me.

Raising my head, I looked at Dion and asked, "So what is this all about? Why do all that for one amulet? An amulet which now seems to have a twin."

"Ah," he breathed, nodding his head. "That is a good question, and one I will answer because you cannot tell anyone about it now."

I knew what that meant as far as my fate was concerned, but I still wanted to know. If I had been put through all this, if Fronto had been tricked into setting me up, and if Circe had really been Dido all along, I needed to understand why.

Dion began what sounded like a rehearsed speech.

"The people of Egypt in general, and Alexandria in particular, long to be free from Roman rule. But we need a spark, a symbol around which we can gather support. We were once a proud nation, with a history stretching back far beyond anything you Romans can conceive of. Now you steal our grain, our treasures and our spirit. It is time for that to end."

"You can't beat Rome," I told him.

"Yes, we can," he smiled back, confident in his own cleverness.

He waited for me to ask him how, but I refused to say anything. I just stared at him until he filled the silence with his explanation.

"If your Emperor is killed, there will be a civil war. That is a proven historical fact."

"You plan to kill Caesar?" I gasped. "You are mad."

"On the contrary," he assured me. "Everyone knows there will be a scrabble for power if the Emperor dies. He has no heir, after all. So Rome will consume itself and, while the various factions squabble and fight, we will rise up behind our own leader."

"You?" I sneered.

He simply laughed at me.

"Not I!" he declared. "No, we will rally behind Alexander."

I followed his gaze and saw he was looking directly at the twins. What had they said a while ago? They had both been Philippos, but now they were both Alexander?

"With the bull amulet, the symbol of sacred Apis, as proof of his identity," Dion continued, "our reincarnated Alexander will rally our people. Macedonia will join us, and perhaps other places too. Parthia will honour him but, above all, Egypt will be free."

I could not help but laugh at him.

"Just because some young, good-looking boy puts on an amulet, it doesn't make him Alexander."

Dion grinned, "It does if the tomb is opened and the body of Alexander awakes."

"What?"

He could not conceal his smugness as he told me, "When your Emperor is slain, we will insist the Tomb is opened. If necessary, we will rouse a mob to smash down the bricks which bar the doors. And when the people go in, they will see Alexander lying there in his crystal coffin, and he will awake. He will be wearing his breastplate and the amulet which all visitors saw before Rome sealed the tomb. They will believe!"

I saw the other men nodding, and the twins were beaming with delight. But the implications of what Dion was saying were too incredible for me to grasp. It seemed obvious that the twins, who might very well have a superficial resemblance to the dead conqueror, would be mere figureheads for Dion and his cronies, but it was the practicalities of their bizarre plan which left me confused.

"How?" I asked. "How can you let people see him reincarnated?"

Dion raised his hands in a theatrical gesture as he said, "Magic! Alexander will be reborn in full sight of the people. And, to prove his divine powers, he will be seen in more than one place. While some will see him here, others will witness his arrival in towns throughout Egypt."

I could follow that last part, of course. Having identical twins would mean Alexander could apparently perform miracles of rapid movement.

"So you've had the amulet copied?" I sighed.

"Exactly so," he grinned triumphantly as he fondled the golden treasures in front of him. "Apis was once a great symbol of Egyptian power. He will soon be so again. The Apis bulls will be worshipped once more."

I knew there was no point in arguing with a fanatic, let alone a religious fanatic, so I was left dumbfounded. In his own mind, Dion seemed convinced he had everything worked out, but he was not inclined to reveal all his secrets.

"I think we have told you more than enough," he decided. "Now we must resume our work. There is still much to be done before we are ready."

My head sagged again. There was still so much I did not grasp. How would they kill the Emperor, and how would they get inside the Tomb to allow one of the twins to replace the mummified body of Alexander? And what would they do with the actual corpse?

But those questions went unanswered because Dion called the meeting to a close.

Signalling towards me, he said, "Agon! Diomedes! Take him upstairs. Lock him in one of the small rooms."

As Agon and Diomedes began the task of untying me, I heard Circe ask, "What are you going to do with him?"

"We have no choice," Dion told her. "But it must wait until this evening. Once it is dark, he can be taken away and dealt with. He can join some other unfortunates at the bottom of the canal."

If Circe made any reply, I did not hear it. Agon thumped me on the head again, then he and Diomedes grabbed me and hauled me out, dragging me up a stairway to an upper floor and flinging me into a small, musty room which was empty except for a few mats of woven rushes and some cylindrical pillows lying on the floor. The window which was set high in the wall had been mostly bricked up, leaving only a small gap to provide ventilation and a little beam of sunlight. When I heard a heavy lock being turned to seal me in, I knew there would be no escape from this tiny cell.

All I could do was sit in the dark, rub my sore head and try not to let feelings of despair consume me.

Chapter 14
In The Shadows

I must have sat in that tiny, lightless place all day. I banged on the door to demand water, but nobody brought me anything to eat or drink. Once, I thought I heard Circe's voice outside, although I could not make out her words, nor the rumbled reply from whoever was standing outside the door. Agon or Diomedes, I presumed.

I tested the door, but it was thick, heavy and had a very stout lock. That struck me as odd, since most people don't have locks on internal doors, but when I searched the room I began to realise what the room was used for.

The search did not take long since the room was very small and practically bare, but I found four rush mats, each large enough for a man to lie on. The room had just enough floor space to accommodate all four mats, but sleeping with that many people inside would have been very cramped. There were four of the cylindrical pillows which I knew some Egyptians still preferred. Instead of laying your head on a soft cushion, you place your neck on the tube when you lie down. This keeps your head clear of the ground.

So the room had been used to house four people who did not warrant blankets, and who were locked inside. It was a slave cell, although locking slaves up for the night struck me as an excessive precaution.

The room was already stiflingly hot, making any sort of physical exertion an ordeal, so I spread out one of the mats, grabbed a pillow and lay down. If I hoped to make any sort of attempt to get away, I knew I needed to conserve my energy.

Lying there, I tried to think of a way to escape. It was clear what they intended to do with me. Dion wouldn't want a body lying around his home, so he'd have Agon and Diomedes take me out after dark, kill me and dump my body. He'd mentioned a canal, so if they weighed me down, I might never be found. The way Dion had spoken, I guessed it would not be the first time they'd disposed of an inconvenient visitor that way.

Whatever they were planning, he'd said they were close to finalising the plot.

I had no idea how they thought they could get close enough to Caesar to kill him, but bribes can be paid, and perhaps they had someone who could slip him some poison or slide a knife between his ribs. I didn't think their chances of success were very high, but you can never rule out how determined an assassin can be, especially if he is a fanatic. Someone who believed in Dion's plan to free Egypt might be prepared to sacrifice his life for the cause.

And how they would gain access to the tomb of Alexander remained a puzzle. What I did know, though, was that they were inventive. Using twins to steal the amulet had been clever.

They were also, as I had always known, ruthless. Killing Aristides without hesitation had shown that. And whoever Circe's mysterious accomplice was, he'd been able to think very quickly and had left incriminating evidence at the scene so that the *vigiles* would look no further. Had it not been for Restitutus reporting the theft of the Emperor's donation to the Juggler, and for him passing the information to Caesar, Dion and his cronies might have got away with it.

I thought about the three other men at the table. Not one of them had said a word, even though I knew they were following what was said. I supposed they were either devout followers of Dion's or perhaps men of standing who had provided financial backing. The plan had certainly required a lot of money to be spread around.

I ran over all these things time and time again, and still I was no closer to understanding how they intended to complete their plan, nor how I could warn Macrinus of what was going on.

It was a long, dreary, uncomfortable day, and I must have fallen asleep at some point, because I woke with a start when I heard the door being pushed open. Light from an oil lamp dazzled my eyes, and I had little chance to evade the two hulking figures who reached down to grab me and pull me to my feet.

It was Agon and Diomedes again, with the slave who had originally attacked me in the alleyway holding the lamp for them.

"Water!" I croaked, deliberately making my voice feeble, although that didn't require much effort.

None of them said a word in response, and I didn't bother asking where they were taking me. I had a pretty good idea.

These two guys were very strong, so I didn't rate my chances of escape very highly. In an attempt to improve the odds, I let my chin slump to my chest and I dragged my legs as if I was too weak to walk properly. I couldn't tell whether they were taken in by this, but it made little difference to our rate of progress as they hauled me along between them.

The slave with the lamp led us downstairs, then out through a door at the back of the house. He unlocked it, then led us out into what turned out to be the oddest rear courtyard I'd ever seen. It may have been night, but the sky was clear, and I could see moonlight reflecting off a pyramid.

I had to look twice before my eyes would believe it. Here, in the courtyard of Dion's home, was a small pyramid built of some light-coloured stone. The structure was probably only around twenty feet tall at its apex, but it was still a wondrous sight.

I had only enough time to reflect that Dion was so steeped in Egyptian lore that he had decided to build his personal tomb in his own courtyard. I had no idea what Egyptian funeral customs were, but that struck me as a decidedly odd thing for anyone to do. In Rome, I'd grown up with the idea that all tombs and graves must be placed outside the city.

But there was no time to consider Dion's odd choices, because the slave had selected a key from among several which hung from an iron ring at his belt, and was now unlocking the large gate in the high wall which surrounded the courtyard. Dion, it seemed, was big on security. This place was like a fortress.

After hanging the ring of keys back on his belt, the slave swung the gate open. Agon and Diomedes, each of them gripping one of my arms with vice-like tenacity, hauled me through, then the gate was firmly closed and locked behind us.

We were in the alleyway, but these two seemed to know exactly where they were going. I couldn't follow the route myself, for it was too dark to make out any real landmarks, and their path involved a great many twists and turns. We crossed a couple of wide streets, but we generally stuck to the darker, narrower lanes and alleys between the houses.

There was hardly anyone about. There are rarely any pedestrians after dark, and it did seem particularly late at night. I had no way of telling the time, but I guessed it was well after midnight. The only people we were likely to run into were patrols of watchmen, but my luck was out, for we were not challenged at all.

Any town at night can seem eerie. It is still and virtually silent, with every home in darkness. The only real sound I could hear was the iron hobnails of our sandals on the paved roads.

I was running out of time. I knew precisely what they were doing, but I was unsure how to escape their intention. Rather than do away with me in the house, they were taking me to the canal or wherever else they had decided to dump me, because that avoided the need to lug a body through the streets. Once we reached their destination, they'd probably say something inane, then one of them would slug me or stab me, and I'd be dropped into the water.

Knowing this didn't help. The hold they had on me was so firm I knew I had no chance of wriggling free. I maintained my pretence of being weaker than I was, but that was the only edge I had in this uneven contest.

We turned another corner and there was an open space ahead of us. In the moonlight, I could make out the regular edges which denoted a man-made watercourse, and I could see the faint reflection of the moon on the dark surface of water which stretched away to left and right.

I was here, and I was going to die unless I did something.

Agon, who was gripping my left arm with fingers of steel, said, "There will be no mistakes this time, Scipio. I don't know how you escaped that sailor we bribed on the ship, but we won't be so careless."

I felt Diomedes adjust his hold on my right arm, and I knew I had run out of time. He was about to do something, so I needed to act first.

I'd been pretending to stagger and stumble with faltering steps as they led me through the warren of streets. Now I planted my left foot firmly on the ground and swung my right leg forwards, then whipped it back as quickly as I could to trip Diomedes. I caught his left shin, tripping him and knocking him off balance. As savagely as I could, I raked my sandal down his bare shin, hooked his ankle and yanked his leg back.

He gave a shout as he staggered, and his grip on my arm loosened. I shook him off and twisted towards Agon on my left, swinging my right arm to land a forearm smash in the centre of his face.

He, too, was taken by surprise. I doubt he even saw my blow coming, and it landed exactly where I had hoped; on the bridge of his nose. I heard the crunch of bones breaking, but I did not stop there. He was probably no stranger to this sort of street fighting, and he was certainly smart enough to hold tightly to my left arm.

So I copied the move I had used on the sailor on the ship. Still turning, I grabbed Agon's right arm with my right hand as I swivelled and backed into him. I felt his left hand flapping around, but I think he was reaching for his own face in an instinctive response to my first blow. Whether that was correct did not matter because by the time he'd realised what I was doing, he was flipping over my shoulder.

He landed with a dreadful thump, and I was pretty sure I heard the back of his skull crack down on the paved walkway. Just to be sure, I stamped on his face as hard as I could, grinding my heel down.

All of this had happened in much less time than it takes to tell. Even so, Diomedes had recovered and was holding a knife as he came for me. I could see it glint in the pale light as he held it low, ready to stab upwards at my belly or chest.

I danced back, leaving Agon groaning on the ground. He was between me and Diomedes, so I had a moment to compose my stance. My arms still felt weak from having been gripped so tightly for so long, but they were strong enough to deal with Diomedes.

At least, I hoped they were.

He skirted round his fallen companion at a run, uttering a curse I did not understand because he'd lapsed into Egyptian.

Fortunately for me, Diomedes may have been big and heavily muscled, but he wasn't very fast. He was, though, fast enough for me to use his momentum against him. That was another of the lessons Hannibal had taught me during those long, painful *pankration* sessions. Diomedes obviously expected me to dodge to his left. After all, the dagger was in his right hand, so most unarmed men would want to move away from that threat. Instead, I darted to his right, letting his wild thrust flash past me. It missed me by a good hand's breadth which may not sound like much but was more than enough for me.

143

I grabbed his forearm with both hands, yanking it upwards while, at the same time, I swung my leg and tripped him again. He flailed around in my grasp, but he was falling, so I rammed my knee into his belly, twisted his wrist to force the knife from his grip, then leaped behind him, taking his arm with me and jerking it viciously upwards between his shoulder blades.

He let out a high-pitched scream as I dislocated his shoulder, but that was cut off when I kicked his legs out from beneath him and he fell to the ground on his belly.

Before he could recover, I slammed myself down on top of him, using my knees to ram into his back and drive all the air from his lungs. Then I grabbed his head with both hands and, in a move I'd never actually used before, but which Hannibal had explained to me, I broke his neck with a single, vicious jerk of his skull.

Diomedes lay still, but I pushed myself up, spinning to see whether Agon was recovering. He was, but barely. Blood marred his face as it streamed from his broken nose, but he had caught sight of Diomedes' dagger, and he was crawling towards it on all fours, his breath coming in painful gasps.

I wasn't quite quick enough to reach the blade before him, but I was in time to slam my foot down on his hand as he reached for it. I ground the iron hobnails into his flesh, again feeling bones crack.

Agon let out a roar of pain, but he could not stand because virtually my entire weight was on the back of his hand.

I kicked him in the ribs with my left foot, then lifted my right foot to smash into his already ruined face.

He flopped backwards, landing on the ground with arms and legs spread-eagled, a low moan coming from his mouth. Then he began to choke on the blood that was running down his throat. As he gasped and spluttered, desperately attempting to stand up, I picked up the dagger, knelt beside him and drove the blade down into his chest.

I stood up, breathing heavily. My pulse was racing and my limbs felt weak as reaction set in. I've never liked violence, and actually killing an opponent was something I had rarely done, but I knew I could not afford to allow either of these two thugs to return with news of my escape. Not that I had much sympathy for either of them. They'd have murdered me without a second thought, so I wasn't going to lose any sleep over what I had done to them.

Taking another deep breath, I looked all around to see whether anyone was coming to investigate the noise we had made. The path was empty, and no lights showed in any of the buildings which backed onto the canal. If anyone had heard, they were clearly not inclined to find out what was happening. I heard no shouts of alarm, and saw no lights appearing in windows.

But I did catch a glimpse of a shadow in the alley at the side of the nearest building. This place had the appearance of a large warehouse, and the narrow lane beside it was the same one down which Agon and Diomedes had dragged me only a few moments earlier. Something had moved there. Or, at least, I thought I saw something move, but it was too dark to be sure.

I looked down at the two dead slaves. With a sigh, I grabbed Agon under his shoulders and began to drag him towards the canal. I grunted with the effort this involved because corpses are, quite literally, a dead weight. It's not easy shifting a body on your own, especially when the cadaver in question is as big a brute as Agon.

Shuffling backwards, I drew nearer to the edge of the water.

Then, because I'm a suspicious sod, I suddenly stopped, released my hold and stood up.

I'd been right. There was somebody there. He was a silent silhouette among the shadows, and he had been attempting to sneak up on me while I was busy moving the bodies.

"Who are you?" I demanded, still unable to make out anything except the vague outline of a man in a long robe, and a pair of eyes studying me.

His voice, though quiet, was confident and had the sound of a man of experience.

"Ah," he sighed. "I see your senses are as impressive as your fighting skills. I did not think you had noticed me."

He had stopped, standing perfectly still, only ten yards away from me. I could see no sign of a weapon, but that didn't mean much. He could have been holding a fifteen-foot *sarissa* and I wouldn't have been able to make it out in the shadowy gloom.

"I asked who you were," I said, flexing my fingers in readiness for another fight.

"Someone who wishes you no harm. Not at present, anyway."

He went on, "I was sent to try to save you, but I see my help was not required. I must say I did not expect you to be able to overcome both of them so easily."

I ignored the compliment. The other thing he'd said was more important.

"You were sent?" I demanded. "Sent by who? Macrinus?"

"Who is that?" he replied.

"Macrinus. The Praetorian Prefect. Did he send you?"

"The Praetorian Prefect! No, not him."

"Then who?"

"Can you not guess?"

"I'm too bloody tired to guess!" I snarled.

"The lady has many names. She wanted you to know she wished no harm to come to you. That is why she tried to keep you away from Dion."

"Circe?"

Inwardly, I cursed myself for the way my heart leaped at that thought.

The man agreed, "That is one name she has."

I frowned, "That makes no sense. Why order her slaves to kill me, then send you to stop them?"

"They are not her slaves," he informed me with a throaty chuckle. "They belonged to Dion."

"But they were in Ephesus with her."

"To watch her as much as to serve her, I think," the shadow man said.

That shed a little light on the power dynamics within Dion's conspiracy, but he had still not answered my very first question.

"And who are you?"

"A man she trusts."

"The man who killed Aristides?"

"And the man who must now take you somewhere until all this is over. She does not wish you dead, but she needs the enterprise to proceed."

"No chance!" I shot back. "I'm not going anywhere except to the Prefect. You go and tell Circe to get out of that house, because I'm coming back with the whole Roman army to sort Dion and his pals out."

"I cannot let you do that," he said softly. "The lady requires the plan to go ahead."

"And how do you propose to stop me?" I asked. "You'll need to kill me."

He paused as if considering his options, then said, "I confess I had planned to dispose of those two just before they killed you, then drag you away to safety. I would have held you captive until events had gone far enough that you could not prevent them, but I confess I thought you were rather more helpless than you obviously are. You tricked me as well as those two."

"Then, unless you have a small army of your own, I'm leaving now. If you try to stop me, I'll do to you what I did to those two."

"But if I let you leave, the lady's plan will be thwarted."

"It would have been thwarted anyway," I told him. "If you had killed them and did manage to tie me up somewhere, Dion would still have known something was wrong."

"I did think of that," he said with what sounded like amusement. "I planned on reporting that the slaves had been caught by a patrol of watchmen just after they had killed you. Sadly, they died while resisting arrest."

I nodded. That might have worked. Dion was obviously a fanatic and would not let the deaths of two slaves trouble him overly much.

I said, "That still leaves your only options as either killing me now or letting me go. I suggest you go back and tell her to get out of the house before the Emperor sends a troop of Praetorians there."

"She will not be happy," the shadow told me. "She has been planning this for a long time."

I wanted to turn and run, but I also knew this man could provide me with much needed information, so I resisted the impulse and kept talking to him.

"A long time? Why does she want Egypt to rebel against the Empire?"

"Oh, Egypt is not her concern. But the people here have provided her with a chance to accomplish her own aim."

"What aim?"

"Her name is Dido," he told me. "What do you think her aim is?"

"I'm not in the mood for guessing games," I replied.

With a sigh, he explained, "The original Dido had a grudge against Rome. My Dido has a grudge against the man who leads Rome."

"What grudge?"

"That is not for me to say."

I almost yelled at him in frustration, but I was aware that time was running short if I were to get the news to Macrinus before Dion realised something had gone wrong.

I said, "Look, I am grateful that she sent you. I don't begin to understand what she is up to, but I will repay the favour. Once again, I'm telling you to get her out of danger. Your only other choice is to kill me, because nothing less will stop me going to the Emperor and telling him what is going on."

There was another long silence. I still could not make out any of his features, but I did know he was a cool customer. He was standing as still as a stone statue in the shadows, and he must have known I might try to rush him, yet he was confident enough in his abilities to stand his ground. I had the uncomfortable feeling that only Circe's orders to keep me alive were preventing him from doing to me what he had done to Aristides.

"Goodbye," I told him. "I suggest you dump those bodies in the canal in case Dion sends someone to look for them."

I spun on my heel and began running, heading along the side of the canal, following it northwards towards the harbour. I knew the canal drained into the lesser harbour, so I had a straight route marked out for me. Once at the harbour, I could follow the main road back to the palace district.

I hoped I'd managed to get a head start on Circe's assassin, but I still expected to hear the sound of his footsteps coming after me. Instead, I heard a splash as something heavy fell into the canal. I didn't hear the second body go into the water, but that was probably because I'd moved too far away by then. Whoever that shadowy figure was, he'd known he had no choice. I hoped that meant he would also get Circe out of Dion's house.

Because I was going to bring the whole wrath of Caesar down on that place.

Chapter 15
Imperial Justice

The pass Macrinus had given me worked wonders, although the first group of soldiers I met took a little bit of convincing since it was too dark for them to read the parchment I showed them. To be fair to them, I must have looked a sight, wandering the streets alone at night wearing only a tunic and sandals, unshaven and with my hair dishevelled. Fortunately, they took me back to the palace district where a junior officer read the pass and had me escorted into the Emperor's residence where one of Macrinus' secretaries was roused from sleep to hear my story. When presented with my pendant, the pass and my urgent tales of a plot to kill the Emperor, the secretary hurried off to wake Macrinus.

While I waited for the Prefect, I sated my hunger and raging thirst, tucking into some kitchen leftovers which the secretary had ordered a slave to fetch in response to my pleadings.

Macrinus arrived, wearing a fancy tunic with its broad stripe of purple, and had a cloak wrapped around his shoulders against the chill of the night.

"Scipio! I thought something serious had happened to you," he said without preamble when he entered the room. "Thucydides waited all day for you."

"Something did happen," I told him.

I gave him my edited version of the previous day's events; edited because I still wanted to keep Circe out of the whole thing. Not only did I owe her that much for trying to keep me alive, it would have overly complicated things if I told Macrinus about her now after previously having omitted any mention of her. So I told him that I'd spotted a slave I'd recognised from Ephesus, a man who had been one of Eteocles' heavies. It was, I hoped, close enough to the truth to be believed, and if it caused trouble for the little freedman, then that didn't bother me one little bit. Eteocles may or may not have been part of the plot, but he was a crook, and he had it coming.

Macrinus allowed me to speak without interruption, but when I was done he fired questions at me like a *ballista*.

"Did they say how they would attempt to kill Caesar?"

"No. Just that it would happen."

"Would you recognise these men again?"

"Oh, yes. Definitely."

"And how will they get inside the sealed tomb?"

"I have no idea."

"What about the slaves you killed? Will they be missed before dawn?"

"That's hard to say," I replied. "I had the impression they'd done that sort of thing before, so perhaps Dion went to bed and let them get on with it."

He rubbed his chin thoughtfully.

"And they used twins to steal the amulet, you say? And now they have made a duplicate. This smacks of a considerable degree of planning, does it not?"

"It certainly does. They have been very resourceful, and they've spent a lot of time and money on it."

"So we must take the threat against Caesar seriously."

Abruptly, he rose to his feet, waving a hand to indicate that I should remain where I was.

"Wait here," he told me.

Then he was gone, hurrying off on some errand or other.

I sat there for a long time, exhausted but unable to rest because so many things were whirring through my mind. Had Circe escaped from the house? Did Dion know I had killed his slaves? And, above all, what would Macrinus do?

Despite my nervous excitement, I may have dozed off in the chair because Macrinus gave me a start when he burst into the room once again.

"Come with me!" he ordered.

Out in the corridor were two Praetorians and a couple of secretaries who had obviously dressed in a hurry having been called from their beds. Walking briskly, Macrinus led us through a miniature labyrinth of passages until we reached a door where two more Praetorians stood guard. On seeing us approach, one of them opened the door and ushered Macrinus and me inside while the remainder of our small retinue waited in the corridor.

There was another secretary inside the room, a middle-aged man who looked decidedly anxious as he hovered near one wall, fidgeting with his hands.

There was another man sitting in a chair. He was wrapped in a cloak, and wore no signs of rank, but I recognised him instantly. Dark-haired, with a neatly trimmed beard, handsome and in his early thirties, his face was on many of the Roman coins I'd handled over the past few years, and statues of him were prominent in every town across the empire. I was face to face with Marcus Aurelius Antoninus Augustus Caesar, Emperor of Rome. From the expression on his face, I guessed this would not be a good time to address him as Caracalla.

"You are Sigma?" he asked me, his voice hard.

I overcame my nervousness sufficiently to respond, "Yes, Caesar."

"Tell me your story. Macrinus has explained it to me, but I want to hear it from you. Begin in Ephesus."

So I went back over my tale, with his dark, brooding eyes boring into me the whole time. I could practically see the rage building inside him as I spoke. That was one of the most nerve-wracking experiences of my life. Angry Emperors are dangerous, and I hoped he was not the sort who would kill the messenger.

When I was done, he gave me a curt nod.

"You have done well, Sigma. I shall commend you to Sempronius Rufus."

"Thank you, Caesar," I mumbled.

The Emperor then turned his gaze on Macrinus.

"Your suggestions?"

"I have already sent orders for a Century of Praetorians to assemble. Sigma can lead them to the house. If we raid it at dawn, we stand a good chance of capturing at least some of the ringleaders."

"Unless they have already flown," Caracalla growled.

"I fear there is not much we can do about that, Caesar," Macrinus said calmly.

The Emperor almost leaped from his chair, grabbing his cloak and holding it tightly to his body. From the brief glimpse of flesh I caught as he jumped up, I realised he must be naked underneath it. The main thing I noticed, however, was that he was not a very tall man at all. In fact, his stature was quite diminutive. Somehow, that should have made him appear ridiculous as he stomped back and forth, but all I could feel was a mounting fear as he began ranting.

"This place must be punished! They made a play mocking me! And those philosophers who follow Aristotle's teachings were laughing at me the other night. Did you not notice that, Macrinus?"

"Philosophers laugh at everyone, Caesar," Macrinus said placatingly.

"Not at me!" Caracalla roared angrily, sweeping his right arm in a gesture of fury. "And don't think I have forgotten how Aristotle poisoned Alexander the Great. I have heard that story and, now that I have met his followers, I believe it!"

I dared not look at Macrinus. That was one of the weirdest theories I'd ever heard about Alexander's death, mostly because Aristotle was hundreds of miles away when the great conqueror died of some mysterious illness. But it did shed a little light on our Emperor's character. His father had sealed Alexander's tomb, and Caracalla himself had embarked on a career of military conquest. Did he see himself as a second Alexander? Was that why the Macedonian king's tomb had been sealed? To prevent anyone seeing the original so that they only had eyes for the new conqueror? It may sound an unlikely theory, but sitting there watching and listening to the Emperor made it all too believable.

He seemed almost beyond reason as he continued to rage.

"And now they plot against me! The people of Alexandria must be shown that such disloyalty does not go unanswered."

"Whatever you plan, Caesar," Macrinus advised, "let us first move against this Dion of Memphis. If he is behind the plot, let us capture him, torture him and discover who else is involved in the plot."

The Emperor rounded on him, his eyes flashing maniacally.

"The entire city is involved!" he shouted. "The city will be punished!"

Macrinus didn't bat an eyelid as he asked, "Then what is your will?"

The Emperor stopped his frantic pacing. He took a deep breath, then began barking orders.

"Have all the leading citizens summoned to meet me as soon as the sun rises. And make sure those Aristotelian fawners are included. And I want my Legions ready to act on my orders."

"The Legions, Caesar?"

"Have them ready to march into the city as soon as I give the word."

"I shall send the orders immediately," Macrinus assured him. "But what is it you wish them to do?"

The Emperor's face became a mask of barely suppressed rage as he snarled, "I want them to punish the city."

I had the sense to remain silent, and Macrinus obviously knew his man. Bowing his head, he simply said, "It shall be as you command."

"Good."

The Emperor turned towards the secretary who stood pressed against the far wall as if wishing he could sink into it.

"Have my slaves fetch my armour."

The secretary bobbed his head and hurried away into an adjoining room, while Macrinus placed a hand on my arm and eased me towards the door which led out into the corridor.

"Come, Sigma," he said. "We have much to do."

Half an hour later, I was dressed in a Praetorian breastplate and helmet, with a kilt of studded leather strips hanging down to my knees, and I had a short sword strapped at my waist.

I felt ridiculous. I'd never been much good with a sword, and I'd never worn the get-up of an ordinary soldier, let alone one of the Emperor's elite troops. The looks of contempt I received from the squad of genuine Praetorians did not make me feel any less awkward.

Macrinus had gone off to issue the orders for the Legions and to have Alexandria's leading citizens summoned to what would probably be their deaths. He had left me in the care of a Centurion named Aelius Caecus, a tough-looking veteran who looked as if he'd been brought up on a diet of raw meat and iron nails.

"I'm told you will take us to where we will find some traitors," he growled at me. "But don't get any ideas just because you're wearing a soldier's gear. That's only to protect you if there's any trouble. You lead us there, then you stand back out of the way. Is that understood?"

"Yes," I nodded, fearing the weight of the helmet would pull my head off as I did so.

153

"I'll have some men assigned to look after you," he went on. "Martialis!"

Another man stamped up to me. Even by the standards of the Praetorians, he was a big fellow, and it was all I could do not to step back in awe as he loomed over me. From what I could make out beneath his iron helmet, he was probably in his mid-thirties, and had a sour expression on his sallow face.

"Sir!"

Aelius turned to me and said, "This is Optio Justin Martialis. You will stay close to him."

I tried to give Martialis a smile, but he simply glowered back at me. These soldier types really didn't like people like me at all.

Aelius told Martialis, "Take three squads. Keep this ..." He paused, looking for the right word to describe me.

"Keep this agent out of danger. The Emperor wants him kept alive. That's your job. His task is to identify the treasonous bastards we are going to catch."

Martialis nodded, then turned away, shouting orders. A few moments later, I was marching at the head of a column of eighty Praetorians and leading them into the city. Well, they were marching and I was sort of walking in approximate time to the tramp of their feet.

It was growing light by this time, the eastern sky behind us tinged with pink. By the time we reached the Sema Square and the tomb of Alexander, there was enough daylight to see perfectly well.

I held up a warning hand, signalling to Aelius to halt his troop.

"That's the house," I told him. "The one with the iron-banded door. There's at least one other way in. Down that alley, there's an equally solid gate in a wall surrounding a courtyard, and then there's another door into the house itself. It's built like a fortress."

Aelius snorted, giving me a disparaging look. He turned, ordering several men to go to the square and return with one of the stone benches.

"That will sort the door," he told me with a satisfied smile. "And walls can be climbed."

While the Centurion was sending another group of men down the alleyway, Justin Martialis pulled me to the opposite side of the street where his squad of twenty-two men waited.

Like the Legions, the Praetorians operate in groups of eight men. This is known as a *contubernium*. When on campaign, the men in each *contubernium* share a tent at nights and train together under the command of one of their number who is a double-pay man. Ten of these units comprise a Century. Of course, no units are ever up to full strength, so the three squads Martialis had assigned to protect me were a couple short of the full complement of twenty-four.

Not that this slight reduction in their numbers made me feel any more comfortable standing beside them. Each of the twenty-two seemed to harbour some resentment against me. Martialis, in particular, seemed on edge, his eyes constantly darting anxious glances at Dion's house in between the hostile looks he was casting in my direction.

While we waited, I noticed a few civilians emerging from their houses to begin another day. Without exception, they hurriedly made themselves scarce as soon as they saw the soldiers blocking the street.

I was watching the house, looking for signs of life, but all the shutters were closed, and the place appeared almost abandoned.

Martialis, standing next to me, demanded gruffly, "So you say there are traitors in there?"

"That's right."

"Do you have any proof?"

"What?"

"Proof. Do you have any proof that they are traitors? Or that they are in there at all? Or are we doing this just on your word."

"They tried to kill me," I told him.

He gave me another of his disparaging looks as he said, "So you say."

"You'll find the proof when you go in," I told him, hoping I was right.

It did not take long for the Praetorians to gain access to Dion's house. Aelius kicked on the door to rouse the duty slave, but that brought no reaction. The door remained resolutely shut.

Smiling grimly, Aelius ordered his men to smash it down using the stone bench they had lugged from the square. They grunted and heaved, gave the door three or four heavy thuds, then it crumpled under the onslaught, and Aelius was yelling at his men to get inside.

I heard shouts and screams as the soldiers stormed the place. My heart quailed when I heard women among those who were screaming. Was Circe still in there?

Beside me, Martialis was in a strange mood, apprehensive yet angry. He kept moving from foot to foot, his hand clutching at the hilt of his sword, his fingers clenching and unclenching. He seemed both eager to get into the house, and worried about what he might find if he did go in.

But our job was to remain outside, so we stood while the noises from inside the house echoed and faded before renewing again.

"What's going on in there?" I wondered.

Eventually, Aelius strode out of the shattered doorway, his face even more full of scorn than before.

He marched up to me, jabbed a finger at my chest and rasped, "There's nobody in there except a bunch of slaves."

I said nothing. There was nothing I could say. I supposed Dion must have become suspicious and fled during the night.

"Can I go in and take a look around?" I asked.

He gave a snort of a laugh, but waved an inviting hand.

"Go ahead. But I don't know what you expect to find. If there ever were any traitors there, they've gone."

He gave me a gorgon stare, then turned to Martialis.

"Stay with him."

We all trooped into the house. The first thing I saw as I clambered past the abandoned stone bench and the debris of the wrecked door was the body of Dion's house slave, the one who had first grabbed me in the alleyway. He was lying on his back, his sightless eyes staring up at the ceiling, with several stab wounds perforating his ravaged body.

Swallowing hard, I went into the first room on the left. It was the reception room where I had sat tied to a chair while Dion revealed his plot, but it bore little resemblance to that memory now. Chairs had been smashed, the table shoved to one side, and the room was full of soldiers and a gaggle of sobbing, almost hysterical, slaves. Most of them were women, and most of those were naked. It didn't take much imagination to know why.

"What are you going to do with them?" I asked Aelius.

"We'll take them to be interrogated," he replied. "They'll tell us where their master has gone."

I knew what that meant. The slaves would be tortured until they told what they knew.

I cast my eyes over them, selecting a young lad of around fifteen who looked terrified but at least wasn't wailing like most of the others.

"Where has Dion gone?" I asked him. "If you tell us the truth, there will be no need for anyone to be tortured."

I heard Aelius snort again, but I held the young man's eyes, imploring him to tell me what I needed to know.

He simply shook his head.

"He was gone when I woke up."

Aelius growled, "Don't worry. We'll get the truth out of them."

I turned away, sick at heart.

"I still want to take a good look around, There may be some clues as to where he has gone."

What I was really looking for was signs of Circe, but I couldn't tell anyone that.

"The place is all yours," Aelius smirked.

While the thought of what would happen to those slaves sickened me, it soon became evident that some of Dion's slaves would never say anything again. There were two more dead men, both of them built on similar lines to the one who lay in the entrance lobby. Dion obviously liked his slaves to be big and brawny, but they'd had no chance against several dozen Praetorians.

There was a dead female slave too, an elderly woman who was lying scrunched against a wall of the kitchen at the rear of the house. I checked just in case it was Helena, but it was not her.

As I continued my search, moving rapidly from room to room, I began to hope that Circe had also got away. There was no sign of her or Helena.

Squeezing past Praetorians who were busy looting any moveables they could lay their hands on, I checked every room. I found stores and cupboards, most of them having already been emptied of anything of value. There was a cellar carved into the limestone beneath the house where food was stored on shelves of stone. Aelius' men had already liberated several *amphorae* of wine from down here, and were sharing it out among themselves. There was nothing else to see in that dark cavern except a few old rugs which carpeted the floor. They had probably been woven on the loom which we discovered in the next room we entered.

Moving on, we found a couple of reception rooms on the ground floor. These were decorated with frescoes in what I assumed must be the ancient Egyptian style. They showed Pharaohs accepting tribute from supplicants, or counting the heads of their victims. There were musicians, dancing girls, bulls, hawks and gods with animal heads, all painted in bright colours that Leonides of Ephesus would have envied. I also saw what I first thought were some dead animals killed by Aelius' Praetorians but which turned out to be a cat and a hawk which had been mummified. It looked to me as if Dion had been trying to recreate Egypt's past inside his own house.

On the next floor I found several small rooms identical to the one I had been locked in. Each had only rush mats and pillows, and each had a very heavy lock on the door, although none of the rooms were occupied, so the doors had been unlocked, saving the Praetorians the trouble of smashing them down.

The upper storey contained more conventional bedrooms, all of which had been ransacked by Aelius' men, leaving slim pickings for Martialis and his squad.

The Optio followed me everywhere, holding his sword in his hand as if expecting to be attacked, and several of his men trailed after us. The rest had joined in the plundering.

I did find my bag. It was lying discarded on the floor of a sparse room which had probably been a slave's sleeping quarters. The bag was empty, so I left it where it was.

"There's nobody here," Martialis told me several times. "Where's your proof?"

"The slaves will talk," I shrugged, trying not to think about the methods which would be used to encourage them.

We had searched all three floors, but there was another flight of stairs which I climbed to a door which led out onto the flat roof.

It was full daylight now, and I saw there was plenty of open space up here. There was a small area set aside where large boxes of earth had been planted with herbs and vegetables, and there was a washing line ready to hold the day's laundry which would never be washed now.

I wandered to the rear wall to look down into the courtyard. From here, I could see the pyramid Dion had built, a gleaming white monument he had constructed as a reminder of the days of Egypt's glory. It was, I saw, built of limestone, the blocks carefully shaped and laid together in steps, each layer narrower than the one below it until the sides met at a pointed capstone.

"Hades!" Martialis breathed. "What's that doing here?"

"He was a fanatic," I explained. "He wanted Egypt to return to the days of the Pharaohs. I expect he wanted to recreate a bit of that for himself. You saw the decorations downstairs. That pyramid is just taking things a step further."

Martialis and his men gaped at the white pyramid in awe. Three storeys up, we were still barely level with its peak. Down below, some of Aelius' Praetorians were clambering around the lower levels, looking for a way into the construction in case it was a genuine tomb containing treasures. They soon gave up when it became clear there was no entrance.

It was then that we heard the distant sounds of alarm.

Martialis turned, cocking an ear to the north-east.

"It sounds like the fun has started," he observed.

I was barely listening. I knew what was happening because I'd been in the room when the Emperor had made his decision. The people of Alexandria were about to be punished, and the Legions were ready to mete out that punishment.

"We should get back so we can help," Martialis told me.

What he meant was that he and his squad wanted their share of the spoils, but I was still staring at the pyramid.

"Where did he get the stone?" I wondered.

"What?" Martialis snapped.

"The stone to build that thing. Where did it come from?"

"A quarry?" he suggested mockingly.

"Or some place closer to hand," I decided, an idea taking form in my mind.

"What are you on about?" Martialis demanded.

Pointing towards the far end of the courtyard, beyond the white pyramid, I said, "Look. There are lumps of stone lying around over there. That's the leftovers from when the stones were shaped. The work wasn't done in a quarry. It was done here."

"So what?" Martialis shrugged. "You said yourself the man was a fanatic. Maybe he wanted to oversee the work himself. Come on, we've searched the house and there's nobody here. We may as well leave."

"Not yet!" I told him with mounting excitement. "I need to check something first."

"What?" he asked, but I was already running for the stairs that led back down into the house.

With Martialis and his men thudding after me, I descended the stairs all the way down to the ground floor, then went deeper, moving into the cellar once again.

"Bring some light!" I called.

One of the soldiers brought a flickering candle he'd taken from the nearest room.

"What are you looking for?" Martialis demanded of me.

"Doesn't this house strike you as odd?" I asked him. "There are cells for locking slaves in, and there's a bloody great pyramid been built in the courtyard."

"Of course it's odd!" he snapped. "So what?"

I went on, "The place was locked up like a fortress, but I don't think that was to prevent people coming in, I think it was to stop people leaving. He had something going on here."

"So you say, but none of that is proof of anything except that he was off his head."

"Here's another odd thing," I told him. "Why have rugs down here?"

"To keep the floor warm?" he suggested.

"In a cold cellar?" I grinned. "The idea is to keep the place cool."

I bent down, lifting one of the rugs and tossing it aside. Below was only the cold, hard stone of the floor.

The next rug produced the same result, but the third, as happens in all the best stories, revealed a wooden trap door.

"And here," I told Martialis, "is what we were looking for."

"It's probably just another store room," he scoffed.

"Open it and take a look, then," I invited.

He had two of his men lift the door. When they pushed it aside and the candle was held over the entrance, we saw steps leading down into darkness.

"You first," I said to Martialis.

Instead, he sent four of his men down. They soon returned with the news that the stairs led to a tunnel.

"It's narrow and only high enough to move in a crouch," one of the soldiers reported.

"A tunnel?" Martialis frowned, clearly confused.

I said, "I think I know where all that stone came from. Dion had slaves dig it out of this tunnel, then they lugged it up to the courtyard and built his pyramid. That would save him having to explain why he had tons of rock lying around outside his house."

Martialis was looking more confused than ever. I was pretty sure he didn't believe me, but I was convinced I now understood how Dion intended to achieve his miracle.

I asked the soldier who had ventured down into the tunnel, "Which direction does it lead in?"

He pointed off to one corner of the cellar.

"And which way is the front of the house?"

We all agreed that the tunnel was heading out under the front of the house in a line that was slightly north of west.

"So what?" Martialis scowled.

"So that leads to the Sema," I told him. "And that's where the tomb of Alexander is. I think we've just discovered how they were going to replace the body of Alexander. This is their way in."

Aelius was sent for. He didn't congratulate me on discovering the tunnel, but he took charge with impressive efficiency, ordering more candles to be brought and summoning as many of his men as could assemble in the confines of the cellar, with the remainder lined up in the corridors above us.

Martialis was now full of eagerness.

"I would like to lead the way in," he told the Centurion. "We've played nursemaid long enough."

With a gesture towards me, he added, "Besides, he will want to see where the tunnel leads."

That, at least, we agreed on.

161

Aelius gave his permission, and Martialis led the way down the steps. I was forced to wait until his entire squad had entered the tunnel, then Aelius signalled for me to go down after them.

"Stay away from any fighting," he told me.

"I will," I promised.

I went down the steps, cursing softly when my helmeted head bumped the roof of the low tunnel. Aelius followed close behind me, and I could hear his men tramping down after him.

It was an awkward journey, walking while bent double, and with very little illumination other than the occasional glimpse of a candle between the dark shapes of the Praetorians. But I felt elated. This was how Dion had planned to raise Alexander from the dead. And we had foiled his plot.

It was then that I heard the noise from the head of the column. Amplified by the narrow tunnel, angry yells and shouts of terror echoed back towards us.

"Move!" bellowed Aelius from behind me.

The Praetorians hurried their pace, and as we drew near to the end of the tunnel I heard the ring of steel as swords were drawn clear of scabbards.

I emerged through a low entrance into a flickering chaos lit by blazing torches set on the walls of a vast chamber. There had been no steps, so I guessed this enormous room must be underground.

I had little time to take it in because Aelius shoved me out of his way, roaring at me to stay out of trouble.

I scurried to one side, peering into the vast chamber while a stream of Praetorians continued to charge into the underground tomb. There seemed to be several niches around the sides, or possibly more tunnels leading off the central space, although those tunnels were considerably more impressive than the one we had scuttled along. Some niches contained huge statues and funerary urns. The closest one I could see had a long inscription in Greek proclaiming that the urn contained the ashes of a long-dead Pharaoh from the Ptolemaic dynasty.

More and more Praetorians were bursting into the chamber, but there was no more sound of combat. Cautiously, I ventured further into the huge room, gazing in wonder at the magnificence of the decoration. Arms and armour decked the walls, huge chests which might once have held gold and jewels sat open around the base of the walls, while funerary urns, statues and inscriptions showed where the Ptolemies had interred their dead.

But in the centre of the wide mosaic floor, drawing the eye because it sat in such splendid isolation, was a low, stepped dais on which sat a bier. And on that bier was a coffin of crystal. I'd heard that Alexander had originally been buried in an enormous coffin made of pure gold, but one of the Ptolemies had allegedly melted it down to pay his troops. The mummified body of the great conqueror had instead been surrounded by crystal so that any visitor to the tomb could admire the perfection of his corpse which had lain here for more than five hundred years.

I looked.

And saw that the coffin was empty.

I hurried to the dais, stepping up to take a closer look, but I had not been mistaken. The coffin was completely empty.

Incredible as it seemed, Dion must have already moved the body in preparation for one of his twins to occupy the coffin and be seen to rise from the dead.

Except that none of them would rise now. From where I stood beside the glittering coffin I could see to the far end of the chamber where Dion and his accomplices had made their last stand.

They lay in a huddle, blood staining their tunics, and they were very dead.

Horrified, I jumped down from the dais and ran round to take a closer look, my heart thumping in my chest at the thought that Circe might be among them.

I pushed past a couple of Praetorians, coming to a stop beside Martialis who still held a bloodied sword in his hand. Dreading what I might see, I looked down at the crumpled bodies. Dion was there, as well as the twins, all of them huddled together. I also recognised two of the three men who had been in Dion's house the previous morning.

The sight of their bloody corpses sickened me, but I also felt a wave of relief because Circe was not there. Her shadowy companion must have managed to get her out of the house in time, but my relief was tempered by the brutal killings of the conspirators.

Glancing at Aelius, I saw that he seemed satisfied with the outcome, but I shot Martialis a dark look.

"The Prefect would have wanted them alive," I told him.

"They resisted us," he shrugged as he wiped his sword clean on Dion's tunic before sheathing it again.

"With what weapons?" I challenged.

He pointed towards a dagger which lay a little way from Dion's mutilated body.

"They won't do any more plotting now," he told me.

I looked to Aelius, but he simply shrugged, "Our task was to catch the men behind the plot. We've done that. We will take their heads to Caesar, and the slaves will give us the names of the other conspirators."

I knew there was no point in arguing. Dion's death had been assured as soon as the Emperor had despatched us on this Mission. It had merely been a question of when and how he would be executed.

But there was one other question that required an answer.

Pointing to the empty coffin, I demanded, "And what about Alexander's body? Where is it?"

Puzzled, both men turned to look at the dais.

"They must have taken it away before we arrived," was all Martialis could say.

I sighed. The Optio seemed inordinately pleased with himself, and I now saw why. The soldiers were searching the chests for any residual treasure, but finding very little of value. Martialis, though, had collected the two golden amulets from the bodies of the twin brothers who would have replaced Alexander if Dion's plan had succeeded.

Giving him my best gorgon stare, I held out my hand.

"Those amulets belong to Caesar. The original was stolen from Ephesus, and he sent me to find it."

He regarded me angrily, and for one horrible moment I thought he was considering plunging his sword into my belly so he could claim I'd been a victim of the fight.

I turned to Aelius for support. I was fairly sure he would have few qualms about disposing of me, but he was a loyal soldier of the Emperor, so I placed my trust in his allegiance and in the knowledge that, with so many Praetorians as witnesses, word of my murder would get out.

"The Prefect knows Dion had the amulets," I informed him. "He'll want to know what happened to them."

Aelius gave Martialis a nod.

"Hand them over."

Reluctantly, Martialis gave me the two amulets. They were surprisingly heavy, but then I'd never held that much gold in my hand before.

"Thank you," I said to Martialis, who turned away from me in disgust.

I did not care. We had thwarted Dion's plan, and Circe had escaped. My mission had succeeded, and I had the evidence in my hands.

So why, I wondered, did I feel so deflated?

Chapter 16
Rome

The sack of Alexandria lasted several days. I had no stomach for witnessing any more of it than I saw on the march back to the palace from Dion's house. That was more than enough for me.

The soldiers were running riot. They plundered wine shops and inns for wine and beer, they smashed down doors to raid private houses, and they killed anyone who dared resist them, whether man, woman or child. Many women were raped, but my pleas to Aelius to intervene and prevent this barbarity fell on deaf ears.

"Keep moving," the Centurion growled at me.

So we delivered the heads of the conspirators to Caesar, and the slaves were led off to be tortured to encourage them to reveal the names of any others who might be implicated. I didn't think it mattered a great deal since the Legions were slaughtering so many people they were probably going to dispose of any wealthy backer Dion might have had.

Over the next few days, I heard many of the Senators, including Cassius Dio, discussing what was taking place only a few hundred yards from where we stayed in luxurious comfort, and I saw wagons being loaded with statuary and chests full of gold and silver, all of this being the Emperor's share of the spoils.

I felt like a coward, skulking out of sight in my room while such horrors were being perpetrated on the citizens of Alexandria, but the reality was that there was nothing I could do. At best, I'd have thrown my own life away if I had dared venture into the town and tried to prevent the legionaries looting. But even knowing that didn't make me feel a whole lot better about myself.

I only saw the Emperor himself once, several days after Aelius had given his report and delighted Caesar by presenting him with the heads of the conspirators. To be honest, I thought everyone had forgotten about me because I was given a small bedroom and left alone while the city was ransacked. Eventually, though, the Emperor summoned me and Macrinus to a private audience where he congratulated me on discovering the tunnel and locating Dion.

"The body of Alexander is gone, you say?"

"I'm afraid so, Caesar."

The Emperor frowned, shooting a glance at Macrinus.

"Make sure the slaves are asked about its whereabouts."

Macrinus nodded, but I don't think they ever found out what happened to the body. Perhaps it, too, was at the bottom of the canal. Dion certainly wouldn't have wanted anyone finding it if his plan was to succeed. Having the corpse turn up when he had two walking, talking Alexanders would not have been part of his plan at all. Still, word of Alexander's disappearance would not have gone down well with the Egyptians, so Caracalla ordered the tunnel to be sealed to prevent anyone ever finding out. As far as I know, this was accomplished by the simple expedient of demolishing Dion's house.

Throughout our meeting, the Emperor had been holding one of the amulets bearing the symbol of the bull's head. I had no idea whether it was the original or the duplicate.

Raising it in his hand, he said to me, "I would ask that you return this to the Temple of Artemis. I want no fuss over it. Simply have it replaced as if it had never gone missing."

He handed me the heavy chain and golden disc, adding as he did so, "Then come and see me again. I think I can use a man of your talents."

That thought made my stomach churn and my knees tremble. The last thing I wanted was to be one of his entourage, but I knew there was no way of avoiding it.

Still, there were other things on my mind as well.

"May I ask a favour first, Caesar?"

I was in his good books, so he graciously nodded his permission.

"Of course."

"Thank you. I would like to return to Rome for a short while. I'd like to visit my mother before undertaking any more missions on your behalf. I have not seen her in nearly ten years. If you would grant me that, I will be pleased to offer you whatever service I can."

I sensed Macrinus' disapproval, although I couldn't tell whether that was at my brazenness in asking such a favour, or at the fact he knew I was lying about being pleased to offer my services to the power-mad Antoninus. Whatever the Prefect thought, though, the Emperor gave a shrug.

"Certainly. In fact, you can travel on one of the fleet's ships. I need messages taken to Rome, and you can report to Sempronius Rufus in person. When you have done that, take a few weeks for yourself, then return the amulet to Ephesus. I shall send word to the Temple as to where you should go after that."

"Thank you, Caesar."

So that was how I found myself an honoured passenger aboard a bireme of the imperial fleet, sailing west along the northern coast of Africa. The voyage was made against the prevailing wind, but the rowers more than compensated for that, and we made good time. We had overnight stops in several cities such as Leptis Magna, Sabratha, Regio Syrtica and Utica, as well as many smaller places, and it was not lost on me that our route would eventually take us close to Carthage. Knowing this, I was tempted to ask the Captain to make a detour so I could visit the place and seek Circe. I knew she had escaped the assault on Dion's house, but I had no idea whether she had managed to leave Alexandria before the massacre. I am not one for praying to the Gods, but I must admit I offered Jupiter some heartfelt pleas to keep her safe.

But Carthage was out of the question. Not only did the Captain have his orders, the fact was I had no idea whether Circe actually lived there, nor under what name I could find her. She may have tried to keep me out of danger by guiding me away from Dion's conspiracy, but she had repeatedly lied to me. Not only that, she was undoubtedly involved, and that presented me with an internal conflict I found impossible to resolve.

So I held my tongue, and the ship veered northwards to Sicily. After another overnight stop at Syracuse, we followed the Italian coast until we reached Ostia, Rome's port at the mouth of the Tiber. From there, a horse ride took me back to the city where I had been born and which ruled an empire to rival any other.

Rome had not changed a great deal in the years since I had left as a proud and horribly inexperienced teenager, but I now viewed the place with a more discerning eye. Like all the other cities I had seen recently, it had public buildings such as temples, libraries, bath houses and theatres, all adorned with magnificent columns and brightly painted statues. There were open spaces, parks and thousands upon thousands of homes, many contained within buildings which rose several storeys. There were wide avenues and narrow lanes, and there was the ancient heart of the city; the forum. I passed through that majestic public space in a sort of daze, then stopped to admire the eye-catching bulk of the Flavian amphitheatre. As I've mentioned, I take little pleasure in watching men fight to the death, or in witnessing animals being slaughtered for the pleasure of the crowd, but the amphitheatre itself is a superb monument to the power and glory of Rome.

My sightseeing did not last long, though. Soon I reached the Palatine hill which is now almost entirely occupied by the imperial palace which sprawls all across the slopes of the original home of Rome's legendary founder, Romulus.

There were Praetorians on guard here, of course, and scribes, slaves and secretaries scurrying in and out of the place, but I knew a quieter way in than the main entrance. Following the side of the hill down towards the Circus Maximus where the chariot races are held, I found a small, unobtrusive doorway where only one Praetorian stood watch. I showed him my pendant and the bag of messages I carried, and he opened the door to admit me into an ante-chamber where I had to explain my visit to an imperial lackey.

"I have messages for Sempronius Rufus," I informed the man. "And I need to see Sestius Fronto."

Once again I showed my pendant, then displayed the seals on the message scrolls. Once he was satisfied with my *bona fides*, he sent a slave hurrying off into the maze of corridors and soon I was being whisked along to the large office where Fronto worked alongside several other members of the Juggler's team. It was a large room containing several desks and more scroll racks than many libraries, although the scrolls here were most certainly not for public reading. This was where reports from all across the empire were read, analysed and filed. There were probably quite a few of my own scribblings stacked somewhere here.

Fronto was astonished to see me.

"Sextus!" he exclaimed with undisguised joy as he rose to his feet. "Is it really you? At last!"

"Hello, Tiberius," I replied, using his *praenomen* in the way close friends do.

Fronto clasped my forearm in the traditional Roman greeting, clapping me on the shoulder with his other hand. I thought he was about to hug me, but the setting was too formal for that.

"What brings you here?" he asked excitedly. "Did you discover anything in Ephesus?"

"I certainly did. I'm here to report to Sempronius Rufus, and I've brought messages from Caesar."

It's not easy to impress Fronto, but that comment made an impact.

"Well, we must take you to see Rufus immediately."

I held up a hand to forestall him.

"I have a favour to ask first."

"Of course. Anything."

"You might regret that," I told him with a smile. "I need somewhere to stay for a few weeks."

Fronto still retained something of the boyish looks he had when I had left Rome nine years earlier, but the expression he gave me transformed him into a man of more years than he carried.

"Aren't you going to stay with your brother?" he asked.

"Don't be daft, Tiberius. You know I can't do that. Can you put me up for a while?"

His smile returned as he nodded, "Of course I can. Faustia will be delighted to meet you at last."

Faustia, I knew, was Fronto's wife, and I felt a pang of guilt when he mentioned her because, although Fronto had been my best friend when we were boys, I hadn't returned to Rome for his wedding. In fairness, I had been in Armenia at the time, sniffing out the always volatile political situation there, but I still regretted missing Fronto's marriage. I'd found out about the wedding long after it had taken place. Yet, for all the years that had passed since I'd left Rome, and despite the fact that I'd only seen Fronto once in the intervening time, meeting him again was as easy as putting on a comfortable pair of old sandals. We knew each other so well, and I knew I could trust him.

"Now we must see Rufus," he told me.

He led me along a corridor to another office, a smaller one from where Sempronius Rufus, the Juggler himself, controlled the Emperor's spy network.

Word of my arrival had already reached him. Anyone bearing messages from the Emperor should go straight to the Juggler, so he was tapping his fingers impatiently when Fronto led me into the room.

Sempronius Rufus is not a big man, although he is running to fat now. As a juggler and acrobat in his youth, he had once had a slim, wiry frame with strong muscles in his arms and legs, but he was definitely too old to do that sort of thing now. His hair was balding, but his eyes revealed the sharp intelligence which lurked behind them.

"Sigma!" he greeted, using my code name as usual. "It is a long time since we have seen you here."

I showed him the bag I carried.

"I bring messages from Caesar. And he asked me to give my report to you in person."

Rufus twitched his head in a signal to Fronto that he should leave the room, but I added, "Fronto may as well stay. I will only have to repeat myself if he leaves."

Rufus gave me a hard stare, then nodded his acquiescence.

"Sit down, both of you."

We sat in the chairs facing him across his writing desk. No slaves were present, so Fronto poured wine and water for each of us, then I began my tale.

I recounted everything that had happened, although I once again omitted any mention of Circe. I know I should have told the Juggler about her, but I could not bring myself to reveal how stupid I had been to trust her. Omitting her presence meant I also had to leave out the attempt to kill me on board the ship, but that was a minor detail in any case. Agon had admitted it had been him and Diomedes who had bribed the sailor to kill me but, since both they and their hapless assassin were dead, I calculated there was little point in mentioning that particular episode.

Other than that, I told them everything.

Fronto let out a soft whistle when I was done.

"You are a lucky man, my friend."

The Juggler said nothing for a while, then told me, "I want you to write all of that down in an official report."

"I've already done that," I told him. "It's included among those scrolls."

"Very good," he grunted. "And well done. I expect Caesar was pleased with you."

I tried not to reveal just how terrified that thought made me as I went on to explain what Caracalla wanted me to do next.

Rufus cocked his head, then held out a hand.

"You'd better leave the amulet with me for the time being," he instructed. "I'll keep it safe until you head back to Ephesus."

The amulet was wrapped in a cloth at the bottom of my pack, but I dug it out and handed it over. The Juggler unwrapped it with care, then studied it for a long moment.

"Is this the original or the copy?" he asked me.

"I honestly have no idea. They look identical."

He nodded, wrapped the cloth around the golden amulet again, then told me, "You can pick it up when you leave. In the meantime, I will read these messages with interest."

He paused slightly, then asked, "Where will I find you if I need you?"

"I'll be staying with Fronto."

He regarded me with that cold stare again, but gave a brief nod. He knew all about my differences with my brother, Primus, so he betrayed no surprise at my choice of host.

His parting words were, "Don't discuss any of this unless you are completely alone. Not even a slave should overhear this."

We assured him we would follow that command, then Fronto decided it was late enough in the afternoon for him to return home. He sent a slave running ahead to warn Faustia that he was bringing a guest, then we set off together on the long walk to the Quirinal hill on the north of the city.

"Primus still lives just along the street from me," Fronto informed me. "It won't be possible to keep your presence a secret for long."

"I'm not bothered about that," I told him. "I intend to see my mother, but I'm going to keep well clear of Primus. That ought to suit him as much as it suits me."

"Will you not even visit his children? You have a nephew now as well as a niece."

"I expect they are better off not knowing me," I replied defensively.

"It is up to you, of course," Fronto said, not pushing too hard, although I knew he would bring the subject up again at some point.

Fronto lived in the house he had inherited from his father. He'd been an only child, his mother having died giving birth to a daughter who had not survived her first year. With no mother and no siblings, Fronto had gravitated towards our house where my mother had made him welcome. He was more of a brother to me than Primus, my natural brother.

The Quirinal is a fair walk from the Palatine, but it is becoming a more prosperous place than it had once been. Like most places in Rome, though, it contained the usual mix of rich and poor properties standing side by side, although I had the impression it was definitely a less squalid neighbourhood than it had been when I had left at the age of sixteen.

Fronto's house was modest but comfortable, the atrium having only two reception rooms, the peristyle garden being about half the size of the one in Circe's home in Ephesus, and the two-storey rear block housing only Fronto, Faustia and a dozen slaves.

Faustia herself was a very pleasant surprise. Most marriages in the upper echelons of Roman society are contractual arrangements designed to create family alliances. In many cases, Roman men regard their wives as vehicles for producing heirs, while their sex life is satisfied by the city's army of prostitutes. Somehow, I doubted Fronto would follow that tradition. There seemed to be genuine affection between him and Faustia who, small, dark-haired and bubbly, was full of lively conversation. She even joined us at the dining table, sharing a couch with Fronto while I lay opposite, tucking into the various dishes her kitchen staff had conjured. Fish and sea urchins featured prominently, with *garum*, a potent fish sauce, being offered in liberal quantities.

We chatted amiably for a few hours, catching up on old times. Fronto had obviously warned Faustia that I would not be able to discuss any of the missions I had been on, so we concentrated on tales of our boyhood and on them bringing me up to date with all the latest scandals in Rome. I did tell them about Alexandria being sacked by the Legions because that was an event which everyone would know about before long, although I pleaded ignorance of the details on the grounds that I'd been sheltering in the palace all through the devastation.

Fronto said nothing, but his expression revealed his distaste for the news, while Faustia muttered, "That sounds quite horrible. Those poor people."

That was about as close to criticising the Emperor as it was safe to go, so we soon changed the subject back to happier things.

It was as convivial an evening as I had ever experienced, and I was feeling very content by the end of the meal.

Faustia made her excuses, giving Fronto a peck on the cheek before leaving us alone. Fronto then dismissed the slaves.

Giving me a keen look, he said, "There's something you want to talk about, isn't there? I can tell something is bothering you."

That's the problem with knowing someone so well. Fronto could read me as easily as one of the reports he examined every day.

"It's a delicate subject," I said cautiously. "I don't want to fall out over it."

"Now you are worrying me," he frowned. "What is it?"

"Who is Circe?" I asked him bluntly, hoping that springing the question would bring a truthful response.

Fronto looked at me blankly.

"Who? The sorceress in the old legend?"

"No. She also goes by the name of Tertullia Tertia. She said she met you some time ago and you told her about me."

Now Fronto looked really confused.

"I don't think I've ever met anyone by that name," he said.

"She has lots of names. Circe. Dido. She claims to be from Carthage and she told me she'd met you a few years ago. She insinuated you had been trying to impress her and you told her about your work. And about me."

Now I saw a blush begin to creep up Fronto's face. He picked up a goblet and drank some wine to cover his embarrassment.

"You do know her?" I pressed.

Putting down his goblet, he gave a wry nod.

"Yes, I think I know who you mean. A tall girl, quite thin. Eyes you can drown in?"

"That's her."

He gave a sigh.

"What has this to do with anything?" he asked.

"A lot, believe me. But I need to know how she knows you and what you told her."

Fronto took another gulp of wine, then recounted, "It was about three years ago, just before my father died and, I must make clear, before I met Faustia."

"Go on," I prompted.

Her name was Petronia Tertia. She came to Rome with her guardian, an older man by the name of ..." he paused while he searched his memory. "Veronius Pulcher, I think."

I nodded, "That makes sense. She said her father was dead and she had a guardian. And she's used the Petronia name elsewhere. I doubt it is her real name, though."

Fronto gave me a look of puzzlement, but went on, "I can't really recall why they were in Rome. But Veronius knew my father and came to visit him. Petronia was with him, and I was asked to entertain her."

I grinned in spite of my brooding.

"Entertain?"

"Not what you think," he said with a soft smile of his own. "Although I admit I tried. And yes, I did try to impress her. Veronius had already told her I worked for the Juggler, so she kept asking questions, and I kept answering."

He held up a hand as he added, "I told her nothing specific, you understand, but I'll admit I was a bit too loose-tongued."

"She has that effect," I agreed. "Did you tell her about the eagle pendants?"

He flushed again, giving a shrug.

"I may have let her see mine."

I told him, "She had a ring with a similar design. I'd guess she had it made from memory to match the official symbol."

Fronto looked crestfallen as he asked, "What is this all about, Sextus? I'll admit I was young and foolish, and trying to impress her, but if you've met her, you'll understand she is very hard to resist."

"Oh, I know that, my friend. She fooled me even worse than she tricked you."

Then I told him the true story, leaving nothing out, not even the fact that I'd shared Circe's bed and fallen helplessly in love with her.

When I had finished, Fronto looked appalled.

"You are taking a huge risk keeping this from the Juggler," he sighed. "And if the Emperor ever finds out ..."

He did not need to elaborate on that point. I knew only too well what Caesar would do to me if he learned I'd been sheltering a conspirator from his justice.

Fronto poured more wine, then let out a sharp breath as he gathered his composure.

"All right," he said with an air of decisiveness, "let us look at what we know."

He pursed his lips, then began, "I suspect she does stay in Carthage. Veronius Pulcher was certainly from there. My father told me as much."

"Her tales of her childhood certainly support that hypothesis," I agreed.

"And she has a vendetta against Caesar," Fronto continued. "Whether that is personal or simply because he is Caesar is not something I would like to say for certain."

"I suspect it might be personal," I said. "Although I don't know what could be behind it."

Fronto pulled a face, lowering his voice as he reminded me, "The Emperor has not been averse to disposing of anyone he believes to be disloyal to him. There are thousands of people who have had family members executed."

Fronto was putting it mildly, and I knew that the executions he spoke of were not public beheadings following a formal court trial. When the Emperor wants you dead, it's more a case of the Praetorians turning up on your doorstep with drawn swords. Since Antoninus Caracalla came to power, he'd kept his death squads very busy indeed.

Gravely, I nodded, "That's true. But it doesn't help us pin down who Circe might be. If she's one of thousands, we might never find her."

Fronto asked, "And what is the purpose of finding her, Sextus? What will you do if you do discover her whereabouts?"

At that, I was forced to admit, "I don't know. I just want to understand why she got involved with Dion and his cronies."

"That's easy," Fronto told me. "If we assume Circe has a personal vendetta against the Emperor, then she may have aided the Alexandrians solely because that was part of their plan. She may have had no interest in the other part of their plot. To be honest, I wouldn't blame her. That Dion fellow sounds completely mad."

"He was certainly a fanatic," I agreed. "But his plan might have worked. The only thing I don't get is why he picked Alexander as his rallying point. I'd have thought he'd have tried to reincarnate someone like Ramesses."

Fronto dismissed that thought with his usual certainty.

"Alexander's tomb was close at hand," he explained. "Many people had seen the body, and Alexandria has always been a hotbed of uprisings. Who better than their local semi-deity to serve as their leader? Besides, Alexander was a Pharaoh every bit as much as any other."

"He wasn't Egyptian, though," I countered.

"He was if you believe some of the rumours about him."

I frowned, "What do you mean?"

Fronto smiled, "I mean there is a legend about a Pharaoh named Nectanebo who fled to Macedonia when he was evicted from Egypt. Some say he was Alexander's true father, or possibly grandfather."

"That's ridiculous!" I snorted.

"Nevertheless, some believed it at the time Alexander was proclaimed Pharaoh. True or not, it makes him a genuine Egyptian hero."

I waved a dismissive hand.

"All right. I'll take your word for that. But we are moving away from the important subject. I want to know how to find Circe. I need to know the truth."

"There is one thing you are overlooking," he told me.

"What's that?"

"She may not have left Alexandria. If she was trapped there, the chances are that she will not have survived."

"I'm not overlooking that," I told him. "I'm trying my best to ignore it. I need to believe she got away."

"Very well," Fronto shrugged. "Then let us assume she did escape. There is no guarantee she would have returned to Carthage."

"No, but it's as good a place as any to start looking for her."

"Well, you can't go there," Fronto told me flatly. "You need to return to Ephesus, and then on to whatever Caesar has in store for you."

I exhaled a long sigh because I knew he was right.

He shot me a grin as he went on, "But I can perhaps make some enquiries. Not about her, because we still don't know her true name, but about Veronius Pulcher. If I can track him down through our local agents, that may provide a lead."

I gave him an earnest look as I said, "That would be a great help if you can do it. Thank you."

"Don't thank me yet," he warned. "It is a long shot which may come to nothing. And I shouldn't need to remind you that the Juggler will not be pleased if he discovers what I am up to."

"Don't put yourself at risk," I said.

He grinned, "Too late for that, my friend. I already know too much. By rights, I should denounce you as a traitor for not having told Caesar the whole truth. By remaining silent, I become your accomplice."

"It's not as serious as that!" I blurted. "The plot has been foiled."

"Not entirely," Fronto argued. "They planned to kill Caesar, so there must be at least one other conspirator who is close to the Emperor but who has not yet been identified. And what if Circe, or Dido as we should perhaps call her, makes another assassination attempt?"

He was right. What was worse, I had no arguments against his point.

Seeing my dismay, Fronto said, "If Faustia were here, she would no doubt tell you to forget this woman. She would say you ought to find yourself a wife and settle down. But I expect that advice would go unheeded, would it not?"

"You know damned well it would," I grunted.

"Then we must act carefully, you and I. We must make enquiries, but we must mask our true intent. And if we do discover that Dido lives and who she really is, you will need to confront her."

He gave a shrug as he added, "What you do then is up to you, my friend, but make sure you choose the right course."

"Just find her," I told him.

We rarely mentioned Circe after that first evening. Fronto sent coded messages to one of his trusted contacts in Carthage, but I waited several weeks and there was no reply. I spent that time relaxing, wandering the streets of Rome and, eventually, meeting my mother.

She came to the house one afternoon when I was sitting indoors, sheltering from the summer sun, idly working my way through Livy's account of the war against Hannibal. That's the original Hannibal, not my friend from Ephesus. I wondered whether that ancient war would provide any insights into Carthage even though I knew the city Hannibal had known had been destroyed centuries ago. It was a Roman city now, with Romanised inhabitants. But reading passed the time, and it was an old hobby I had found little time for in recent years.

When a slave interrupted me to announce that my mother had come to see me, I was not sure how to react.

She gave me little choice. Sweeping majestically into the room, she spread her arms wide, then embraced me passionately, kissing my face and repeating my name over and over again. When she broke free, I saw tears had dampened her cheeks.

She soon recovered, of course. My mother is as tough as they come. She'd been through a great deal in her life, not least of which was being whisked away from her home in Syria to be brought to Rome as a young trophy wife by my father who had just retired from the army. But she'd learned Latin, had become almost as Roman as most local women, and had raised two sons. In spite of that, she'd never forgotten her roots, and she had taught me how to speak Aramaic while filling my head with tales of the east.

She was still striking in appearance despite being in her late forties now. Her dark hair and olive skin shone with vitality, and her brown eyes were as keen and lively as I remembered. I was much taller than her now, so she had to look up at me when we stood facing one another, but I still felt like a small boy as I tried to explain myself to her.

It was she who told me to sit down, and she who commanded a slave to bring wine and sweetmeats. I knew Faustia was in the house, but she had obviously decided to be discreet, and she left us alone in the small study overlooking the garden.

At first, my mother did most of the talking. She told me all about Primus, his wife and their two children, but she did not chastise me for not visiting. She knew the rift between my brother and me was too deep to be easily healed, but she did bring me up to date with how the family was progressing.

Then, naturally, she scolded me for rarely writing to her.

"It is not right that I must ask Fronto for news of you," she told me in a tone which suggested I deserved a whipping.

"It is not always easy to write," I told her. "And I cannot use the official messengers for private correspondence."

"Excuses!" she snapped. "But since you have not written to me, you must now tell me everything that has happened. Fronto told me much, but I wish to hear it from you. I want to understand your life."

So I spent the rest of the afternoon giving her an account of my life. How, after I'd demanded my meagre share of the inheritance my father had left me, I'd purchased passage to Athens, squandered most of my cash, then travelled to Ephesus because I'd heard about the Temple and wanted to see it for myself. I told her how I'd been down on my luck, and how Hannibal had befriended me, giving me an introduction to the High Priest, Restitutus, and how the old man had, for reasons I don't think I'll ever really understand, offered me the post as head of the Temple security when the previous incumbent had died of fever.

That job had led to Fronto discovering my whereabouts and suggesting to Restitutus that he send me to meet the Juggler who was in need of spies who could pass as Parthians or Syrians. Since I spoke Aramaic and had my mother's dark looks, Fronto reckoned I was ideally suited to the role.

"You came back to Rome?" my mother exclaimed. "And you did not come to see me?"

"I was under orders not to tell anyone," I explained feebly. "And then I was sent back to the east."

"And what jobs do you do for the Emperor?"

"Oh, this and that. Nothing very exciting. Writing reports on local events, mostly."

She was not fooled. I could tell by the look she gave me, but she said nothing except to ask, "And what brings you back to Rome now?"

And then, because she was my mother, and because I needed her to understand, I told her all about my mission to

Ephesus and Alexandria, including my hopeless infatuation with Circe.

She listened in silence, then reached forwards to clasp my hand.

"You must find this girl," she told me.

"I am trying to," I replied. "Or, more correctly, Fronto is trying to. But I don't know what to do. She is an enemy of the Emperor, and that makes her dangerous."

"You should follow your heart," she told me decisively. "Being an enemy of the Emperor does not make her a bad person. He has many enemies, and most of them feel justified in their hatred of him. You said yourself he ordered the deaths of thousands of people in Alexandria. From all I have heard about him, he is a monster."

"You cannot say that!" I warned, flapping my hands to silence her.

She paid no attention.

"He killed his own brother," she went on. "And they say he sleeps with his step-mother. She is just as bad, for she sided with him against her own son. The two of them are evil."

"Mother! Say no more!"

She stared into my eyes as she said softly, "You know I am right. You serve a monster."

"He is an Emperor," I replied. "And I don't have much choice. It's not easy to leave the imperial service once you are inside. Not if you want to stay alive, anyway."

"That has not always been the case," she countered. "There have been good emperors before now, although I dare say most of them had blood on their hands. But this Emperor has more blood than most."

I managed to get her off that subject before any of the household staff overheard, but she had made her point, and I knew she was right. Yet what could I do?

Fronto returned home that evening, giving me a brief shake of his head to let me know there was no news from Carthage, then he and Faustia made a great fuss of my mother and we all had dinner together, talking about old times. My mother regaled Faustia with stories of the antics Fronto and I had got up to when we were young, and we all laughed at the memories.

When my mother returned home, she departed with a smile and a whispered word for me to seek out Circe.

"I will try," I promised her.

I meant it, but what I did not know was how I would ever be able to keep that promise.

Chapter 17
Intrigues

I stayed in Rome long enough to celebrate my birthday. My mother came to Fronto's house, bringing gifts of new tunics and sandals.

"If you are working for the Emperor," she told me, "you need to look your best."

I did not tell her that most of my jobs for the Emperor required me to look anything but my best, but I had already begun the process of replacing the belongings I'd lost in Alexandria, so her gifts were just what I needed. So was the company, and we spent another excellent evening of food, drink and laughter which ended with me promising to write to my mother more frequently. The look she gave me suggested she did not really believe me, but I felt closer to her then than I could ever recall, and it was a wrench knowing I would need to leave her again.

I presented Fronto and Faustia with some small gifts I'd purchased; bolts of cloth and some perfume, and then, after a stay which had been longer than I'd expected, I prepared to say farewell to Rome once again. To tell the truth, I would not be sorry to depart. Other than my friends and my mother, I had no real reason to stay in Rome. It was too big, too crowded, too full of intrigue for my liking, and that's not even taking account of the high risk of catching malaria which still kills more Romans than just about anything else.

My only reason for lingering was that I was desperate to hear what Fronto's agent in Carthage had discovered. So I made excuses to delay my departure for a few more days. And, just when I was giving up hope, Fronto returned home with news.

"We need to talk," he told me, his face bright with expectation.

That evening, the two of us sat alone in Fronto's study with the door closed so nobody could overhear us. Fronto then produced a small wax tablet on which he had jotted some notes.

"I burned the original report once I had read it," he informed me.

That was sensible. It would not do to be found carrying a report on a matter like this.

"So tell me what it said," I urged.

"I'm afraid you won't like it."

"Just tell me!"

"Very well. Our agent in Carthage has been there for a considerable time. He knew Veronius Pulcher by reputation, but he was very thorough in his investigation, which is why it has taken so long for him to reply."

Glancing at his cryptic, coded notes, Fronto went on, "It seems Veronius Pulcher died last year. His family history is rather complicated, but our agent managed to provide a lot of details. Pulcher was married three times. His first wife died years ago, he divorced the second, and his third is still alive. There were no children from the first marriage, but he has two children by his second wife; a son and a daughter. The son is serving with the Twentieth Legion in Britannia, and the daughter is married. She has two sons of her own, both in their early teens."

"What about the third wife?" I asked, my breath catching in my throat in case he named Circe.

"She is only sixteen," Fronto told me with a shake of his head. "The daughter of some wealthy local official, I believe. Her physical description does not match Circe at all."

"So Circe wasn't part of Pulcher's immediate family," I nodded. "But she claimed he was her guardian."

"And that is where the trail goes cold," Fronto sighed. "Our agent could find no trace of Pulcher ever having been guardian to anyone at all, let alone a wealthy young woman. He even obtained a copy of Pulcher's will and is certain the man left nothing to anyone outside his family. Other than the usual donations to the city and a bequest in favour of the Emperor, there were no other beneficiaries."

"So it was another lie," I sighed. "But there must have been a connection between him and Circe. She came to Rome with him."

"Yes, and I still don't know why. Our agent could learn nothing of the purpose of that trip. Indeed, he found no record of it at all."

"Which means what?" I wondered.

Fronto cleared his throat before saying, "It could mean a number of things. The most obvious one is that Circe, or whatever her real name is, was having an affair with him, and he brought her to Rome to impress her."

I shook my head.

"Then he would have left her something in his will, wouldn't he?"

"Not if he didn't want his wife to find out. More likely he gave Circe expensive gifts while he was alive."

I asked, "Do we know why his second wife divorced him? Was it because she found out about an affair?"

"No. The divorce was Pulcher's idea. He wanted to link himself to an important family, and his second wife did not have sufficiently wealthy connections."

That was not unusual in Roman society, so I moved on, desperately seeking a connection between Pulcher and Circe.

"Do we know what he died of?" I asked.

"A riding accident. He was out hunting with friends when his horse stumbled and threw him. He broke his neck."

I ran my hand over my face, trying to see how Circe could have fitted into the dead man's life. Had she been nothing more than a lover? Somehow, that didn't fit the picture of the woman I knew.

Fronto pursed his lips before continuing, "I have, however, found a link between my father and Pulcher."

I shrugged, "I presume they knew one another when they were younger?"

"They did indeed. I remember my father brushing aside my enquiries as to who Pulcher was when he came to visit that day. But I asked one of the older slaves who informed me that Pulcher used to be my father's patron."

I nodded. Most wealthy Romans act as patrons to many people of lesser rank. A patron will dispense money and support for his clients who, in turn, back him in any election or other social or political venture. Rome is built on patronage, with some very important men having a whole train of clients following in their wake when they walk out in public.

"So what?" I asked.

Fronto now cleared his throat and lowered his voice before telling me, "Well, our agent says Pulcher moved to Carthage about ten years ago, just after the plot of Fulvius Plautianus was discovered. He is not certain, but Pulcher may have been one of Plautianus' clients."

I tried to think back that far. Ten years earlier, I'd been a restless, angry boy chafing under the restrictions placed on me by my older brother who had inherited everything from our father and who treated me little better than a servant.

"Plautianus? Wasn't he executed for plotting against the old Emperor?"

"That's right. He was a former consul and was Praetorian Prefect at the time he was denounced. His daughter was married to our current Emperor who, incidentally, was the one who uncovered the plot. He had Plautianus killed on the spot, and he sent the daughter into exile. If you believe rumour, she was quietly disposed of a couple of years later."

That sounded like Antoninus Caracalla, but I couldn't remember much about the case, and I said as much to Fronto.

He shrugged, "There's not much more to tell. Whether there really was a plot, or whether our current Emperor merely wanted rid of Plautianus and his own wife, nobody seems very sure."

"How do you remember all that? I can't recall any of the details at all."

"I've been asking around," Fronto admitted. "Very casually, of course. Some members of our team have been working at the Palatine for a while. They're pretty close-lipped about it, naturally, but I can read between the lines."

"So Antoninus discovers a plot, kills the Praetorian Prefect who happens to be his father-in-law, and banishes his wife who is also killed once a suitable time has passed. Is that right?"

"That seems to be what happened."

Fronto's voice dropped to a barely audible whisper as he confided, "There was apparently a rumour that young Antoninus was already sleeping with his stepmother at that time, and that his wife objected. Plautianus allegedly threatened to tell the Emperor, so Antoninus had him killed."

My mother's words about Antoninus Caracalla being a monster rang inside my head. Whether or not this scandalous rumour was true, the story was plausible. Our Emperor had always had a way of responding to threats with violence.

The connection was obvious.

I asked, "And Pulcher was a client of Plautianus?"

"I think so. Our agent wasn't able to be absolutely sure of that, but it seems probable."

It certainly made sense. If a wealthy man is discovered plotting against the Emperor, his clients are in very real danger. It was no wonder Pulcher decided to quit Rome if he really had been a client of Plautianus.

"I suppose your father broke his connection to Pulcher when he left?"

"He must have done, but this theory explains how they knew one another, and why Pulcher went to Carthage."

"But there's still no link to Circe," I pointed out. "I suppose she might have a reason to want revenge if she had some connection to Pulcher, but it seems a bit extreme to want to kill an Emperor for forcing someone into voluntary exile."

"I agree," Fronto nodded sombrely. "Which brings us back to having no idea why she would want Caesar dead, and the only possible link between her and Pulcher being that she was his mistress."

"It's not impossible, I suppose," I conceded grudgingly.

"Whatever the connection is, we have lost the trail," Fronto pointed out. "Our agent even went so far as to try to find any wealthy young women who owned a villa outside Carthage. There was nobody who even came close to matching Circe's description."

"It depends how far he looked," I frowned. "Africa is a big province."

"Yes, it is. And we do not have the resources to search it. Not unless we make this official. Which we cannot do."

And that, it seemed, was the end of my search. Circe, or whatever she was really called, had vanished. I had visions of her lying dead in Alexandria, and those haunted my dreams for many nights, but I still clung to the belief that she had escaped. Whether that would have been a good thing or not, I still could not say.

But she was gone, and I had no more excuses to delay completing the mission Caesar had given me.

Chapter 18
The Mosaic

By the time I returned to Ephesus, it was late in the sailing season. The weather was still mostly dry and hot, but occasional storms had blown up, and rain had fallen, turning the land's summer browns to vibrant greens.

This time, I rented a room in a more salubrious establishment near the north gate, not far from the stadium. The racing season was already underway, and that always brought large crowds to the city, but I was fortunate enough to find decent accommodation.

Not that I planned on staying long. I had retrieved the golden amulet from the Juggler, and now had it buried at the bottom of my pack. It was quite a weight to carry around, and not only in the physical sense. Knowing I had one of the Emperor's trinkets in my sole possession had made me nervous throughout the voyage. I couldn't wait to get rid of it, but I had another task I wanted to undertake before I headed out to the Temple.

I walked through the familiar streets until I reached the large house where Circe had stayed. I knocked on the door which was opened by a smartly dressed young slave.

"I'm looking for Tertullia Tertia," I told him.

He looked confused as he replied, "I'm sorry, Sir. There is nobody of that name here."

"Oh? She used to live here. Only a couple of months ago, in fact."

"Ah!" he said with a smile as understanding dawned. "That would be before my master bought the house."

"That must be right," I agreed. "Can I ask who owned the house before your master acquired it?"

As I spoke, I withdrew a silver *denarius* from my belt pouch and twirled it between my fingers.

Being the door slave, it was his job to know about his Master's business and who he had dealings with. Ephesus may be a city, but the number of people who could afford to purchase a house of this size numbered in the tens, not the thousands.

"The former owner lives in Rome now," the slave informed me, his eyes flicking towards the silver coin in my hand.

I waited a moment, then he went on, "The local agent who handled the sale was a banker by the name of Julius Bastianus."

"And where would I find him?" I enquired, digging out a second coin.

"I believe he has a home in the northern district, sir. Somewhere near the stadium."

I thanked him and gave him the coins, then retraced my steps back to the north gate. A few enquiries soon led me to the ostentatious dwelling of Julius Bastianus. Luckily for me, he was at home, and he agreed to see me when I mentioned I was there on imperial business.

His slave led me to a large, bright and airy room where I was served wine and olives while Bastianus assured me that he would be only too happy to assist me.

"It's very confidential," I told him. "Very confidential indeed."

"I am a man who knows how to hold his tongue," he promised me.

I smiled, although it was hard to like this man. He was large and fat, with heavy jowls and pudgy fingers which held several gold rings. Lending money obviously paid well.

"It's about a house sale you recently arranged," I told him. "I am interested in the former occupants."

He continued to smile, so I told him which house I was talking about.

"Oh, yes! I recall that very well. A most superior property."

"What can you tell me about the people who owned it?"

A slight frown creased his podgy brow as he sighed, "It had formerly been the home of a very prominent local citizen, a man who was a long-standing member of the City Council. After he died, his son, who moved to Rome some years ago, sent instructions that the house should be sold. Unfortunately, there was little interest in the property. It was, as you might imagine, beyond the resources of most people. Fortunately, I did eventually locate a buyer who moved in only a few weeks ago."

"But the property was not empty the whole time, was it?"

That brought another scowl.

189

"No," he admitted reluctantly. "Back in January, I was still seeking a buyer, but there had been no offers. Indeed, I was considering suggesting that we should put the place up for auction, although that would have resulted in a very low sale price."

"So what happened?"

He sighed, "I was approached by a young lady who offered to rent the building for six months. I would not normally have agreed, but she offered a ridiculous amount of money."

"Can you describe her?"

"Young and pretty. Dark hair, very slim and quite tall. She said she was from Carthage."

I found it difficult to resist smiling. Piecing together all the strands of this case was like designing a mosaic floor but not knowing where all the pieces were. I'd just found another small piece.

"Did she give a name?" I asked.

Bastianus scratched his cheek while he tried to remember.

"Tertullia Tertia," he decided.

That piece fitted, but would the next one? It was time for the big question.

"And where can I find this young woman now?"

He spread his hands in a gesture of helplessness.

"I'm afraid I do not know. She vanished a few months ago. Just left the place empty with no word that she was going."

He scowled as he grumbled, "It was most inconsiderate of her."

"Do you have any way of contacting her?"

"None at all."

There was not much more I could ask him, so I thanked him and left. I'd put one more piece into position, but there were still huge gaps in the mosaic.

I made the long walk out to the Temple. Restitutus, the High Priest, was only too glad to welcome me, especially when I dug the amulet out of my bag and handed it over to him.

"You found it!" he gaped. "Where? How?"

"I'm afraid I can't really tell you," I replied apologetically. "All I can say is that it was taken to Alexandria, and those who stole it were caught and punished."

Restitutus may be old, but he's no fool. His eyes narrowed as he asked, "Would that have had anything to do with what the Emperor's soldiers did in Alexandria?"

"It was related," I confirmed.

"Well, no matter. I am sure the Emperor had his reasons. The important thing for us is that you have recovered the amulet. I shall see that it is put in its proper place."

"Caesar wanted it done with no fuss," I told him.

"Of course. We have no wish to advertise that anything was stolen. We shall replace it without any fuss. If anyone should ask, which I doubt, we will simply say it was being cleaned."

We had a celebratory drink, and he invited me to dine with him. Pomponius Niger, his head of security, joined us. Like Restitutus, he was suitably impressed at my success in recovering the amulet.

"They used twins?" he gasped when I explained how the theft had been accomplished. "There were two Philipposes?"

"That's right. Identical twins. I saw them, and I couldn't tell them apart. It's no wonder the theft seemed so miraculous."

"And they are both dead, you say?"

"That's right."

"Serves them right," he grunted with the attitude of an ex-soldier.

None of us dwelled on what had taken place when the Emperor had unleashed his Legions on Alexandria. Niger, I guessed, would feel the citizens deserved their fate, while Restitutus, like me, regretted it while understanding the effect it would have on any other city which might be considering any sort of uprising. I could tell what they were thinking, but nobody would make any comment out loud. That sort of conversation was dangerous.

When it was almost time for me to return to the city if I wanted to get back before dark, I said to Restitutus, "I was told the Emperor would send instructions here as to what he wants me to do next."

The old man smiled, "I have a sealed message scroll for you. I would not let you leave without it."

I wondered if he knew what the scroll said, but he was too wily to let it slip if he did. He rose from his chair, moved to a locked set of drawers, took out a small key, then located a scroll which bore the Emperor's own seal. I was so amazed that I feared to break it open, but I was aware of Niger's jealous gaze, so I unrolled the parchment and read it just to spite him.

"I am to go to Antioch," I told them. "The Emperor wishes me to report to his mother."

Niger's expression barely concealed his envy, but Restitutus merely smiled.

"You are going up in the world, Scipio," he told me. "I wish you well."

Which was, I guessed, his way of telling me to be careful.

The sun was low in the sky when I said farewell to Restitutus, but I asked Niger if he would accompany me as far as the road to the city.

"I need to do my rounds anyway," he agreed.

So we ambled past the huge Temple, its glory still majestic enough to draw my eyes even though I'd seen it a thousand times. But I had a reason for asking Niger to walk with me, because I thought I'd identified another piece of the mosaic.

You served in Africa, didn't you?" I asked him.

"That's right."

"Where, in particular?"

"I moved around a bit, but mostly around Leptis Magna."

I felt my heart beat a little faster. Another piece of the mosaic had just slotted into place.

"You told her I was coming, didn't you?"

He shot me a hard look.

"What?"

"Tertullia Tertia. Or Circe, or whatever other name you know her by. She came to Ephesus and rented a house. I'll bet she came out to the Temple and she saw you. Or you saw her and recognised her."

"I don't know what you are talking about," he growled defensively.

"I think you do. She spun me a story about being sent to help me by the people I work for in Rome, but I've just come from Rome, and nobody there knows who she is. Which means somebody else told her. And the only other people who knew I was coming were Restitutus and you."

He was silent for a moment, his tread heavy on the gravel path we were following.

"So what?" he eventually snapped.

"I think you knew she had something to do with the theft," I told him. "At the very least, she asked you to let her know if anything came of the investigation."

Niger remained silent, his expression dark.

"Don't worry," I said, hoping to pre-empt any thoughts he might have of doing away with me. "I haven't told anyone about her, so you are in no danger. If I did report you, I'd be in even more trouble because I've kept her out of the investigation."

He snorted, a response I was becoming accustomed to as far as he was concerned.

I asked him, "So who is she? What's her real name?"

"I can't tell you," he replied. "That's not a secret I am prepared to give up."

"Why not?"

"Because it could end her life. I owe her enough loyalty to prevent that harm coming to her."

"But she's in Leptis Magna?"

He hesitated too long before saying, "I don't know where she is."

"But her home is in Leptis Magna?"

His silence confirmed it.

By this time, we had reached the edge of the Temple grounds. The road ahead of me was still fairly busy with the last of the visitors beginning the long walk back to the city. The shadows were lengthening, and it was time for me to go.

I stopped for a moment, turning to face Niger.

I told him, "I don't know how much you were involved in what went on. I'm prepared to believe you only had suspicions, and that you made sure you went nowhere near her when you were searching for the stolen artefacts. But if you do see her again, let her know I'm looking for her."

He hissed, "I'll warn her. If I see her. Which I doubt I will."

I gave him a curt nod of farewell, then turned my back on him and began the long walk to the city.

The mosaic was taking shape. I was fairly sure Fronto's theory that Circe had been Pulcher's lover was wide of the mark. At least, if she had been having sex with him, it was to use him as she had tried to use me. She wanted vengeance, and she had planned this for years. Somehow, she'd persuaded Pulcher to take her to Rome. There, she'd goaded Fronto into showing her the design on his pendant, and she'd heard all about me. I doubt she was counting on me being the one who was sent to Ephesus to investigate the theft, but that had been a lucky bonus for her. Knowing Fronto's name and having had a ring made with a copy of the eagle design, she'd have been able to convince most imperial agents that she was one of them. She'd certainly fooled me easily enough.

And yet, for all the things I now understood, I still had no idea why she wanted to kill the Emperor. The answer, it now seemed clear, lay in Leptis Magna, another of the great cities of Africa. The only problem was that I had no excuse to go there, because I now had orders to go to Antioch.

To serve the Emperor's stepmother.

Chapter 19
The Cabal

Antioch is an ancient city. It lies on a bend of the Orontes river, the bulk of the city being on the south bank where the river deviates from its southerly course to bend westwards towards the sea. There's a smaller part of the settlement on the north bank, but the place I was heading to was a large island in the middle of the wide river which is connected to both northern and southern sections of the town by several bridges. This island is where the government administration and the palace buildings are to be found, and it was here that I also found the Emperor's stepmother, Julia Domna.

She had once been a striking woman. That much was obvious the first time I met her in the large room she used as her principal place of work. She was the sort of person who had an aura about her, a way of compelling people to pay attention to her every word, and to use that power to exert her authority.

She still retained that power, although it was much diminished by the illness that was ravaging her body. She was quite open about it, for she could not conceal the pallor of her skin, nor the increasing frailty of her body.

"I have a cancer," she told me bluntly. "I found a lump in my breast a few weeks ago. The physicians say it will kill me eventually, but I am not going to let that stop me living my life."

She had been the wife of an Emperor, mother of another and was stepmother to our current Caesar. Rumours about their actual relationship abounded, but I never did learn the truth of the matter. All I know from the year and a half I spent working closely with her is that she was extremely clever and could be utterly ruthless. I suppose I should have known about that last attribute since she had been the only witness to the occasion when our Emperor, Antoninus, had killed his brother, Geta. It had happened in Julia Domna's own bed chamber, where Geta had reputedly called for a meeting to settle the increasing acrimony between the two half-brothers. Their father, the Emperor Septimius Severus, had decreed that they should rule as joint Emperors after his death, but it soon became clear that this was unworkable. Antoninus was several years older and vastly more experienced than Geta, and his nature was such that he could not bear to have an equal.

Nobody really knows what happened on that fateful night. Antoninus insisted afterwards that his brother had drawn a sword and summoned guards to kill him. He claimed he had been unarmed, so he had been forced to grab the weapon and stabbed Geta in self defence. The younger man had bled to death in his mother's arms, while Antoninus had run through the palace screaming about a plot to assassinate him.

In the aftermath, thousands of people who had been known supporters of Geta had been put to death, the Praetorians wreaking bloody justice in a spate of blood-letting. That mass slaughter was carried out so quickly and on such a vast scale that many people whispered it must have been planned in advance, but only Antoninus Caesar knows whether that is true.

Oddly, amidst all the killing, Julia Domna had said nothing. She had buried her son, then acted as if nothing had happened. She remained an important and highly esteemed member of the imperial family, and I soon discovered that Antoninus, who had been sole Emperor for four years now, trusted her implicitly. Make of that what you will. I suppose she had perhaps become so accustomed to holding a position of power that she did not want to give it up no matter what had happened, but I certainly wasn't going to ask her any questions about her choices.

I'd been a bit worried about what it was she wanted me to do, but I soon discovered that my role was to help her keep track of what was going on all across the empire. Many of the reports which found their way to the Juggler on the Palatine were copied and sent to Julia Domna who would then decide which ones needed to be passed to the Emperor in person. The reason for this was that, as the ruler of such a vast empire, the Emperor did not have enough time to handle everything himself. He relied on the army of imperial scribes and secretaries to ensure the smooth operation of most matters, but there were only two individuals in particular who were trusted to make the really important decisions. One of these was the Praetorian Prefect, Opellius Macrinus, whom I'd encountered in Alexandria, and the other was the Emperor's stepmother, Julia Domna.

Despite her illness, she worked incredibly hard, and she made sure I did as well. I read reports, summarised most of them

196

for her in short notes, passed her the really important ones, and checked over the replies which were drafted by her small army of scribes. She had her own copy of the imperial seal, and would often dictate replies as if they came from the Emperor himself. She was not governing the empire, but she certainly had a hand on the tiller while the Emperor fought his campaigns.

I soon learned that Antoninus Caesar had been busy during my absence in Rome. Having overseen the sack of Alexandria, he had turned his attention to the Arab people to the south-east of that city. They had a habit of raiding merchant trains, and this had been disrupting trade. The fact that killing thousands of people in Alexandria had devastated local trade did not seem to have mattered overly much, but then our Emperor rarely needed anything other than a flimsy excuse to go to war. After several months of campaigning, he claimed he had subdued the Arab tribes, although I wasn't convinced that was entirely possible. Our troops had to march or ride across endless miles of shifting, trackless sand to hunt down an enemy who was so elusive they were rarely seen. With few permanent settlements to destroy, the Legions' usual tactic was bound to be ineffective.

But, with the Arabs allegedly subdued, the Emperor had headed back north, venturing into Armenia where he had settled the perennial squabble over who should be king by imprisoning one candidate and placing another on the throne at the point of a sword.

And then, inevitably, he had turned his eye towards Parthia.

I confess I had mixed feelings about the seemingly endless war between Rome and our neighbouring empire. I'd ventured deep into Parthian territory on my earlier mission and I had come to like the people and to admire many aspects of their culture. It seemed to me that the two empires could have lived side by side in peaceful cooperation rather than expend energy and hundreds of lives in fighting over vast swathes of territory, much of which was desert. The ordinary people certainly would not have objected to that.

But Emperors don't think like ordinary people. They see the borders of their territory and believe that, because the people on the other side of that often imaginary line are different from them and, equally importantly, pay taxes to someone else, then those people must, by definition, be hostile.

Perhaps I was too idealistic, for it must be said that many of the German tribes who lived in their forests beyond the Rhine and Danube borders were frequently very hostile, but I do think it might have been possible to come to some other arrangement than slaughtering them for not being Roman.

But warfare existed long before the Roman empire was created, and I dare say it will continue long after it has fallen and become nothing but a memory.

War with Parthia was certainly a consistent theme, but the highly complex political situation in Parthia and neighbouring Armenia was often baffling to outsiders. My own experience in Parthia had lasted only a few months, but that still provided me with more insight than many Romans ever achieved. That, I discovered, was another reason Julia Domna wanted me on her staff.

"What do you know of Artabanus?" she asked me one morning.

"I know he rebelled against his older brother who was the recognised king," I replied. "And he's turning himself into the dominant power. Things may have changed since I was there last, but I believe Artabanus is a much more dangerous foe than his brother, Vologases. He's clever and he seems to be a good general."

Julia Domna had frowned at that, then handed me one of the scrolls which had been sent personally to her. It was a private letter from the Emperor himself, although there was little personal content. Mostly, it contained the news of a battle between himself and Artabanus in which he admitted our side had come off worst.

"Perhaps my son should appoint you as a military adviser," she said with a half-teasing smile.

"I'm no military man," I said quickly. "I can only report what I learned from others while I was in Parthia."

"Read on," she told me.

I unrolled the next section of the scroll to discover that a marriage proposal was back on the Emperor's agenda. Artabanus had apparently rejected the initial approach, but Antoninus, having failed to defeat him in war, had once again asked the Parthian king to provide one of his daughters as a wife.

Julia Domna said, "Our Emperor has decided to seek peace, and this will cement the treaty. If Artabanus agrees. What is your opinion on that?"

I thought about that for a few moments before saying, "Well, he's turned it down once already, but I think it depends on his position at home. All the reports we have suggest Vologases is still holding out against Artabanus. I'd guess a peace treaty with us would serve Artabanus well. It would allow him to turn all his attentions against his brother."

"My thoughts precisely," she said approvingly. "That is what I will tell my son."

I had a momentary worry that she was about to suggest I acted as one of the envoys to Artabanus, but I managed to avoid that fate, and she kept me as one of her closest advisers all through that long, hot summer and beyond.

That was a happy enough year for me. Compared to the events I'd recently lived through, there was very little to tell. The weather was hot, Antioch provided all the things a young man could wish for, and I was well paid for the work I did. Even though I worked hard, I still found plenty of time to explore the great city and sample its many wine shops, bath houses and gymnasia. I must say, though, that I still preferred Ephesus to Antioch. This Syrian city might be a thriving centre of culture, but it was a bit too much so for my liking. Conspicuous consumption was the order of the day, with the wealthier people going out of their way to dress in extravagant clothing, bedeck themselves with ornate jewellery, and decorate their homes with expensive ornaments from exotic lands to the east. War with Parthia would have disrupted a lot of the trade which brought such luxuries, so most people were happy to learn that a peace treaty had been arranged. I, for one, shared that view.

The worst thing about this new job the Emperor had selected for me was that it brought me into close contact with the imperial family and all the political and diplomatic intrigues this entailed.

That's because the Emperor's stepmother had other relatives staying in the palace complex. I knew a little of their family history, but I soon learned a lot more about the individual members.

This is where it gets a bit confusing, but these people were important players in the highly political atmosphere of Antioch, and it wasn't possible to completely avoid them no matter how hard I tried.

Julia Domna's father had been a High Priest of an eastern god called Elagabalus. Thanks to some ancient history dating back to the time of the Emperor Augustus, the High Priests of this cult were virtual kings in their home city of Emesa which lies about two hundred Roman miles, or sixteen hundred Greeks stades if you prefer, south of Antioch. The role of High Priest was hereditary, but Julia Domna's father had not been followed by a son because his wife had given him only two children, and both were girls. Naturally, they were both called Julia. Domna was actually the younger sister, but I soon encountered her older sibling who was known by the *cognomen* of Maesa.

Like Domna, Julia Maesa had married a high-ranking Roman senator. Both women had risen to prominence within the empire, but it had been Domna who had struck really lucky with her choice of husband because Septimius Severus had seized the greatest prize of all when he had become Emperor.

Maesa, though, was hardly inconsequential. Already inordinately wealthy from her own family, she had grown even richer thanks to her marriage. That marriage had, however, again failed to produce sons and had resulted in another two girls in the next generation of the Julius family. Oddly, but perhaps because they wanted to preserve their links to the line of High Priests of Elagabalus, these girls were also named Julia instead of taking their father's familial name.

So there were four women named Julia I needed to watch out for. Domna, for whom I worked directly, was certainly extremely intelligent and accustomed to wielding immense authority, but I quickly learned that her sister, Maesa, was also very clever but far more cunning. Where Domna would tackle any problem by the fastest and most expedient course of action, Maesa would go about things in a more subtle way. Generally, this did not affect me directly since I did my best to keep out of her way, but I know the two women often discussed matters of state, and I think Maesa had far more influence than many people realised.

As for the next generation of Julias, Maesa's daughters were hardly alike at all except in their deference to their mother.

The older girl, Julia Soaemias, was widely known to be hot-blooded and passionate. She'd had a string of lovers which had resulted in her divorcing her husband and returning from Rome to the eastern part of the empire where she had grown up. She had brought her young son with her. This boy was officially named Verius Bassianus, but everyone referred to him as Elagabalus because, as the oldest male member of the family, he had been declared High Priest of that sun-worshipping cult. Since he was only twelve years old at the time, it was clear that his mother and grandmother had been responsible for his appointment. Family name and inordinate wealth counted for a lot when it came to such things, and Julia Maesa was always willing to use both in order to get her way.

The boy was a very odd character. He was obviously effeminate, for he usually went around with his face painted like a girl, and his main accomplishment was dancing and prancing around to the music of drums, cymbal and flute. I was told by one of the other court officials that he even did this as part of the temple celebrations whenever he was taken to Emesa to perform in one of the cult's rituals.

As I say, he was an odd child who seemed to live in some sort of dream world. Personally, I couldn't care less what his sexual orientation was, but the thought of having such an empty-headed youth as a local king seemed likely to create a great many problems. Fortunately, his mother, Soaemias, and his grandmother, Maesa, kept fairly strict control of him, but Soaemias' own lifestyle wasn't exactly free of scandal. Several people whispered to me that I should avoid her advances if she ever turned her attentions towards me because those men she tired of soon found their careers ruined. I have to say that I sometimes felt this would not be such a bad thing but, as it was, Soaemias had taken up with her son's tutor, a freedman named Gannys. Like many former slaves, he had clearly decided that the best way to achieve high status in society was to attach himself to a member of the imperial family. I've always distrusted people like that, so avoiding contact with Gannys was another skill I soon developed.

As for Soaemias' younger sister, the second daughter of Maesa, she was known as Julia Mamaea. She was generally regarded as the most personable member of the family. She was quiet, composed and usually very polite, although she was very much under the influence of her scheming mother. I suspect she was just as cunning and ruthless as the older woman but managed to conceal it rather better.

Mamaea also had a son, a boy of around eight years old named Alexander. In contrast to his cousin, Elagabalus, this lad seemed much brighter and more intelligent, although any boy growing up in that family of dominant, ambitious women was bound to develop some character flaws in time.

As far as possible, I had as little to do with these women as I could. It wasn't always easy, because Maesa frequently came to speak to Domna, and her daughters were highly visible around the palace. They often had visitors calling to see them, usually prominent Romans who were visiting Antioch and deemed it a wise move to pay their respects while in town. But there were other visitors too, and the palace often had a queue of merchants and local politicians coming to seek the patronage of one or other of the imperial family.

I didn't pay a lot of attention to any of this, although it was hard not to be aware of it. There was, however, one occasion when I encountered a visitor who intrigued me.

Domna had sent me to deliver a message to her sister and nieces about an idea she'd had for arranging an official temple sacrifice which would be held to seek the blessing of the gods for the Emperor's marriage. I remember being a little put out about being sent on a trivial errand which any slave could have carried out, but Domna had taken a bad turn with her health and had needed to retire to bed. As I was with her at the time, she gave me the task.

So I went off in search of the three women. I eventually found them sitting under the shade of some fig trees in a pleasant little garden which overlooked the river.

As I approached, I saw that they already had a visitor who had been engaged in what had obviously been a very serious discussion. The three women were leaning forwards in their seats, their heads close together as they carried out a hushed conversation with the man who sat in front of them.

I hesitated at the entrance to the garden, not wishing to interrupt, but Julia Soaemias noticed me and signalled to the others to stop talking. They all looked at me as if I'd caught them in some illicit act, but Maesa said something to their guest who rose from his seat, bowed to them, then left. He walked briskly past me, bowing his head in acknowledgement of my presence, but saying nothing as he left the garden.

I was puzzled by the way the women had dismissed him so abruptly. This made me curious about him, but I only managed to catch a brief look at his face as he passed me. He was middle-aged, tall, with tanned features and a narrow face. The brown eyes which had briefly scanned me were set above a hawk-like nose, and he was clean-shaven, revealing a firm jawline below a strong mouth.

I can't say why I paid so much attention to him, but his presence was unusual. I'd certainly never seen him before, even though he wore a very expensive tunic which suggested he was a man of some means.

Julia Maesa, the matriarch of this little group, dragged my attention away from the man by calling me over and demanding to know what I wanted.

I delivered my message, in response to which they all happily confirmed they thought it was an excellent idea to seek divine approval of the Emperor's wedding. Again, their reaction struck me as being a little odd, as if they were eager to get rid of me. This made me curious as to what they had been discussing with the tall stranger, so I decided to probe a little deeper.

"Might I ask who that man was?" I asked. "He seemed familiar."

"He is a merchant from Emesa, our home town," Julia Maesa told me.

The look she gave me made it plain she was not about to say any more to the likes of me, so I smiled, wished them a good day, and left the garden with as much dignity as I could muster.

Naturally, I followed up my suspicions. Working for the Juggler had taught me never to take anything at face value, so I hurried through the corridors of the palace to the main entrance. I did not manage to catch up with the tall stranger who must have made a very quick exit. When I checked with the guards who stood at the main doors, they confirmed that a man who called himself Acrocles had come to visit Julia Maesa.

"He's a merchant from Emesa," they informed me.

But whoever he was, the man had disappeared into the thronging streets of Antioch, so I returned to my duties none the wiser about his visit.

A few days later, the sacrifice was duly made on the front steps of the local temple of Olympian Zeus, and every notable person in Antioch attended to watch a bull and a ram being struck on the head to stun them, then having their throats slit so that their blood soaked the altar which had been placed on the temple steps. Priests then slit the beasts open, examined the entrails and announced that the omens favoured the Emperor's upcoming marriage to a Parthian princess. It wasn't an announcement which surprised me. Even a senior priest would think twice before telling Julia Domna that the omens were bad.

I suppose I ought to mention another woman who was in attendance at the ceremony. I had become acquainted with her because she, too, lived in the palace. In my opinion, she was much more approachable than any of the four Julias. Her name was Nonia Celsa, and she was the wife of Opellius Macrinus, the Praetorian Prefect. To me, Nonia appeared rather lonely, for none of the Julias would have anything to do with her, which meant few other palace residents wished to be seen to be friendly with her. As a consequence, she spent most of her time with her seven-year-old son, who was also largely friendless. I must admit I felt sorry for them, so I always tried to be as friendly towards them as my lowly status allowed. Perhaps that was why Nonia fell into step beside me as we returned to the palace after witnessing the sacrifice.

To my surprise, she said, "My husband told me about you, Scipio. He was very impressed by what you did in Alexandria."

"I only did what I had to," I replied with what I hoped was suitable modesty.

She smiled, "My husband likes you, you know. He says you are a man who can be trusted, and he is a good judge of character."

"Thank you for the compliment. Your husband was very helpful to me when we met," I told her.

"And I am sure he would be pleased to help you again in the future," she said.

I wondered where the conversation might be going, but we had crossed the bridge back onto the island by this time, and she simply smiled, wished me a good day, then went on her way.

I was left feeling more than a little nervous. I was, I knew, becoming too well known to very senior people in the Empire. I would have preferred to remain in relative obscurity, but I was becoming ensnared in imperial politics and I could see no way out.

Several times, I considered asking permission to go to Leptis Magna, but I could never find a suitable excuse. I certainly couldn't tell Julia Domna that I wanted to look for a woman whose name I did not know and who had been part of a plot to assassinate the Emperor. So, while Circe still tormented my dreams, I did my best to get on with my new life.

"Are you not travelling to join your son?" I asked Julia Domna as the summer waned and the time appointed for the wedding drew nearer.

"I am not well enough to travel," she told me. "It is a long and difficult road, and my physicians advise against it."

I couldn't argue with her on that, for she certainly suffered a lot of pain, but I noticed that, although Nonia set off on the long journey to meet up with Macrinus in the army's encampment, none of Julia Domna's relatives went to join the celebrations. It was only when an exhausted messenger galloped into town bearing yet another personal message for the Emperor's stepmother that I learned the true reason why they had all remained in Antioch.

The scroll was a hastily scribbled note from the Emperor. Domna smiled when she began reading, then frowned and clucked her tongue. Eventually, her frown became a deep scowl, and she let out a sigh of frustration as she let the scroll fall into her lap.

I stood in front of her chair, wondering what had caused this reaction. She was normally difficult to read because she rarely displayed emotion, but it did not take a great deal of perspicacity to see that she was angry about something.

"I hope it is not bad news," I said rather inanely in the circumstances.

"I must speak to my sister," she said irritably before sending one of the slaves hurrying off to fetch Maesa.

I stood silently, waiting patiently for her to let me know whether I should stay or go. Eventually, she thrust the scroll into my hands.

"Read it yourself," she snapped. "Everyone will know soon enough."

I took it with some trepidation, and when I read the message, I felt sick to the core of my being.

"I thought the wedding was to seal a peace treaty?" I gasped in bewilderment.

Domna regarded me as if I were a simpleton.

"There can be no peace with Parthia," she told me. "The wedding was a ruse."

I could not deny the truth of her words. The evidence was there in the ink and parchment in my hands. Like everyone else, I had been fooled by the Emperor's overtures to Artabanus of Parthia. With a peace treaty agreed, the Parthian king and all his nobility had come to meet the Emperor of Rome, bringing the king's daughter to what was supposed to be her wedding feast.

And then Antoninus Caesar had loosed his troops on the guests, massacring hundreds of them.

I suppose I should not have been surprised. The Emperor had done a similar thing in Germania, inviting tribal leaders to a peace conference then having them killed when they thought they were protected by a treaty. Now he had attempted the same trick against Parthia.

But, while this devious tactic had worked in Germania, it had not entirely succeeded this time. According to the report I held in my limp hand, Artabanus and a large group of his followers had fought their way clear and managed to escape. They had left hundreds of their party behind, but the king had wriggled clear of the trap.

And now he would never trust Rome again.

Julia Domna was annoyed, but it was the failure rather than the subterfuge which had irritated her, and I realised she had known the true intent all along. Knowing her as I now did, I could not rule out the possibility that it might even have been her idea. Or, more likely, her sister's idea. It was just the sort of thing Maesa would have proposed.

But, whoever had thought of it, the plan had failed, and what Domna said now showed she felt no remorse.

"I expect the war will resume," she frowned. "We had best discuss how we can raise more troops, or perhaps bring some forces from elsewhere."

I regained my composure in time to say, "The other frontiers have already been stripped to the bone. The commanders on the Rhine and Danube frontiers have already asked for reinforcements themselves."

"Then we must recruit more men," she decided.

The campaigning season was almost over. That, I reflected, had been a mistake on the Emperor's part. He should have arranged the wedding earlier in the year so he could have marched into Parthia and taken over once he had snared Artabanus. But he had failed to kill the king, and now he would need to wait several months before he could resume a full scale invasion. Artabanus was hardly likely to waste those months, so the next year's campaign promised to be another bloody and brutal confrontation.

I felt utterly sick, and it was all I could do to conceal my disgust from Domna. Fortunately, she seemed distracted, and when her sister burst into the chamber I was dismissed. I returned to my room and wrote out a coded letter to Fronto, rolling it inside a letter to my mother. She would know to take it to him, and he would tell her what I had learned. I could put no criticism of the Emperor in my personal letter in case it fell into the wrong hands, but my coded note would allow Fronto to tell my mother she had been right all along.

Our Emperor, Antoninus Caracalla Caesar, was a monster.

Chapter 20
Prophecy

My heart went out of my work after the news of the massacre at the wedding. I did my best to conceal it from Julia Domna, but I think she knew how I felt. Whether she would have done anything about it became irrelevant as she grew more and more frail, often spending entire days in bed while her physicians poured pain-killing drugs down her throat. For all my disgust at how she and her son had plotted to murder Artabanus of Parthia, I could not help feeling a grudging admiration for this strong-willed woman who refused to give in to the cancer that was killing her.

"I am not dead yet, Scipio," she assured me one morning as we sat together in her large, airy study. "I suspect I will not live to see another Saturnalia, though."

We had just celebrated that ancient tradition which was a time when slaves were allowed some freedom and their masters served them at table for a day, but things in the palace soon got back to normal while those in the city continued the celebrations for several more days.

Saturnalia marked the ending of the year, and now we were into the sixth year of Antoninus' reign as Emperor. It was the year in which he was determined to test his strength against Parthia and bring that proud empire to its knees.

Personally, I had no great hopes of success. Rome and Parthia had been battling for centuries, and Parthia had often come out on top. Even when Emperors like Trajan had extended the borders of Rome as far as the Euphrates, the gains had not lasted long. History should have taught us that neither great power was strong enough to overcome the other, but our Emperor, who was increasingly being referred to as Caracalla, was determined to try. I've heard soldiers say he was a great general, and I can't deny that he seemed to know what he was doing on a battlefield, but I don't think he was in the same league as Alexander or even Julius Caesar. Still, he was going ahead with his plans, and his army was growing every week. He'd recruited men from Greece and Macedonia, equipping them with the enormous *sarissa* pikes which had won so many victories for Alexander centuries ago, but he'd also changed other things. Instead of the traditional short *Gladius* the Legions had used since the days of the Roman Republic, his men were now armed with the longer, heavier *Spatha* which had once been viewed solely as a cavalry sword. And he had thousands of archers training every day in preparation for dealing with the famous Parthian horse archers who were so skilled they could shoot accurately from horseback even when galloping away from their target. The Parthian shot is no myth, and those horse archers had defeated Rome's Legions before. This time, Julia Domna informed me, things would be different.

"We have many more cavalry than we've ever had," she explained. "And war elephants too. But it will be the combination of heavy infantry and archers that will win battles this time. That is what my son says."

Who was I to argue?

While those preparations for war continued, the weather brought cold and rain. The Orontes river was in full spate for some weeks, the water frothing and bubbling beneath the piers of the bridges which connected the island to the rest of the city. This strong current made communications more difficult than usual because the river is the quickest way to get from Antioch to the coast, and small boats are forever plying up and down.

Upstream, though, it is a different matter, for there are rapids, narrows and cataracts which mean the river is not navigable by boat even in summer. This means that there is a constant stream of traffic coming in by road, with mules, horses and camels laden with all sorts of foodstuffs and luxuries.

I often sat and watched these caravans arriving while I sipped at a goblet of wine and mulled over the course my life was taking. I longed for a return to obscurity, sometimes even for the danger and excitement of a spying mission. Above all, I wanted to escape the confines and machinations of the palace. After some weeks of thought, I decided there might soon be a way. The impending war would no doubt last all year, then yet another peace treaty would be agreed, new borders finalised and gifts exchanged by the two rulers. I doubted Julia Domna would let me leave until then, although everything might change when her cancer eventually overcame her. When that happened, I decided, I would take my leave. I'd need to think of some excuse, but I was determined to go to Leptis Magna and look for Circe. I still didn't know what I would do if I ever found her, but that was a problem to worry about once I'd tracked her down.

But, as I should have known, life is never that simple.

It was just past the *kalends* of April when a message arrived and threw everything into turmoil.

It came along with other scrolls from the Juggler, but this one was marked with the priority code which signified that it was extremely important. I spotted it as soon as I'd taken the bundle of scroll cases from the messenger who had brought them upriver from Seleucia, so I shoved the others aside, broke the seal on the case and tipped out the contents. There were two scrolls inside, one addressed to the Emperor in person, the other marked as a copy to be read by Julia Domna. But she was very ill, and had told me to deal with everything that day, so I snapped the scroll open, unwound the first panel and began to read.

"From Sempronius Rufus to Her Imperial Majesty Julia Domna, greetings. This is a copy of a letter I have written to your son, Antoninus Caesar. I urge you to send it to him as soon as possible.

"News has reached me from the temple of Herakles in Tingis. The High Priest sends word that a local prophet has made an announcement which bodes ill for our Emperor. This prophet, a wild-haired man from the hinterland of Africa, proclaimed in the forum at Tingis that he had been granted a vision by the gods. He announced to a large crowd of people that Opellius Macrinus was destined to be Emperor of Rome, that he would overthrow your son and proclaim himself Emperor within the year."

I had to read that a second time before the words sank in. It was a sign of how seriously the Juggler had taken this news that he had not bothered to use his favourite code names for the individuals concerned.

With a sour feeling in my stomach, I read on.

"The prophet has, I regret to inform you, disappeared. As soon as the High Priest heard of his prophecy, he sent soldiers to arrest the man, but he had left the city and returned to the wilderness. All attempts to trace him have proved fruitless."

"I cannot speak for the true intentions of the Prefect of Praetorians, but my agents confirm that word of this prophecy has spread rapidly throughout the provinces of Mauretania, Numidia and Africa. I fear it is too late to contain it. I only hope that this message reaches you before the rumour of the prophet's words arrive in Caesar's camp."

Rufus then signed off with the usual formal flourishes which I read automatically, my brain already galloping.

For one moment, I was tempted to burn the scroll. I could throw it into the brazier which was warming the room, and I could place the still sealed original message with it. Nobody need know, I tried to tell myself.

But if the rumour was already spreading, it would soon reach Syria, and then what would happen? Questions would be asked, and I would find myself as the last person known to have held the message scroll.

So I took the copy and the original and went to Julia Domna's chambers where I shouted at the guards, priests and physicians until they let me see her.

She was lying on her bed, her face pale and her hair damp with sweat, her frail form covered by a single sheet. Her eyes were dulled by the drugs she had taken, but she retained enough alertness to take the scroll from me and read it.

I had said nothing to her. I had simply handed her the copy while I clung onto the sealed original.

She read it slowly, her eyes sometimes wandering, then she rolled the scroll shut and handed it back to me.

With a wave of her hand, she ordered everyone else to leave the room. Once we were alone, she looked me in the eye and asked, "What is your opinion?"

Her voice was weak, and I could see she was not able to think as clearly as she did when she was well.

I said, "Macrinus is originally from Mauretania, so it is no surprise that this rumour should have begun in Tingis, the capital of the province. I expect the people there will naturally wish to believe such a prophecy, but I do not think he is capable of plotting against your son."

"Why not?" she asked in a near whisper.

"Because he would need the support of the army. Your son has that, and any man who raised a rebellion against him would find little support. I think this so-called prophecy is either the ravings of a madman or part of a plot to sow dissension in our camp. Parthian spies could be behind it."

"You may be right," she agreed wearily. "But it must be my son who makes the decision as to what must be done. Go and warn him. Go yourself. Do not trust this message to anyone else. And burn the copy. I want nobody to read it."

I did not want that task. I knew how the Emperor was likely to react, and I rather liked Macrinus. I had no wish to see him being executed as a traitor on the word of some mad prophet from Africa. But I had been given a direct order, so I packed a few belongings in a bag, and sent word for a small escort of cavalry to ride with me. I requisitioned a horse from the stables and, with half a dozen mounted soldiers to keep me safe from bandits, I crossed one of the bridges to the northern section of the city and the gates that led out to the north and east. Once beyond the city, we headed eastwards at a fast canter.

I knew from the reports I had read that the Emperor had pushed his army forwards from their winter quarters. He had sent several detachments to destroy some of the Parthians' forts and watchtowers, but the bulk of his army was still concentrated on our side of the border.

Even so, it was at least a five day ride to reach the last known location of Caesar's camp. We rode hard, changing horses whenever we reached one of the staging posts of the *cursus publicus*, but we were out near the frontier now, and such facilities were few and far between, so we needed to conserve the strength of our horses as much as possible.

The fortified camp, when we located it on the morning of the sixth day, was enormous. I knew the Emperor had at least five Legions here, along with vast numbers of auxiliary troops, archers and cavalry, but the scale still astonished me. Row upon row of leather tents were arranged in precise lines, soldiers were marching, running and leaping as they worked on their fitness, horses were wheeling and charging on the plain outside the camp, while archers fired volley after volley at targets which had been set up at varying distances from their closely packed line. There were wagons for transporting supplies, mules tottering under the weight of water sacks, and an entire village of camp followers sprawled outside the official camp.

My imperial pass gave us access with no problems. I left my horse in the care of my escort, then hurried through the vast encampment to the *Principia*. There was no possibility of getting lost because, even in a huge camp like this one, the layout remained the same as every other Roman army fort, so I simply followed the *Via Principalis* until I came to the wide square of the *Principia* and found the *Praetorium* which housed the command centre. This was a very large tent outside which were planted the standards of the various Legions, each one bedecked with brightly coloured ribbons and guarded by a soldier of the Legion whose honour it represented.

I approached the *Praetorium*, gave my name and told the duty Centurion that I had an urgent message for Caesar.

"The Emperor isn't here," he told me, giving me that hard stare which seems to be part of a Centurion's standard equipment. "He left a couple of hours ago. You'd best see the Prefect."

I hesitated, then said, "I was told to deliver it to the Emperor in person."

The Centurion's gaze was as hard as stone as he told me, "The Prefect reads all messages first. No exceptions. That's Caesar's command."

I hesitated, torn between obeying the order Julia Domna had given me and wanting to warn Macrinus of the danger he was in. I was edging towards the latter anyway, but the Centurion gave me no choice.

"Come with me," he ordered.

He pushed aside some of the internal hangings which divided the tent into sections, and showed me into the tiny area which served as an office where the Praetorian Prefect was sitting at a folding table which was piled high with scrolls, maps and tablets, while two secretaries sat with poised styluses.

"Scipio!" Macrinus greeted me warmly. "How good to see you! What brings you out here?"

"I have an urgent message for the Emperor," I told him, my nerves on edge. Seeing Macrinus again had reminded me how much I admired this man. And I held a scroll in my satchel which would bring about his execution.

"Caesar has gone to the temple of Luna at Carrhae," Macrinus informed me. "He will be away for two or three days, I expect."

I knew the Emperor would not be visiting a temple out of piety. Carrhae was close to the border with Parthia, and I was certain he would be going there to collect messages sent by spies who were doing the same sort of thing I had done during my secret mission there.

Macrinus held out his hand.

"The Emperor gave me full authority to read all his messages," he said with a smile.

Not this one, I wanted to say, but I handed it to him anyway.

As I did so, I told him, "I think it best you read it in private."

A look of concern briefly flashed across his features, but he dismissed the secretaries and the Centurion who had continued to stand close behind me. Once they had left the compartment, he looked at me with a serious expression.

Speaking softly so as not to be overheard by anyone in the adjoining areas of the huge tent, he asked me, "What is it? Do you know?"

I felt weak and terrified.

"May I sit?" I managed to ask, my throat suddenly dry.

He waved his permission, so I parked myself on one of the chairs vacated by the secretaries. Slowly, feeling the weight of history on my shoulders, I gestured towards the sealed scroll case.

"This message ..."

My voice failed me. I could not find the words to tell him he was facing a death sentence.

With a calm smile, he said, "Perhaps I should just read it."

He broke the seal, tipped out the thin scroll, and grasped the small wooden spindles around which the parchment was wound.

I saw his expression change as he read the fateful words. His face paled and there might even have been a slight trembling in his hands.

"I am sorry," I told him. "For what it is worth, I do not believe you harbour any ambitions to become Emperor."

He forced a smile, then he began to laugh.

"Of course I don't!" he said. "The idea is ludicrous."

"Nevertheless, some people will believe this. And one person in particular will soon get to hear of the prophecy whether this message is delivered to him or not."

I was stating the obvious. Macrinus had begun his career as a litigator, so his mind was as sharp as anyone's.

Still, he took a few moments, sitting back in his chair and clasping his hands in front of his chest while he pondered what to do.

"Why do you not believe this warning?" he asked me.

"Because you would need the support of the army to succeed," I told him, giving the same response I had given to Julia Domna. "With respect, you are not a soldier. You may command the Praetorians, but it is more an administrative role than a military one. The army would never back you against Antoninus Caesar."

"Not if he were alive," he agreed. "But if he were dead? Men have attained the Purple before now by merely offering a sufficiently large bribe to the troops."

Calmly, he continued, "But there are other reasons why it would be difficult for me to become Emperor. The problem is convincing Caesar of that."

"At least you have a couple of days before he gets back. That gives you some time to work out what to tell him."

Macrinus gave me a sad smile.

"No," he told me. "I must tell him as soon as possible. Word of this will leak out, and I do not want him returning here to find a camp in turmoil."

He waved a hand to take in our surroundings, and I understood what he meant. I could still hear some voices from other parts of the great marquee, so even our low tones were perhaps being listened to by inquisitive ears. Then there were the men of my escort who, while they did not know the contents of the scroll, were well aware that it was an important and urgent message. Even if we did nothing, rumours would soon begin to fly.

Macrinus went on, "Things are reaching a climax as it is. Artabanus is gathering a great army, and we expect to encounter him within a week or so."

Tapping a finger on the scroll, he added, "So this must be dealt with one way or another. Caesar only left a couple of hours ago, so it should be possible to catch him."

"I could …" I began, but he held up a hand to silence me.

"We shall go together, Scipio. The only person who can persuade Caesar of my innocence is me."

"And if he does not believe you?"

"Then he will have me executed."

After his initial shock, he seemed to have recovered his poise. He spoke of his own death as if it was of little consequence.

He went on, "If that happens, I would ask one favour of you."

"Of course."

"If possible, and I confess it may not be possible, please try to see that my wife and son are kept safe. See that they are taken back to Mauretania. I still have a house there."

"I will do that if I can," I promised.

Then Macrinus was grinning again, rising to his feet and reaching for his cloak which lay folded on top of a small chest.

"But let us think positively," he told me. "We must ride quickly and catch up with the Emperor. There is no point in sitting around here waiting for the gods to decide my fate."

He patted me on the shoulder as he added, "Do not look so worried, Scipio. I know the Emperor better than most men. He is not immune to reasoned argument."

I had my doubts about that, but I followed Macrinus out of his screened cubicle and waited while he issued a series of commands to the staff who manned the central area within the tent. His attention to detail was impressive as he gave instructions to the senior Legate, then organised a small escort for us.

"Two squads will do," he told me as we went outside. "The Emperor has taken one hundred men of his personal guard with him. To turn up with a similar number might inflame a delicate situation, so I will take only sixteen men."

Those sixteen men were commanded by another familiar figure. Centurion Aelius Caecus had collected a livid scar on his cheek since I had last seen him on the day we had found the tunnel that led to Alexander's tomb, but he looked every bit as dour and tough as I remembered.

He gave me nothing more than a nod of acknowledgement when Macrinus said, "You two know each other, of course. You foiled a plot to kill Caesar. Now we must thwart another one."

Aelius didn't bat an eyelid. Macrinus had not told him why we were hurrying to catch up with the Emperor, but the reason did not matter to an old soldier like Aelius. What was important to him was obeying orders.

We left at a gallop, pounding out through the eastern gate and chasing our Emperor.

"He won't have been travelling fast," Macrinus called to me as we rode alongside each other. "So we should overtake him before too long."

We did. It was a little after mid-day when our tired mounts crested a low hill. Ahead of us, in a narrow valley between low, wooded hills, we saw the men and horses of the Emperor's escort. They had stopped beside a stream, and the horses were being fed and watered, the men also taking the opportunity to refresh themselves. Most were sitting under the shade of some trees while they ate and drank out of the harsh glare of the sun.

Their sentries saw us coming, but relaxed when they recognised Macrinus at the head of our little column. We rode amongst them, slowing to a trot, and saw that the Emperor was sitting apart from the soldiers, having perched on a rock near the stream. He saw us coming, but he remained where he was, casually chewing on some bread. His silver-trimmed cloak, one of the *Caracalla* type that had given him his nickname, was cast back from his shoulders, and he appeared relaxed even though the sight of his Praetorian Prefect riding after him must have told him something serious had happened.

Macrinus gave the order to dismount.

"Take care of the horses," he told Aelius. Then, to me, he said, "Come. Let us give the Emperor our news."

He seemed incredibly calm as we walked to where the emperor sat. For my part, I wanted to climb back on my horse and gallop away as fast as I could. This, I thought, must be what it is like for men who are sent into the amphitheatre to face a pride of starving lions.

Antoninus Caesar smiled in greeting. He looked fit and alert, his hair and beard still neat despite him having been on the road all morning.

"Macrinus! And young Scipio! What has happened to bring you here?"

He remained seated on the rock while we stood facing him. I had a sudden horrible worry that Macrinus might, after all, have decided that the best way to save his own life would be to fulfil the prophecy and strike Antoninus down. Did he have a dagger concealed beneath his long cloak?

His hand moved beneath the dark fabric, but came out holding the scroll.

"I brought this to you in person, Caesar. I want you to know that the claims it makes are false."

The Emperor frowned as he took the proffered scroll. He tossed aside the last piece of bread, unrolled the parchment and read the Juggler's message. He remained icily calm as he did so, then he looked up at Macrinus.

"Tell me why this is a false prophecy," he said in a disturbingly quiet voice.

Macrinus did not hesitate. The tension hung so thickly in the air I felt I could have touched it, but the Prefect made his case as eloquently as any lawyer.

"First, Caesar, you know I have served you loyally these past few years. I have never done anything that was not to your benefit."

The Emperor's expression did not alter. He continued to stare implacably at Macrinus. He held no weapon, only the scroll which dangled loosely in his hand, but he had a hundred Praetorians within earshot. One shout and Macrinus and I would have been cut to ribbons.

Macrinus went on, "Secondly, I come from an equestrian family. Nobody from such a background has ever been Emperor. The people of Rome might accept someone of lesser nobility, although I doubt it. The Senate would certainly not approve."

I saw Antoninus nod slightly, but I could also detect the anger in him. As usual when faced with any sort of threat, his reaction was to lash out. He was holding that response in check, but it was not easy for him.

"Thirdly," Macrinus continued, "and most importantly, the army would never back me as Emperor. Their loyalty is to you, Caesar. I am no general. I am an administrator. A good one, as you know, but leading an army into battle is something I have never done, and the troops know it."

He paused to take a breath, then gestured towards me.

"Scipio, as you know, foiled the last conspiracy aimed against you. I do not think I speak out of turn when I say that, although he brought this message as quickly as he could, he does not believe the claims either."

The Emperor looked at me, his eyes challenging.

218

Swallowing nervously, I nodded, "I think this may be a Parthian plot to create dissension, Caesar. I do not believe Opellius Macrinus would ever seek to overthrow you."

Macrinus put in, "You will recall, Caesar, that we both agreed Sempronius Scipio is a man who can be trusted. I value his judgement."

I felt even more guilty when I heard that. Macrinus trusted me, but that was because he did not know I had withheld information about Circe from him. But I certainly wasn't going to bring that up now. The only thing I felt like bringing up was my breakfast.

The Emperor chewed his lip for a moment, then signalled for me to leave.

"I wish to speak to Opellius Macrinus in private," he told me brusquely.

Grateful to be released, I bowed my head and turned away. It was a few moments before my racing heart began to slow to its normal beat.

Most of the soldiers were sitting on the grass or standing in small groups. Their horses were tethered in lines a few yards away, all of them still saddled. This had obviously been intended as a short break in their journey. All of the men, I knew, were watching what was taking place between Caesar and Macrinus. They knew without being told that something unusual must have happened to bring the Praetorian Prefect chasing after the Emperor.

I wasn't sure what to do. I could see no sign of Aelius Caecus or his men in the crowd, and I had no wish to engage in conversation with any of the other Praetorians. Some of them, I noticed, were probably Germans. Their large build and long, fair hair made them stand out even among the elite Praetorians.

And then I saw another man I recognised. Wearing his heavy chainmail and an iron helmet, he was engaged in an animated conversation with a stooped civilian who wore baggy, flowing robes and an Arab head dress. This man's straggly beard was bobbing as he nodded his head, but I could not see his face as he was turned away from me. But the soldier was facing me, and he noticed me at the same time as I recognised him.

It was Justin Martialis, the surly Optio who had led the assault on Dion's conspirators in the tomb of Alexander.

When he saw me, he slapped the civilian on the shoulder with the back of his hand, dismissing the poor fellow. I caught a glimpse of a tanned, narrow face as the man scuttled away, then Martialis was stomping over to confront me, his own face deathly pale.

"Hello," I said as calmly as I could in the circumstances. "Having trouble?"

"Just trying to get sense out of our guide," he growled. "What are you doing here? What's going on?"

I couldn't tell him the truth, but I was struggling to find an excuse that might be even part way believable, so I simply said, "We brought a message for the Emperor. It's from his mother."

"From Antioch?" he hissed as if the very thought appalled him.

"That's right."

"And it's so important the Prefect needs to bring it himself? What is it? Have you discovered another plot against the Emperor?"

His guess was so close to the truth that even my years of experience operating as a spy did not allow me to completely conceal my reaction.

"I'm not allowed to say," I said rather feebly. "No doubt the Emperor will tell everyone soon enough."

That answer had a surprising impact on the moody Optio. He glared at me for a moment, his eyes wild and his nostrils flaring, then he turned on his heel and stalked away.

I gave a shrug. I had no idea what had caused the antipathy between Martialis and me, but he still seemed to hold some sort of grudge against me even though we hadn't met during the two years since we'd foiled Dion's plot.

I sighed, looking around. Centurion Aelius had appeared, walking briskly through the clustered Praetorians until he was only a few paces from me.

"What's up with Martialis?" I asked him, nodding towards the retreating Optio.

"He thinks he should be a Centurion," Aelius shrugged. "He was posted to Caesar's personal guard, but the Emperor doesn't seem inclined to promote him."

That figured. I had no idea what sort of a soldier Martialis was, but he was not a pleasant person. His attitude was never going to impress someone like Antoninus Caesar.

At that moment, Martialis turned back again. He saw the two of us looking at him, and he stared back at us for a long moment, his face as stiff as a death mask.

"I don't think he likes me," I murmured.

Aelius, to his credit, didn't point out that he didn't like me either. Instead, he nodded over my shoulder to where Macrinus was still standing in front of the Emperor.

"I think they have finished talking," he informed me.

I turned to see the two men clasping forearms in a gesture of friendship. Then Macrinus bowed his head before turning and striding back to join the main group.

He was smiling broadly as he told me, "Let us return to the camp. Caesar is satisfied with what I have told him."

I think I was more relieved than Macrinus himself. I felt a weight lift from my soul as I exhaled a long sigh.

Macrinus said to Aelius, "Gather our troop. We are returning immediately."

Aelius saluted, planting his fist on his chest, then turned away and went to fetch our escort.

Quietly, Macrinus said to me, "Caesar agrees this could be a Parthian plot. He wants you to go to Tingis to see if you can find this so-called prophet. It seems very odd that he was not apprehended at the time, and Caesar wants to have him brought here for questioning."

I gaped at him. If the army had failed to track down the mysterious preacher, I was hardly likely to be successful. But then it struck me that, to reach Tingis, I would need to sail along the entire length of the African coast. Which meant I would be passing Leptis Magna. Perhaps, I thought with a rush of excitement, I could stop over there for a few days.

"I will be happy to," I told Macrinus.

I glanced to where the Emperor was still sitting on the rock. He seemed deep in thought, but at least he had not ordered Macrinus' execution. Only time would tell whether he would change his mind about that.

221

Then he rose to his feet, turned and began fumbling with the ties of his long riding breeches. I looked away when he began to urinate against the trunk of a nearby tree.

As I turned, Martialis came back into my line of sight. He was striding purposefully towards the Emperor as if he was about to demand the promotion he had been denied. All I could think was that his timing was not good. But perhaps he reckoned Antoninus would be in a more relaxed mood once he'd emptied his bladder.

I could not help but keep my eyes on Martialis as he approached the Emperor. Caesar refastened his breeches and turned to face him, a puzzled expression on his face.

It was Macrinus, who had turned to see what had attracted my attention, who realised what was about to happen.

"Stop him!" he yelled.

But it was too late. Even as soldiers turned to see what Macrinus was pointing at, Martialis had drawn a dagger and lunged at the Emperor. He stabbed him in the chest, then repeated the blows several times even as Antoninus fell to the ground. Martialis knelt, plunging his blade into the body time and time again.

There was a moment of stunned disbelief as we all stared at the incomprehensible scene in front of us. Then I was surrounded by chaos. Men were yelling, drawing swords and running towards the scene of the attack, disbelief mingling with fury as they closed on Martialis.

He stood up, still holding the bloody dagger, and turned to face them.

"It is done!" he shouted, holding the blade high as if it were a trophy.

Then he seemed to realise what was about to happen as one of the big German guards rushed at him.

"No! I was promised …"

But we never learned what he had been promised, because the Praetorian cut him down with one savage slash of his long sword, cleaving deep into Martialis' chest, screaming in fury as he avenged his Emperor. The Optio fell to the ground beside the body of the man he had just assassinated. He was clearly dead, but other soldiers began to hack at him as they vented their rage at his betrayal.

I was shocked to immobility. I could not summon the energy to move. Macrinus ran to join the soldiers, calling, "Caesar!" over and over again as if he could not believe Antoninus was dead. He pushed his way through the Praetorians who were clustering around the two bodies, and he fell to his knees as he reached out to hold the Emperor's ravaged corpse.

I could not watch. I felt I needed to sit down. Antoninus was a monster, but he had left no heir and I knew what that meant. Dion had foretold it when he had outlined his plan to me in Alexandria. The empire would dissolve into chaos as powerful men staked claims for the right to wear the purple robes of the Emperor.

And all I could think was that Circe had, somehow, gained her revenge.

As I turned, seeking some physical support for my trembling legs, I saw someone riding away. It was the civilian guide, the man who had been talking to Martialis. He was moving quickly but calmly, heading into the wooded hills. He glanced back over his shoulder, and I am sure he saw me watching him. I saw a brief flash of white teeth as he grinned, then he jabbed his heels to his horse and galloped into the woods, vanishing from my sight.

I had caught only the briefest glimpse of his face, but I suddenly knew where I had seen him before. He had been better dressed then, and he had been clean-shaven. He had walked proudly and erectly, not with the stooped shoulders and shuffling gait of the guide who was now leaving the scene of the assassination.

He had been the tall stranger who had been speaking so conspiratorially to Julia Maesa and her two daughters.

I was sure of it, but by the time I gathered the strength to find Macrinus in the crowd of devastated Praetorians and made him understand, the guide was long gone.

And he had left behind an empire which would descend into chaos.

Chapter 21
Aftermath

We took the body of Antoninus back to the camp, but Martialis' mutilated corpse was left for the crows and the foxes. Our arrival cast a pall of stunned disbelief over the entire army, for the man the soldiers affectionately called Caracalla had been immensely popular with the Legions. He had fulfilled his father's command to look after the army and ignore everyone else, and he had massively increased the soldiers' pay. He had also, until the recent setback against Artabanus of Parthia, led them to victory after victory over Germans, Arabs and Armenians.

And now he was dead, and the army mourned him. For an outsider like me, it was strange to see grown men who were accustomed to death weeping like children at the sight of the body of their dead Emperor, so I tried my best to remain in the background, sticking close to Macrinus without intruding on the collective grief.

Naturally, there was a great deal of discussion about what had motivated Martialis to murder the Emperor. Aelius shared the common view that the man was angry at having been denied promotion despite asking several times.

"Caesar put him in his place last time," the Centurion informed us. "He wasn't happy, and thought he had been humiliated. And don't forget Caesar had his brother executed a couple of years ago for being mixed up with some other conspiracy."

"I didn't know that," I said. "What happened?"

Aelius shrugged, "Nothing much. According to Martialis, his brother did nothing more than get mixed up with a bunch of loudmouths who were overheard criticising the Emperor. Someone reported it, and that was enough to earn them a death sentence."

I sighed. That was a familiar story in recent years. Most emperors are touchy about criticism, and Antoninus had been almost paranoid about such things.

But, while most of the soldiers agreed with Aelius' assessment, I was not so sure.

I told Macrinus about the guide and what I suspected were his links to Julia Maesa.

He frowned, "That makes no sense, Scipio. What reason would the Emperor's aunt have for wanting him dead?"

"I don't know. But I'd like to take a look at Martialis' belongings."

So, with Aelius escorting me, I was taken to the tent Martialis had shared with the men of his squad. His pack was still there, but it was obvious that his comrades had already plundered it for any valuables.

"How much money did he have?" I asked them in exasperation at their eagerness.

One of the soldiers looked me full in the eye as he replied, "Only a few *sesterces*. Hardly enough for us to get drunk on."

I was fairly sure he was lying, but his comrades backed him up. I was tempted to ask Aelius to have all their packs searched, but the mood in the camp was so tense I knew that would be a bad idea.

I rifled through the rest of Martialis' belongings, but there was nothing out of the ordinary, only the usual change of clothes and personal kit.

"There were no incriminating letters," I reported back to Macrinus. "Although I hardly expected to find something as obvious as that."

"Then we are no nearer understanding what motivated him," Macrinus said wearily.

I could tell it had been a difficult day for him. His normally calm and confident manner was fraying slightly under the pressure of events. I could hardly blame him, but I needed to ask the big question which was on everyone's mind.

"What will happen now?"

"I don't know," he admitted. "The empire needs an Emperor, but there is no obvious choice to succeed him."

"One of the provincial Governors or Legionary Legates might put himself forward," I suggested.

Macrinus shook his head.

"I doubt any one of them could garner enough support. Caesar made sure that nobody of genuine talent was ever promoted high enough to present a threat to him."

That was as close as I could ever recall Macrinus saying anything disrespectful towards Antoninus, but that did not make the statement any less true.

"Perhaps some rich man in Rome will offer the army a bribe large enough to gain their support?"

"Perhaps, but the bulk of the army is here, and Rome is far away. And we have a Parthian war host heading towards us."

I looked at him keenly. To be honest, I was surprised that he was being so open with me. There was a considerable difference in our ranks and standing in society, but I suppose he needed someone to talk to, and I was the man on the spot. Besides, he knew I understood the events which had brought us to our current predicament.

A predicament to which there was, as far as I could see, only one solution.

"You could do it," I told him. "The prophecy said you would."

"The prophecy said I would overthrow him. I did not do that. And I never wanted to rise that far."

"Nevertheless," I told him, "somebody needs to take the throne. Who else is there?"

"Nobody," he sighed. "But, as you yourself pointed out, the army is unlikely to support me either."

We sat in solemn silence for a few moments. I could tell that Macrinus understood the situation as well as anyone. He also understood that, like fabled Odysseus, he was, metaphorically at least, caught between Scylla and Charybdis, facing deadly danger no matter which course of action he followed. He could risk being eaten by the monster or being sucked down into the deadly whirlpool, but there was no safe path ahead of him.

"The rumour of the prophecy will spread," he sighed. "Men know you brought me the message and that I saw it before Caesar did. They will say I murdered him out of fear for my own life, and that I then had the assassin killed to conceal my involvement."

I supposed he was right. Whatever had actually happened, a story like that was too scandalous not to spread far and wide. No matter how often he denied it, people would still have their suspicions that the story might be true.

"So what will you do?" I asked, glad that I was not the one in his position.

"I will think on it," he told me.

To prevent any word of the Emperor's death spreading beyond the camp before he had decided what should be done, Macrinus ordered that everyone be confined to the fortress for two days. That included me, so I bunked down in the *Praetorium* for two nights until he had sounded out the senior officers and they had, in turn, spoken to the men under their command. The upshot was that, after he agreed to pay each soldier a handsome sum, Macrinus was proclaimed as Emperor. As he himself knew, this was not because the soldiers held any affection towards him, but because there was no other viable candidate they would all support. He was, from the soldiers' point of view, the least bad option.

For my part, I thought Macrinus would make a good Emperor, but that was probably because I liked him as a person. At any event, he quickly threw himself into the task, beginning an exhausting round of meetings and letter writing. To my surprise, though, he still found time to summon me for a private word late that evening.

We sat in the same tiny cubicle in the Praetorium, screened from the other occupants by the great sheets of heavy cloth which divided the tent. I dare say men were trying to listen in but, as we sipped at cups of watered wine, Macrinus and I made sure to keep our voices low and confidential.

"I have sent letters to all the provincial Governors, major cities and Legion commanders," he informed me. "And, most importantly, I've sent a letter to the Senate in Rome asking them to confirm my position."

This, I knew, was important. It might have been a mere formality, for the army normally selected the man they wanted to lead them, but the Senate remained a symbol of Roman power, and having that assembly of rich men officially name him Emperor would ensure that the constitutional niceties had been properly observed.

"I've sent back all the Senators who have been following us around for the past couple of years," he told me. "And I entrusted the letter to Cassius Dio. You remember him? You met him in Alexandria, I believe."

I nodded, "Yes. He's writing a history of Rome, I believe."

"So he says. The man is a boor, but he's not stupid. I believe he will ensure the Senate supports me despite my lowly birth."

He gave me a wry smile as he added, "I try not to think about what he will say of me in his history."

I smiled at that. Macrinus may not have come from a senatorial background, but he had hardly been one of Rome's poor. Still, a snob like Cassius Dio would no doubt view things differently. To him, Macrinus was probably an upstart.

"If the army backs you, the Senate will agree," I said.

He nodded, "I know. But the soldiers only elected me because I offered them an enormous bribe. It is, sadly, the expected thing nowadays."

I nodded. Bribing the soldiers was a tradition which had been established long ago, and Macrinus could not have retained power without following the custom.

Rubbing his chin wearily, Macrinus went on, "They all know I have no military experience. And yet I now face a war with Parthia."

I stiffened. Was he about to ask me to undertake another mission into enemy territory? Was that why he had invited me here?

I waited, on edge at the thought, but then he reached beneath the voluminous folds of his purple-trimmed robe and pulled out a bulging purse.

"This is for you," he told me as he passed it to me. "It is only fair you should have some reward if the soldiers are to be enriched simply for shouting my name."

The purse weighed heavy in my hand. I did not think I deserved any reward, but such a handsome gift was not something I could afford to turn down.

"Thank you, Caesar," I said.

He smiled, "Caesar? I haven't got used to hearing that yet."

Then he looked at me more keenly as he went on, "I am not sure what to make of your claims that Julia Maesa and her daughters were behind the killing, but I trust you, Scipio. I have sent word that they are to be returned to their home town of

228

Emesa. They can play at being rulers there, and that boy of theirs can dance in their temple all he likes."

That was a sensible precaution, and I was grateful he had paid some heed to my warning.

"As for Domna," he sighed, "I have sent orders that she is to be confined to her room. I doubt that will make much difference since I hear she is virtually bed-ridden now. I doubt she will live much longer."

"And what would you like me to do, Caesar?"

The question had to be asked.

He looked at me gravely as he said, "I trust you, Scipio, but I need proof if I am to take any more drastic action than that. I will not begin my reign by becoming a tyrant and having women executed for little reason. Do you understand?"

I said I did. I did not waste my breath by pointing out that some men had not bothered with such scruples when they had first seized power. Macrinus was not that type of person. Not yet, at any rate. Whether holding absolute power would transform him into a tyrant remained to be seen.

He went on, "But I would like you to discover the truth behind the murder. If Julia Maesa really is plotting something, I'd like to know what it is. If I am to accuse her and her daughters of treason, I need some justification."

"It will not be easy, Caesar," I replied. "I doubt any of those women will ever say anything incriminating if questioned, so I will need to look elsewhere."

"Finding that guide would be a good start," he told me.

The same thought had occurred to me, and I was able to tell him, "I have already been asking questions about him. The trouble is, nobody seems to know where he came from. The soldiers of our former Emperor's personal guard all say that it was Martialis who found him."

"That does not surprise me," Macrinus sighed. "In which case, it brings us back to the mission my predecessor set for you. Find that prophet in Tingis. It all began with him."

"I will leave tomorrow," I promised.

"Good. Do whatever you feel you need to. I shall write you a pass so that local commanders will provide whatever help you need."

He was as good as his word, which made me feel as if I was betraying him again, because I knew I would not begin my hunt in far away Tingis. Instead, I would go to Leptis Magna.

Chapter 22
Aurelia

The journey took a few weeks. My first stop was Antioch where I delivered a personal letter from Macrinus to his wife.

Nonia Celsa gaped at me in astonishment when she read the scroll.

"Is it true?" she asked me.

"It is, Augusta," I replied, calling her by her new official title.

She sagged in her chair, disbelief etched in every line of her face.

"My Marcus? The Emperor of Rome?"

As I had promised Macrinus, I told her everything that had happened. He had not wanted to write all the details in a letter, so it fell to me to explain, although I don't really think Nonia Celsa took it all in. I left her still stunned by the unexpected news, then went to collect my few personal belongings.

I wondered whether I should pay a visit to Julia Domna. It would be churlish not to, even though I knew it would be a difficult visit. I eventually plucked up the courage and went to her rooms, but the physicians turned me away.

"She is very ill," one of them informed me. "She has been given a lot of drugs, and she is sleeping."

I never saw Julia Domna again.

I had no excuse, nor any desire, to stay in Antioch any longer than necessary, so I took a boat downstream to Seleucia. From there, I sailed to Leptis Magna via Cyprus on a couple of merchant ships. I suppose I could have used Macrinus' letter to commandeer a bireme from the imperial navy, but I thought that might be an abuse of the trust he had placed in me. Besides, I wanted my mission to be low key.

It was nice to fall back into the role of a solo investigator. The months in Antioch now seemed like a dream in which I'd been trapped, but now I was free.

And I was going to find Circe.

Even so, I had felt a little guilty about leaving the army camp. The soldiers knew they were about to engage in a battle which could result in many of them dying. It could also settle the future course of both Rome and Parthia, depending on how it turned out. But I was no soldier, so I swallowed my pride and rode away, leaving the fate of Rome in the hands of Macrinus and his Legions.

I arrived in Leptis Magna one hot afternoon. I'd never visited the place before except for a brief overnight stop on my earlier voyage from Alexandria to Rome. This time, I was able to see more of the place and I was impressed by its scale and grandeur. Of course, this city had been the birthplace of our former Emperor, Septimius Severus, and he had lavished a great deal of money on the place, so it was no wonder its public buildings rivalled those of any other city.

I strolled under a long portico which sheltered the main walkway from the harbour up to the forum. Here, where grand temples fringed the open space, was an enormous, four-gated archway decorated with statues of Victory to commemorate Septimius Severus. It looked fairly new, and it seemed ironic that it had probably been completed not long before that warlike Emperor's dynasty had come to a sudden and brutal end with the assassination of his only surviving son. I dare say it will outlive other dynasties too.

The immediate difference I noticed was that everyone here spoke either Latin or a tongue I presumed was Punic. That was a clear sign I was no longer in the eastern part of the empire.

It was easy enough to find the local temple to Serapis as it was just across the forum. I had no idea whether Macrinus would maintain the network of spy communications Caracalla had established via the temples, but the High Priest was the man I needed to see in any case.

I showed him my pendant and the letter from our new Emperor.

"Is it true, then?" he asked me. "The prophecy was fulfilled?"

"Only in so far as the Emperor was assassinated," I told him.

I explained briefly what had happened, but I don't think the old man believed me. Word of the prophecy had spread, and a religious man like a High Priest was always going to believe in pre-ordained fate no matter how many times I told him the facts.

Eventually, I was able to get down to business.

"I am looking for a young woman," I told him. "She may go by the name of Tertullia. All I know is that she probably lives in a villa some way out of town, and that she owns the villa herself because her father died some years ago. Do you know anyone who matches that description?"

He smiled benignly as he said, "There are a great many villas on the edge of town and beyond, but most are owned by male citizens. However, I believe there is one young woman who does own an extensive property in her own name. But that name is Aurelia, not Tertullia."

Another name? That didn't really surprise me.

"Can you describe her?" I asked.

He pursed his lips for a moment, then said, "I have only seen her once, and that was very briefly. She rarely comes into the city, but she does have a freedman who is of Berber stock. He frequently carries out business on her behalf."

Trying to restrain my growing excitement, I said, "Then I suppose she might be the woman I am looking for. Can you tell me where I can find her?"

"Of course. But may I ask why you are looking for her?"

"I just need to deliver a message to her," I lied.

I doubt he believed that either, but he gave me directions anyway.

I needed to hire a horse, for the villa was a good fifteen miles inland from the city. There was a paved road for much of the way because there were several small settlements and farmsteads along the route. The land I rode through was rich and fertile, with olive groves, vineyards and meadows where sheep, goats and cattle grazed on grass and scrub. But even here in the fertile strip of land which lay between the sea and the desert, the temperature was bakingly high. I was hot and thirsty, but I kept moving even though I was sorely tempted to stop at some of the village taverns I passed, but the afternoon was wearing away, and I needed to reach the villa before nightfall. What I would do if it turned out this woman named Aurelia was not Circe, I did not know.

I found the place easily enough. The High Priest had told me to look for an ancient monument which was reputed to be a Phoenician temple but was now little more than a low pile of rubble. Opposite this, off to the left of the road which had now degenerated into an unpaved trackway, was another rutted path which led between stands of fig trees to a low hill.

I turned the horse onto this secondary path and urged it on. The sky was beginning to darken, and I knew how quickly night would fall. I needed to find the villa soon if I did not want to be stranded alone in the darkness, and that was not a pleasant prospect. Other than these trees, nothing much seemed to grow out here. The land was changing from green to sandy brown, the earth hard and dry. Off to the south I could see low, scrub-covered hills. Beyond them, I guessed, would be a desert of sand and rocks.

I was beginning to wonder why anyone would make a home so far out of the city when I crested the low rise and saw a very different landscape. Here was a wide plain which was criss-crossed by irrigation channels. In stark contrast to the encroaching desert, lush grass and trees held sway here. I could see a wide expanse of fields, and beyond them was the unmistakable outline of a large villa.

I urged the horse on. Some of the fields I passed were planted with wheat, others sprouted the first green shoots of vegetables, while others were fenced off and contained cattle and a great many horses. A shepherd boy was guiding a flock of sheep back into a pen from the meadows where he had been watching them all day, while other slaves were slowly trudging back towards the main villa complex, their day's labours ended.

My horse was tired, but it trotted gamely along the path towards the buildings. I could see long barracks-type buildings where the slaves were heading, a large barn, stables and several other outbuildings whose purpose was unclear. But, above all, there was the villa.

It was two storeys high, the front façade painted in blue and white, with statues of nymphs and satyrs adorning the pediment around the tiled roof.

A dark-skinned Nubian stood near the wide entrance. He was finely dressed, so I took him to be a freedman, possibly the *major domo* of the house. He had certainly seen me approaching, and he was clearly there to greet me.

"Good evening, Sir," he said in perfect Latin. "Are you expected?"

"No," I told him. "I am looking for a lady named Aurelia. Is this her home?"

"It certainly is, Sir. Can I tell her your name and the reason for your visit?"

"Tell her my name is Sigma. I hope she will understand the reason I am here."

His smile did not waver at all, but he did not invite me inside. I dismounted, but was forced to wait several minutes before he reappeared through the large double doors which led into the villa.

The shadows were lengthening by now, and I knew it would be full dark in moments. Already, I could see lamps being lit beyond the partly open doors. This was clearly the home of a very wealthy person, but had my gamble paid off? Was Aurelia the woman I knew as Circe? If she was not, I would need to beg a room for the night, then return to Leptis Magna with my tail between my legs.

The Nubian returned, bringing another slave with him, a teenage lad whose tunic was nevertheless of good quality.

"My mistress says you are welcome," the dark-skinned man informed me, his smile still in place. That, I supposed, was a promising sign, but I tried to restrain my excitement at the thought I had found Circe at last.

Gesturing to his companion, he said, "Carpo will see to your horse. Come, the lady has invited you to dine with her."

The slave took my horse and led it away to the stables, while the Nubian showed me in. All this formality and politeness seemed unreal, but I followed him through the doors, under the narrow tunnel formed by the second storey of the front of the villa, and stepped out into a wide courtyard which was surrounded by a columned portico. The villa was built in a square around this courtyard which contained a garden of small shrubs and flowers. Understandably in light of the thoughts racing through my mind at that moment, it reminded me of the garden in the villa in Ephesus where I had sat with Circe in what I had imagined was the beginning of a love affair.

Slaves were busy lighting oil lamps around the courtyard, but none of them paid any attention to me as the Nubian led me under the portico to one of the many doors which led into the building.

Inside, more lamps illuminated an elegant antechamber and long corridors. Busts of men and women I did not recognise stood on plinths against the white walls.

A young slave woman was waiting for us, holding a towel and indicating a bowl of warm water.

"The mistress says you might like to wash," the *major domo* suggested.

I certainly did. My body felt clammy from sweat. This was not the sort of place to strip off my tunic, but I used the bar of tallow soap the slave proffered to wash my arms and face. The slave handed me the towel, and I patted myself dry.

"Thank you," I said to her as I ran my fingers through my hair in a vain attempt to smooth my travel-worn appearance.

Silently, she gathered up the bowl and towel and walked off down the corridor, her sandals flapping softly on the tiled floor.

"Leave your bag here, Sir," the Nubian told me. "I will make sure it is kept safe."

I smiled my thanks. As usual, my bag contained little of value, and I had lost my personal possessions so many times in the past couple of years that it would not have bothered me overly much to lose another set.

"Come this way, Sir," he invited, moving towards another stout door.

My throat felt parched and my heart was racing as I followed him into the next room. This was a typical Roman dining area, with three large couches set around low tables in the centre of the room, with another door leading to the kitchens beyond. I could smell the wonderful aroma of cooking food, a sensation which added to the welcoming atmosphere of the room. Frescoes denoting wildlife themes were painted on every wall. Trees, birds, foxes and other smaller animals abounded, but there were none of the usual scenes of hunters pursuing lions. Heavy shutters barred what I presumed was a large window which would make the room light and airy during the day.

I took all of this in even as I stood stock still, my movement arrested by the sight of the two people who were waiting for me.

One was a tall man, his lean, narrow face dominated by a hawk nose. He wore flowing robes of the type popular among the

Arab and Berber people, and I could see the ivory hilt of a dagger protruding from a wide, red sash he wore around his waist.

I knew him instantly. I had seen him in that garden in Antioch, and again in the shabby robes of a guide when he had worn a beard. And now I knew I had first met him on the bank of a canal one dark night in Alexandria.

As if that revelation were not enough to stun my senses, the sight of Circe held me rooted to the spot. She was as lovely as I recalled, wearing a dress of the finest white and blue cloth, and with her hair partly piled on her head but with strands falling about her face in curls which must have taken an age to create. Just like the first time I had seen her in that wine shop in Ephesus, she was wearing several bangles on her bare forearms, and her ear rings were miniature copies of the statue of Artemis. I doubted she wore them as everyday items of jewellery, so she must have spent the past few minutes hurrying to find them. Was that some sort of signal she was trying to send me?

She gave me a smile, although I thought I detected some concern behind her expression as she said, "Hello, Scipio. How did you find me?"

All the things I had imagined myself saying to her fled from my mind as I gaped at her. All the protestations and accusations I had rehearsed deserted me. If I had not been so dazed by actually seeing her again, I think I would have crossed the room and wrapped my arms around her.

She waited, cocking her head and lifting her delicate eyebrows when I did not answer.

Eventually, I found my tongue.

"Niger," I told her. "Pomponius Niger."

She frowned, "I did not think he would give me away."

"I tricked him," I told her. "I'd worked out he must have been the one who told you I was coming to Ephesus, so I asked him where he had served in Africa."

She seemed very formal as she stood there, her body stiff and tense.

She said, "Collinus told me you might find me eventually."

As she spoke, her hand fluttered to indicate the tall Berber beside her.

"Collinus?" I asked, doing a rough translation in my head. "The man of the hills?"

"It is a name I was given some years ago," the tall, tanned man told me. "I am pleased to meet you properly at last."

I wasn't sure I shared that emotion. His right hand was not far from the hilt of that dagger, and I knew he was very capable with the weapon. He'd murdered Aristides with it, after all, and he'd had no qualms about the prospect of tackling Agon and Diomedes on his own.

"So what happens now that I have found you?" I asked Circe.

"That depends on why you have come," she told me.

Her words sounded harsh, but the expression in her large, doe-like eyes held something of an appeal. What, I wondered, was she really trying to say? Was she afraid of what I might say next?

"I came to see you," I responded rather lamely. "I want to understand why you did what you did. And who you really are."

"I thought you would have worked that out by now," she said evasively.

"No. I've figured out how you did things, or at least I think I have. But I still don't understand it all."

Collinus interrupted, "And what will you do if you learn these things? Do you have a troop of Praetorians ready to ride here? Or will you run back to Macrinus to claim a reward for discovering the truth?"

The hard look in his eyes told me precisely what would happen to me if he suspected I might do either of those things. Was that what Circe feared; that Collinus might feel the need to kill me?

I tried to reassure her on that point.

"I have never told anyone about you," I told her. "Only Fronto and my mother, and neither of them will say anything. To do so would place them in danger themselves. Nobody else even knows you exist. But I need to know the truth."

It was not the speech I had intended to make, but it seemed to convince her. She visibly relaxed, her shoulders sagging with relief, and the smile she now gave me seemed almost genuine, although I reminded myself she had lied behind her smiles before now.

"If I tell you," she said solemnly, "I want you to swear an oath you will not tell anyone else."

I hesitated, wondering how I could keep that oath and still convince Macrinus I had discovered the truth behind Julia Maesa's plot.

Then I decided I could not afford to tell him about Circe in any case.

"I swear it," I told her. "By any god or goddess you care to name, and on my mother's life, I promise I will not mention you to anyone."

I saw her shoot a quick glance at Collinus.

He nodded gravely, "I believe Sempronius Scipio is a man of his word."

And this time, Circe's smile was as bright as the morning sun as she said, "Then let us talk over dinner."

She moved towards me at last, placing a hand on my arm. The touch of her fingers set my blood boiling, and I am sure my face flushed when she reached up to plant a soft kiss on my cheek.

"I am glad you found me," she whispered. "I just hope you don't hate me once you know the whole story."

Chapter 23
Answers

Circe stretched out on the couch which was placed at the head of the long, low table. Collinus moved to lie opposite me, while I propped myself on my left elbow and lay down on the nearest couch. As with most formal Roman dining couches, each of these luxuriously upholstered benches could easily accommodate three people, so we had plenty of space. By taking a couch each, though, we could all see one another without needing to twist our necks.

Circe addressed the Nubian servant.

"Julianus! Have the food served."

Julianus, the *major domo*, quietly left through the second door, no doubt to instruct the slaves to bring the food. They must have been waiting, for the first dishes arrived almost immediately.

None of us spoke while the food was being placed on the table. I was still searching for the right words to say in any case, but Circe and Collinus obviously wished our conversation to remain private. Many Romans speak quite openly in the presence of their slaves because they view them as little better than dumb animals, but Circe obviously held her household staff in higher regard.

Under the watchful eyes of Julianus, several slaves delivered platters of food to the table, spreading them efficiently and then departing. Wine was poured, with plenty of water added, and my hunger got the better of me. There were eggs of several sorts, fish, thin slices of lamb, two or three varieties of roasted bird, honeyed dormice, and all accompanied by plenty of fruit and vegetables.

We began to eat, and only when all the slaves except Julianus had left the room did Circe open the conversation.

"So what would you like to know first, Sextus?"

That was easy.

"Your real name," I told her. "Is it Aurelia? You have so many names, but I do not know who you really are. Then I'd like to know why you were so determined to kill Antoninus Caesar."

She hesitated, delicately chewing on a rib of lamb. Then she said, "The answer to the first should explain the second."

I waited patiently while she paused to consider her next words.

After a moment, she said, "Aurelia was my mother's name. I always liked it, even though I hated her. That is the name by which people in Leptis Magna know me."

"It's a nice name," I told her. "But I always think of you as Circe."

"I like Circe too," she agreed with a warm smile. "But my original name was Fulvia."

She looked across the table, her eyes fixed on mine as she added, "My father was Gaius Fulvius Plautianus. He was once the Praetorian Prefect."

I stared at her in amazement.

"The man who plotted against Septimius Severus?"

A flash of anger crossed her face as she snapped, "He did no such thing! He was a friend of the old Emperor. They grew up together in Leptis. He was killed because Severus' monster of a son was jealous of my father's influence."

This was obviously a sensitive subject, and Circe's anger was very real.

She continued, "Antoninus also wanted rid of his wife. My older sister. She had discovered he was sleeping with his stepmother, the Emperor's wife, and she had threatened to tell the Emperor."

I took a moment to take all that in.

"So Antoninus had your father executed, and he banished your sister?"

"Executed? It was murder. He stabbed my father himself, right there in the audience chamber in front of the Emperor. My sister told me all about it."

I could hear the rage in her voice as she recalled those events from long ago, but she took a deep breath and calmed herself before continuing her story.

"Actually, Fulvia Plautilla was my step-sister, my father's daughter from his first marriage. But I was always close to her even though there were twelve years between us. She had always made a point of spoiling me and was more like a mother to me than my real mother."

She smiled sadly as she recalled, "When I learned she was to be banished, I insisted on going with her."

Her smile became a twisted grin as she explained, "My mother and my other sister stayed in Rome. My mother was quick to distance herself from the memory of my father, you see. She claimed he had been a traitor in order to ingratiate herself with Antoninus. But I screamed and yelled until my mother gave in and allowed me to accompany Fulvia Plautilla. I think, in truth, she was glad to be rid of me. I had always been a trial to her."

"I can't imagine why," I said.

That broke the tension which had been hanging over us. Collinus laughed aloud, and Circe herself could not help but join in.

"I suppose I probably was a difficult child," she admitted. "Anyway, Plautilla and I came back to Leptis Magna because my father owned this estate. But I think Plautilla always knew Antoninus would not let her live. I think it was his father who had held him in check, for Antoninus sent a troop of Praetorians to kill her as soon as he became Emperor himself."

"But you obviously escaped," I remarked.

"I was not here. Plautilla had sent me away to Carthage to stay with one of my father's former clients."

"Veronius Pulcher?" I guessed.

"Very good," she smiled. "I presume Fronto told you about my visit to Rome a few years ago?"

"He did. That was when you saw the eagle pendant design and heard about me."

"It was. Pulcher took me to Rome because I was already trying to work out how to have Antoninus killed. But I knew he had a secret army of spies, and I needed to understand how they operated. Pulcher knew that your friend, Fronto, was working at the Palatine for Sempronius Rufus, the spy master. Fronto's father had told him as much in a letter. So Pulcher agreed, reluctantly I might add, to help me."

"So you had already taken on the role of Dido by that time?"

"I vowed to avenge my sister as soon as I was able," she nodded, her face showing her grim determination. "I know it meant deceiving people, but it was the only way I could accomplish my goal."

"You certainly deceived poor Fronto," I said.

She gave a soft shrug.

"I did him no harm. And it did not take much to get him to talk. He was trying to impress me by telling me how important his job was, and all about his clever friend, Scipio."

Collinus put in, "Which makes me wonder whether you can rely on him to keep silent about Aurelia."

"Fronto learned his lesson well," I assured him. "He will not make that mistake a second time."

Collinus' face was as solemn as a statue, but Circe accepted my word.

She said, "That is good to know. But we are getting too far ahead in the story. We were talking of my sister. Plautilla had expected Antoninus might try to kill her. It had been a few years since she had been exiled from Rome, but that man never forgot a grudge. So she sent me to Carthage with Collinus to look after me. Pulcher arranged some accommodation for us, and we hid there for several months."

I looked across the table to the tall Berber whose eyes never seemed to stop watching me.

"What is your story, then?" I asked him.

He replied, "I did a service for Aurelia's father when I was a boy. He took me on as a free member of his household. I have served the family ever since."

"Collinus is a true friend," Circe told me. "I trust him implicitly. He is extremely talented in a number of fields, and has been the most loyal of guardians to me ever since I was a young girl."

I gave the Berber a nod of acknowledgement. I'd certainly known he was a very capable man even before I knew exactly who he was.

Returning to the main thread of the unfolding story, I said to Circe, "So you escaped Antoninus' killers?"

"I did. Plautilla had been very clever as well as cautious. I don't think Antoninus knew or cared of my existence, but my sister did not want to take any chances. She made sure that Collinus had access to most of our family fortune. So, when our family home fell into the hands of the imperial treasury after my sister was murdered, Collinus was able to buy it from the local Procurator on behalf of an orphaned girl named Aurelia."

"And then you assumed the name of Dido and set about planning your revenge?"

She nodded.

"That man was a brute. He had tens of thousands of people murdered simply because they supported his younger brother, or for having the temerity to question his rule."

I wasn't going to argue with her about that. Antoninus had a mean streak, and he hadn't been afraid to display it. I'd witnessed that at first hand in Alexandria.

I asked her, "So how did you get mixed up with Dion and his Alexander conspiracy?"

"That was just a stroke of luck," she told me. "We breed horses here, you know. Collinus had visited Alexandria to talk to a potential buyer. While there, he met someone who mentioned Dion as a radical who was always coming up with schemes to make Egypt great again and who wanted to be free of Rome."

"So you gave Dion the idea of resurrecting Alexander?"

She gave me a self-deprecating smile which made her look incredibly seductive.

"I went to talk to him," she explained. "I soon discovered he was a fanatic, but he had a lot of followers, including those twins, and he had contacts with important people in Egypt. His problem was that his ideas were all very vague and idealistic, so I made some suggestions."

"So the theft of the amulet was your idea?"

"It served two purposes," she admitted casually. "It struck at Antoninus because it had been donated to the Temple by his father, and it provided a symbol which Dion's false Alexander could use to convince people of his return. We wanted something memorable, but there was not a great deal of treasure left in the tomb because so many Emperors had taken mementoes over the past centuries."

"Then you became Julia Petronia and lured Leonides away to Athens so Aristides could place one of your twins at the Temple?"

"That's right," she said.

Shooting a look at Collinus, I said, "But Aristides got greedy, and you killed him."

The Berber did not bat an eyelid as he agreed, "Yes. He was threatening to tell the authorities if we did not double his reward."

He spoke as if killing the old crook had been nothing more than a business transaction. That made me shiver. Circe might trust this man, but it would take a lot more than that for me to warm to him.

I turned back to Circe.

"So why did you go back to Ephesus after the theft?"

"Oh, that was simply a precaution. Collinus and the twins had to leave the city in a hurry after Aristides was killed. They took the amulet back to Alexandria, but I returned to Ephesus as soon as I heard about it. I stayed on in the house we'd rented to keep an eye on what happened next. Dion was scared that someone might discover his plan before he was ready, so I promised to monitor the situation for a couple of months. Having Niger as a contact proved useful for that."

"Did you know beforehand that Niger was working at the Temple?"

"No. That was a happy coincidence. I met him when I visited the Temple to check on the layout and the security."

"And, after the theft, he told you I was coming, and you remembered about my friendship with Fronto?"

She had the good grace to look slightly guilty as she confessed, "It was a surprise when Niger told me your name, but I decided I should do my best to mislead you. Fronto had been quite expansive in explaining how effective you were in discovering things."

There were a lot of things I wanted to say to her, but I could not bring myself to talk about the way she had betrayed my trust in her.

I simply said, "I fell for it."

"Yes. I'm sorry about that. But I did not want you discovering the truth."

"So it meant nothing to you?" I challenged, unable to conceal the hurt I felt. I had told her I wanted to hear the truth, but the recollections were now bringing back the pain.

"I did not say that," she replied softly, lowering her eyes.

Then, with a spark of temper, she added, "I did not plan to sleep with you, if that is what you meant. That was ..."

She shrugged, unable to complete her sentence.

"... I just wanted to keep you away from Dion. I knew what he was like. It was all I could do to persuade his thugs, Agon

245

and Diomedes not to kill you. Even so, they bribed that sailor to get rid of you when we were sailing to Alexandria."

She held my gaze as she added, "I shouldn't need to tell you I knew nothing of that."

I must admit I wasn't entirely sure how I felt about hearing this. Like me, Circe seemed to be very confused about her emotions.

"I'm glad to hear that," I nodded. "So your idea was to abandon me in Alexandria?"

"Yes. I knew Dion was getting close to finalising his part of the operation, and I wanted to keep you out of it. But you blundered right into his house. How did you find us?"

"I saw Helena doing some shopping, and I followed her."

Circe nodded, "I thought it might be something like that. But at least you escaped Dion's thugs. Those two brutes were very unpleasant, but Collinus says you killed both of them."

"I got lucky," I told her.

Collinus said, "I think it was more than luck."

"Whatever it was," Circe said, "you ruined Dion's plan. But at least we were able to leave the city before the killing began."

"I was worried about that," I told her. "But things were out of my control by then."

Her large, expressive eyes fixed on me as she said, "I was very angry with you. We were so close. I had no interest in Dion's plans for Egypt, but I wanted Antoninus dead. Because you foiled the Alexander plot, our assassin refused to carry out his part of the plan."

I was glad we were moving away from the emotive part of our discussion. The past few minutes had been difficult for both of us, I knew, but now we were nearing the critical part.

"That's the bit I haven't figured out yet," I admitted. "Who was your assassin?"

"You don't know?" she asked, her astonishment plain.

"Should I?"

"It was Justin Martialis," she informed me. "He was supposed to get close to Antoninus during a public outing, stab him, then Dion's mob were supposed to whisk him away to safety. In the confusion, Alexander's tomb would be opened, and the new

Alexander would have risen from the dead to take control of Egypt."

She pulled a face as she added, "That part was mad, of course, but all I wanted was for Martialis to kill Antoninus."

"Instead, he killed Dion and all the others," I frowned, remembering the eagerness with which Martialis had slaughtered the conspirators. "I suppose he decided to get rid of them once he knew their plot was bound to fail."

"That is what he told us later when Collinus made contact with him again."

I shot the Berber an accusing look.

"You had some nerve, my friend. You walked right past me in that garden in Antioch."

"What else could I do?" he smiled. "I didn't think you would recognise me since you had not seen my face properly that night beside the canal. And I would have denied knowing you even if you had challenged me."

"But why were you there? I still don't understand that part."

Circe put in, "It's quite simple, really. Julia Maesa is desperate for real power. She has more wealth and influence than almost anyone else in the empire, but she wants more. I think she is jealous that her younger sister had married a man who became Emperor. But she saw an opportunity when Antoninus failed to produce an heir. So she kept asking him to nominate her grandson, Elagabalus, as his successor, but Antoninus had consistently refused her."

"So she wanted to kill him?" I frowned. "What would that achieve?"

"Actually, she wanted Macrinus killed," Circe informed me. "She believed, rightly I think, that it was Macrinus who had persuaded Antoninus to refuse to acknowledge Elagabalus."

"I can't say I blame him," I muttered. "The boy may look like an angel, but he's not cut out to be any sort of ruler, let alone Emperor."

"That would not matter if Julia Maesa controlled him," Circe said.

"So you got involved with her in order to dispose of Macrinus?" I asked, my gaze flitting from one to the other.

Then another tiny fragment of the mosaic fell into place.

247

I looked at Collinus.

"Don't tell me you played the part of the prophet in Tingis?"

He grinned at me.

"That was one of my better performances, I believe. Certainly one of my most effective."

"But things did not work out," Circe said, regarding me with an accusatory stare. "How did you get involved? We thought a message would be sent to Antoninus and, knowing his temper, he would have had Macrinus executed."

I told them about my job in Antioch, how I had come across the message, and how Macrinus had come to read it thanks to Antoninus ordering that he should deal with all correspondence.

Circe nodded pensively, but Collinus took up the discussion.

"Your arrival certainly terrified Martialis. We had told him Macrinus would be executed and then he could take his own revenge on Antoninus. But when you and the Prefect turned up with a scroll and talked about discovering another plot, he thought you were about to denounce him."

"Did he think that because you persuaded him that was about to happen?" I guessed.

In response, Collinus returned another of his smooth smiles.

I leaned back on my couch, taking a sip of the excellent wine. When I put the goblet down, I said, "So Martialis was spooked into killing the Emperor too soon. And I suppose he'd been promised he would be kept safe?"

"He may have been given that impression," Collinus agreed.

"Which would leave the throne empty, Macrinus out of the way, and Julia Maesa could have bribed some of the Legions into supporting her grandson as Emperor."

"That wasn't exactly how Maesa intended it," Circe told me. "She wanted Macrinus out of the way so she could persuade Antoninus to proclaim her grandson as his heir before he died. She had a couple of Senators lined up to push the boy's claim. He is, after all, the oldest surviving male of the Severan line."

"But why did you need Maesa at all?" I asked. "Why not just bribe Martialis and have him kill the Emperor?"

"Because Martialis wanted protection. A powerful woman like Maesa could offer that. We couldn't. It didn't matter to me whether he survived or not, but we needed Maesa's promises to convince him."

"So it has worked out for you but not for Martialis or Maesa," I remarked. "Aren't you worried she might try to get some revenge on you for killing Antoninus too soon?"

Collinus put in, "She will not do that. I told her what had happened. She was furious, of course, but I put the blame on Martialis."

A horrible thought struck me then.

"Did you mention my part in what happened?"

"She worked that out for herself," Collinus informed me. "It was, after all, her sister who sent you with the message. But you need not fear. Domna had assured her that you were loyal to Antoninus and that you could not be blamed for Macrinus' involvement."

I wasn't entirely reassured by that. Julia Maesa, I knew, could be as vengeful as any Emperor.

"I suppose I'll need to watch my back anyway," I muttered darkly.

"Not if you disappear," Circe told me.

"Disappear?"

For a moment, I feared she might be about to order Collinus to use his dagger, but she smiled and said, "Change your name. It's easy to do. Maesa has no idea who I really am."

"It's not that simple," I argued.

"Why not? Who will mourn Scipio if he vanishes? Your mother, perhaps, but you can send her a letter as long as you do not reveal your new identity."

I felt lost. I had come here in search of a lost love, seeking answers to a mystery but still not knowing what I really wanted to accomplish. I had the answers now, but I was left feeling more confused than ever.

I wanted Circe, of course, but I still did not know whether I could fully trust her. I certainly wanted to escape the intrigues of the imperial court, but I had no desire to simply vanish and leave my mother grieving.

I closed my eyes for a moment, pinching the bridge of my nose between thumb and forefinger.

When I looked back up, I said, "I need to think about all this."

Collinus told me, "I think your choice is simple. Either you return to your life as an imperial spy, with all the risks that entails, or you become someone else and quietly make a new future for yourself."

"It's more complicated than that," I told him, although I suspected he had summed up my situation very concisely.

The issue, I knew, was my relationship with Circe. Where did I stand with her? And where did she stand with me?

I looked at her, seeking some indication that what had passed between us in Ephesus had been more than an attempt to distract and fool me. Some of the things she had said and done since then gave me hope, but her scheming had nearly brought the empire to its knees, and I was a good Roman. At least, I thought I was, but having seen at first hand how Antoninus had acted as Emperor, I wasn't entirely sure what a good Roman was any more.

Circe returned my gaze as if reading my thoughts. Then she turned to Collinus.

She said, "There is something else I need to show Scipio before he makes up his mind."

Standing up, she told me, "Come with me. There is someone I need you to see."

Collinus watched me, his expression unreadable. As I rose to my feet, I realised that the Nubian, Julianus, had been standing behind me the whole time. He, too, gave no indication of what he might be thinking. But he was already reaching for an oil lamp to light our way.

I followed Circe out of the room and along a corridor which I guessed ran all the way around the square building. Julianus was in front, holding the lamp high, and I was all too aware that Collinus was only a few paces behind me.

I was also aware of Circe's perfume. I was walking close beside her, and the fragrance from her reminded me that, no matter what she had done to me, I could not deny that I still wanted her. I knew now how and why she had done what she had, and I suppose it seemed reasonable from her perspective. But she had been involved with murder and the assassination of an Emperor. Could I ignore all that?

But the worst feeling of all came from the thought of how I would feel if I walked out of this villa and never saw her again.

We turned, climbing some stairs to the upper level. There was an ante-chamber with two doorways leading off on opposite sides, each one closed by a heavy curtain. One of these curtains was pulled aside at the sound of our footsteps, and I saw the plump, elderly figure of Circe's maid, Helena, appear. She exchanged a few words in Punic with Circe, then she looked at me and, to my surprise, regarded me with a knowing smile. She bobbed her head, then watched as Julianus approached the other doorway. He stood aside, allowing Circe to quietly pull the curtain aside, revealing a room which was lit only by a solitary candle.

There was another woman in the room. She was sitting in a chair, busy spinning wool on a hand-held spindle, but she put down her work, rose to her feet and bobbed her head to Circe.

"Is he asleep?" Circe asked in a whisper.

The woman nodded again.

Turning to me, Circe placed a hand on my arm. Gently, she ushered me forwards to where a small bed was placed against the far wall.

The slave woman brought the candle closer, and its flickering light showed me the tiny figure of a baby boy sleeping soundly in the bed, his arms spread wide. He was dark-haired, his skin bearing a slight olive tint.

"He is nearly fifteen months old now," Circe told me. "He began walking when he was just past his first birthday."

I looked at her, trying to make out her expression, but all I noticed was the reflection of a tiny droplet of a tear at the corner of her eye.

"His name," she told me, "Is Sextus Sempronius Scipio."

The final piece of the mosaic slotted into place. I looked, disbelieving, at the tiny boy fast asleep in his bed, and I looked at Circe who was smiling back at me, sniffing away the tears which were now rolling down her cheeks.

"Why did you not tell me?" I asked, my throat constricting with emotion.

"You worked for the Emperor," she said with a tearful sniff. "I did not know what you would do if you found out."

I had no answer to that. I did not know either. But I knew what I needed to do right then.

I reached for her, putting my arms around her, and pulled her close so that I could kiss her.

I don't know how long we stood there, our mouths recreating the bond we had felt in Ephesus, our bodies clamped together by our entwined arms, but when we eventually broke off the kiss and Circe was wiping away her tears, we were alone in the room.

Alone with our son.

Hoarse with emotion I said, "You are right. I will need to change my name if I am to stay here."

"A name can be changed easily enough," Circe laughed. "What would you like to be called?"

"Your husband?" I suggested.

"That will do for a start," she agreed.

Author's Note and Acknowledgements

The assassination of Marcus Aurelius Antoninus, better known nowadays as Emperor Caracalla, was the spark which plunged the Roman Empire into what has become known as the Third Century Crisis. There are, however, conflicting versions of what actually happened.

The only consistencies in the tale are that the Praetorian Prefect, Opellius Macrinus, did have authority to read Caracalla's correspondence, and so learned of a prophecy which he realised would result in the paranoid Emperor having him killed. Conventional history tells us that Macrinus then hired a soldier named Martialis to carry out the killing. Martialis, according to the few sources we have, had a grudge against Caracalla, although whether this was over a denied promotion or the death of his own brother depends on which source you read. The assassination itself has several variants, from Martialis being killed by a German bodyguard, shot by a Syrian archer or killed by a thrown javelin as he tried to make his escape. One version even says his attempt was bungled and that Caracalla was only wounded, but was then killed by two Tribunes who were also in Macrinus' pay.

Nearly every modern historian agrees that Macrinus was behind the plot, but that does not square with the fact that it took him three days to proclaim himself Emperor. That delay adds a little doubt to the story, and I have tried to use it to paint a very different picture to the one most history books portray.

There is also some confusion over Caracalla's life. Most historians say he was close in age to his brother, Geta, and that both were the sons of Julia Domna. There is, however, a minority view that Caracalla was much older than his brother and could have been the son of Septimius Severus' first wife. Whatever the truth of it, and whether rumours of the sexual relationship between Caracalla and Domna are true, her reaction to the violent death of Geta is certainly a strange one. She seemed devoted to Caracalla in the years that followed Geta's death, although it is, of course, impossible for us to know her motivations.

Whatever the truth of this confusing tale, it provides sufficient uncertainty for me to have created this story.

Much of the rest of the tale is invention. There was no stolen amulet, nor was there any plot to have Alexander the Great reincarnated. There was, though, a wholesale massacre in Alexandria which was carried out on Caracalla's orders. The reasons for this remain dubious, with a simple parody play often being cited as his justification for sacking the city. Even for an Emperor like Caracalla, that was an extreme response, and there may have been more to it.

The theory that Caracalla used temples as part of a network of communications is also a minority view, but it must be admitted that he often carried out purges of alleged traitors after visiting a temple and claiming to have been granted a revelation by the gods. Perhaps this was merely an excuse for him to get rid of people he did not like, or perhaps the priests were indeed gathering information on his behalf. Again, we will probably never know.

In 2010, my first novel, *In the Shadow of the Wall*, was published. I try not to think about it too much since I know if I ever read it again I will want to make changes to it. I have, I hope, learned a lot about writing stories since then. But I still have a soft spot for the principal character, Brude, and people have often asked me when I am going to write a sequel. My answer has always been that I will write that sequel when I come up with a decent plot idea. I had never been able to come up with that idea. The only event in the years following the Brude story which I could ever think of was the sack of Alexandria. Unfortunately, I could never devise any excuse for a Pictish warrior to abandon his new-found happiness and travel to Alexandria. Then, out of the blue, I had the idea of creating a new character who could fit into that timeline, and the concept of Scipio gradually evolved into the current story. So, for those who have asked for a follow up to Brude, this is the best I can come up with. Let us leave Brude in peace. For Scipio, on the other hand …

As always, I owe many thanks to a dedicated team of friends and family. In particular, my brother, Stuart Anthony, spent a lot of time looking at maps of ancient cities so I could add some authenticity to the background to Scipio's adventure. He also created the design of the book cover.

Stuart, along with Moira Anthony, Ian Dron, Stewart Fenton and Liz Wright, helped with the proof reading and between them they sorted out my many typing errors. I owe them all my thanks.

GA
October, 2019

ABOUT THE AUTHOR

Born in Watford, Hertfordshire, in 1957, Gordon's family moved to Broughty Ferry in the early 1960s. Gordon attended Grove Academy, leaving in 1974 to work for Bank of Scotland. After a long but undistinguished career, he retired on medical grounds in 2008 without having received any huge bankers' bonuses.

Registered blind, Gordon had more time on his hands after retiring so, with the aid of special computer software, he returned to his hobby of writing and had his debut novel, "In the Shadow of the Wall" published in 2010. Gordon's books are now being read by a world-wide audience. As well as his historical adventure stories, he has ventured into crime fiction with some spoof murder mysteries in the "Constantine Investigates" series. He is also kept busy with speaking engagements, visiting libraries, schools and community groups to talk about his books.

In addition to his novels, Gordon devotes some of his time to raising funds for the RNIB. As well as visiting schools and social clubs to talk about his sight loss, he has self-published a charity booklet titled, "A Walk in the Dark", a humorous account of his experiences since losing his eyesight. The booklet is available from Amazon Kindle Store. Gordon will donate all author royalties to RNIB.

Now completely blind, Gordon continues to write stories and, in his spare time, attempts to play the guitar and keyboard with varying degrees of success.

Gordon is married to Alaine. They have three children and one grandchild. The family lives in Livingston, West Lothian.

You can contact Gordon via his website or by sending an email to ga.author@sky.com

Other Books by Gordon Anthony

All titles are available in e-book format from the Amazon Kindle store. Titles marked with an asterisk are also available from Amazon in paperback.

In the Shadow of the Wall*
An Eye For An Eye*

Home Fires*
Hunting Icarus*

The Calgacus Series:
      World's End*
      The Centurions*
      Queen of Victory*
      Druids' Gold*
      Blood Ties*
      The High King*
      The Ghost War*
      Last Of The Free*

The Constantine Investigates Series:
      The Man in the Ironic Mask
      The Lady of Shall Not
      Gawain and the Green Nightshirt
      A Tale of One City
      49 Shades of Tartan

The Hereward Story:
      Last English Hero*
      Doomsday*

A Walk in the Dark (Charity booklet)

Printed in Poland
by Amazon Fulfillment
Poland Sp. z o.o., Wrocław